Boot
Camp

GINA MUSA

Boot Camp

wattpad books **w**

wattpad books **W**

An imprint of Wattpad WEBTOON Book Group

Copyright © 2023 Gina Musa

All rights reserved.

Published in Canada by Wattpad WEBTOON Book Group, a division of Wattpad WEBTOON Studios, Inc.

36 Wellington Street E., Suite 200, Toronto, ON M5E 1C7 Canada

www.wattpad.com

First Wattpad Books edition: November 2023

ISBN 978-1-99885-408-0 (Trade Paper original)
ISBN 978-1-99885-409-7 (eBook edition)

Library and Archives Canada Cataloguing in Publication information is available upon request.

Printed and bound in Canada

1 3 5 7 9 10 8 6 4 2

Cover illustration by Jay Flores-Holz

Cover design by Niko Lerman Dalcin

Typesetting by Delaney Anderson

To anyone who woke up one day and
decided to change their life for the better.

Give yourself a pat on the back.

CHAPTER ONE

"I look like I teach Pilates for seniors in the basement of a gym that converts to a church on Sundays."

Standing in front of the full-length mirror in my room, I smooth out the wrinkles around my hips in my bright-blue leggings, wincing as it makes them worse. It's my fault for buying them yesterday without trying them on, but I figured these were a one-size-fits-all kind of attire. With the way the material bunches up around my hips, bags at the crotch, and is missing three inches at the ankles, it looks like I got the three-sizes-in-one deal.

"If that's the long and oddly detailed way of saying absolutely freakin' *adorable*, then you're right."

My best friend, Ava Farzan, climbs off my bed and adjusts the visor I stole from her collection on my head, tipping it up to reveal my unplucked eyebrows and the permanent dark circles around my green eyes. When my frown doesn't budge—and neither do I—she sighs.

"Oh, come on, it's leggings and a tank top, Whitney."

"It's not just the clothing, Ava." I tug up the neckline of my tank top, only for it to sag again and reveal the same polka-dot sports bra I've had since seventh grade, debatably before I ever needed to wear one. "It's that me being here, dressed like this"—I gesture from my head to my toes and then let my palms fall to my side—"goes against everything I stand for."

"You mean . . . exercise?"

"No, not exercise," I say, but that's a lie only because I can't admit that to the future professional athlete standing in front of me. "I'm talking about spending my Sunday morning at a 5K race organized by the mother of the girl who's literally made it her mission to torture me all through high school. How do you tolerate Willow again?"

"*I* don't tolerate her. Our *mothers* tolerate each other. And because my mom signed me up for this 5K because she can't come, you have to come with me."

"Failing to see where my obligation is here."

"Come on, Whitney," she huffs. "Even if I wasn't roped into this to save face for my mother, I'd still want us to go. The charity Willow's mom is raising money for"—she pauses to google the forcibly clever name "Girl (Em)Power" and sprinkles some enthusiasm into her tone as she reads—"'has helped *thousands* of girls across the country meet positive role models, embrace their bodies, and harness their inner confidence to become changemakers in today's society.'"

She looks up at me with those big brown eyes that usually work wonders when trying to win male attention, but I've known her too long, and they're powerless against me.

"Damn, those are some great buzzwords, but Willow has also helped *hundreds* of students at Greene Hill Academy feel bad about themselves, so that evens things out."

Even Ava can't argue with me, because whether she wants to

admit it or not, everyone at our school hates Willow—the teachers, the students in other grades, and even her best friends. A couple of drinks in, even Willow herself would probably start rattling off a laundry list of her terrible qualities, but I stand a better chance at becoming the next woman in history to get hit by a meteorite in her own home before she ever changes her ways.

"One day we're going to be free of her, you know?" Ava says in that distant, wistful way after a moment, like Willow is Stage IV cancer. "*One* day."

Before I can rattle off another excuse for why I can't run this 5K—and there are many—Ava drags me down the wooden spiral staircase, across the foyer, and into the kitchen, where my parents are chatting. Sunday is the only day of the week they can spend any quality time together, and I'm surprised they're wasting it indoors on this balmy late-April day, until I realize the thought comes too soon.

"Mr. and Mrs. Carmichael, *loving* the tennis looks for the day," Ava says, gesturing at their all-white Lacoste apparel. "I would've loved to join, but Whitney and I are already running late to a 5K."

Mom stands up to pull her into a hug. "You know we would've loved to have you, Ava." She then turns to me and plants her hands on my shoulders, the same green eyes I have creasing up at the corners with her wide smile. "Gosh, Whitney, you look adorable. It's always great to see you trying new things."

"Real great," I say through my teeth as Ava updates my dad on her last tennis match.

He gives her his full undivided attention, like he always does with my older sister, Poppy, and that creeping sense of inferiority eats at my brain, making me wonder if he's secretly wishing I was more like them both. Maybe Ava, and not me, was supposed to be the fourth member of the Carmichael family, given its athletic legacy going three generations strong.

It all started with Dad's dad, Grandpa Tom, who, although now retired in a beach house in Fort Lauderdale, was once a star wide receiver and the coach of three different NFL teams over the course of his illustrious forty-six-year career. Dad had been poised to follow in his footsteps until a hamstring injury during his senior year of high school shattered his college football dreams. From then on, he put all his effort into making as much money as possible, which translated into a finance career over-working him from New York City to the nearby Connecticut suburbs, where I've lived for most of my life.

He met Mom on a six-mile run in Central Park, a morning habit lingering from her days as a track and field star at Penn. Although she prefers Pilates, tennis, and golf now—or as I like to call them, rich suburban mom sports—she kept up the morning runs until I was a toddler, taking me out in a jogging stroller around the park on any at least partly sunny day.

Then there's my older sister, Poppy, the only logical child for my two athletic parents. I'd probably be out of breath if I tried to list the number of sports she played growing up, but currently, she's a golfer at Columbia, where she met her boyfriend, Levi, also a golfer. If it wasn't for the two of them, I wouldn't even believe anyone under the age of fifty enjoyed the sport.

And then came me, Whitney. How their genes combined to create a literal walking (emphasis on the walking part) disaster at all things sports, I'll never know, but usually, I embrace my role as the nonathletic black sheep of the family by *not* participating in 5K races.

Especially those turkey trots on Thanksgiving morning. Those are the worst.

"Have fun, girls!" Mom calls as Ava and I head out the garage door. "You're gonna kill it!"

Yeah, in the bad way, Mom.

Ava and I climb into her Audi convertible, and thirty minutes later, we make it to the sprawling college campus where this race is being held. It looks like it does on any day of the school week, except instead of students, the grass and sidewalks are flooded with a mix of teenage girls, their mothers and grandmothers, and young children. They yell at each other over the sound of pop music blaring from speakers on the quad, decorated with booths sporting bright signs, making this 5K race feel more like a holiday bazaar.

Ava and I stop by the registration table to grab our numbers and complimentary neon-green Girl (Em)Power T-shirts before deciding to circle the dewy grass of the quad. A group of middle schoolers call us over and drop two gel pens into our hands while pitching their petition to implement a girls' football league in our public school district. Considering I'll neither play football nor be a middle schooler again in my lifetime, I sign it and move on to the next table, advertising a summer camp.

"Hey, girls," a young woman with blue-tinted hair greets us. "Interested in learning about Camp Campbell?"

Neither Ava nor I can keep a straight face at the name, but I manage to make the smile look sincere as I nod. "Yeah, sure. Why not?"

She gives us a brief rundown on the camp: a five-week fitness program for young women located about an hour from where we are now. My attention wanes as she throws around terms like *running*, *rope climbing*, *boxing*, and *hiking*, but she loses me with one tidbit of information.

"The woman who organized this 5K, Cindy, is joining the camp as a coordinator this summer," she says, referring to Willow's mom. "She's going to be such a great role model for all the girls in the program."

"Oh, we're not int—"

"Here," she says, thrusting a brochure into my hands. "Take one."

I notice she doesn't hand Ava a brochure before we turn away. I figure it's because we seem close enough to share one, but as we keep walking, my self-consciousness blossoms.

Does it *look* like I need a fitness camp?

"Hey, Whitney." Ava snaps me out of my thoughts, and I nod. She juts her thumb behind her, continuing, "I'm going to go begrudgingly tell Cindy my mom says hi and that she can't *wait* for brunch again next weekend, then I'll join you, okay?"

"Good luck," I say dryly, and she mouths *shoot me* before jogging away.

Now alone, I speed through the rest of the booths, earning myself more and more free goodies, which I shove into a tote bag advertising an inclusive fashion brand. My shoulder sags as I walk, despite its contents barely weighing a couple of pounds, making me rethink the brochure crumpled inside. As I'm about to text Ava, a bright-blond head enters my peripheral vision, and Willow leaps in front of me on her long, lean dancer legs.

She settles her hands on the hips of her purple biker shorts, which match the sports bra that gives her the illusion of boobs. "Whitney, didn't expect to see you here today."

"Could say the same to you," I grumble, trying to walk around her, but she blocks my path. Driving my teeth into my bottom lip, I force myself to remain calm only because I don't need half the mothers in our town witnessing a long-overdue catfight. "What now, Willow?"

"Nothing really. I wanted to say this is a charity event more than anything, so don't feel obligated to run the actual race. There are a lot of"—she swivels around and points to the benches lining the perimeter of the quad—"*old* people and babies who would appreciate your company."

If I had any doubts about running this race, Willow wipes them away with that snide comment. But before I can make one back, not that I can think of anything that would remotely hurt her, her mother's voice erupts through a microphone, and she darts away, while Ava joins me again.

"*Hello*, friends!" Cindy calls, standing in the middle of the quad. As I take in her blown-out caramel-colored hair, matching white workout set, and full face of makeup, I question if she'll actually run this race herself. "We're so glad you could be here for our first-ever Girl (Em)Power 5K. As those close to me know, female empowerment is at the core of all the work I do, as a Pilates instructor, wellness coach, and of course, a mother." Willow doesn't return her mother's bright-white smile. "In a few minutes, the race will begin, but I want you to know you are *all* winners for being here and supporting the future changemakers of society."

Just like your daughter loves doing, I think before tuning out the rest of her meaningless speech.

As Ava and I head towards the rear of the starting line, I warn her, "I won't be offended if you run faster than me. Don't feel like you have to hold back."

She looks up mid-toe-touch. "Come on, Whitney. I'm the one who dragged you into this, so we're running together."

At least she can't say she *wasn't* warned when the race begins, and I creep ahead at a pace somewhere between a walk and a jog. I pick it up a little when I notice everyone passing me is old enough to receive Social Security benefits, but within minutes, my thighs start cramping, and phlegm clogs my throat.

"You good?" Ava asks, taking one effortless stride after the other.

"Sure," I say through a wet cough, "just peachy."

For the first third of the race, I alternate between walking and jogging, unable to maintain a continuous pace for longer than thirty seconds at a time. Knowing it's nearly impossible for me to keep up with Ava, I encourage her to speed ahead, while I blend into a crowd of powerwalking elderly women.

"Honey," one of the women says. One of her friends called her Carol before, or maybe Marjorie. Or was it Barbara? I'm not thinking straight. "What's wrong?"

"What's *wrong?*" I ask.

"No, no, I didn't mean it like that. It's just, the youth like you always have so much energy. Are you sick? Injured? Maybe"—she cups her mouth, leaning into my personal space—"*pregnant?*"

Pregnant? I glance down at the inconspicuous curve of my stomach and then back at her curious expression, waiting for the director to cut the cameras and let me know I'm being punked.

"Don't be so nosy, Marj," another woman chides, elbowing her. "Not every young person is athletic. You certainly weren't, for one."

Heat engulfing my cheeks, I bolt ahead, and the gothic-style buildings on campus all blend into each other. As much as I don't want to admit it to myself, those nosy old women are right.

I *should* have more energy.

I *should* be more athletic.

I should be more like my family.

My burning lungs and quads paint a different picture as I struggle my way through the next chunk of the race, but at least I'm finally running next to people close to my age. I allow myself to revel in the rare feeling of fitting in for once, but the experience is short-lived when I try to suck in a breath and my lungs barely expand.

Seeing stars, I stop to the side of the race and double over at the waist, my fingers digging into my knees as I finally spit out the phlegm clogging my throat. I need to sit down on the sidewalk and blink nearly five times before the world becomes less pixelated. In the meantime, two frazzled volunteers run towards me with a bottle of water, yelling questions I can barely hear over the pounding of sneakers against pavement.

I lose track of how many times I tell them I'm okay after chugging half the water bottle, but they don't let me get up. I tell them I *need* to when a runner decked out in purple invades my peripheral vision.

"*Whitney!*" Willow calls, making multiple heads turn my way. Despite being a lap ahead of me in the race, not a drop of sweat trickles down her foundation-caked forehead. "Whitney, oh my gosh, are you okay?"

"I'm fine, Willow," I grumble, looking anywhere but at her eyes. "Go finish your race."

"Oh no. I could *never* do that when you're clearly not okay."

She shoos the volunteers away and drops down next to me.

Looping an arm around my damp back, she tugs me closer to her, while the fingers of her left hand disappear into the side pocket of her shorts. I try to yank out of her grasp as she pulls out her phone, but I can barely blink before she's lifted it up into the air, thumb hovering over the camera's shutter button.

"Don't forget to smile!"

I try to pull away again, but it's too late. "You freakin' bit—"

She jumps up and disappears into the crowd of runners, grinning like she's already won the race.

—

By the end of the week, the soreness in my legs has faded to a dull ache, making my journey up the stairs to my last class of the day, AP Stats, slightly less arduous.

"As we've already covered, the chi-square goodness of fit test should only be used for categorical or nom—" Mr. Meyers whips his head to the doorway as I accidentally slam the handle into the wall, his thick brow furrowing. "Oh, it's you, Whitney. Glad you could join us."

"Sorry for being late, Mr. Meyers," I say sheepishly, clutching the strap of my old blue backpack.

"No, no." He waves me away to my seat by the window and turns back to the whiteboard. "Always a pleasure to have you in class."

This year's salutatorian, Isaac, folds his beefy arms across his sweatshirt and scowls at me as I plop into my seat, but I ignore him. I know he's still bitter that I was named valedictorian and not him, that being a recruited swimmer at Stanford doesn't make up for his GPA being a hundredth of a point lower than mine is, but it's how the system works.

Besides, can't a girl have *something* in life?

With no friends and surprisingly no enemies—apart from Isaac—in this class, I sit back and copy down the formulas I missed from the board, finally in my happy place. If high school had no social aspect to it, I'd never want to leave, but the buzzing of phones across the classroom reminds me exactly why my mental countdown to the last day is still going strong.

Thirty-eight days, I tell myself as I tap my phone screen, already knowing it's the newsletter: a recap of all the events and gossip at school every week, sanitized and packaged up in a format both students and parents alike can read. Trying to be a part of newsletter club at this school is like rushing a sorority; the more people you know and the more popular you are, the better likelihood you get the privilege of one of the fifteen coveted seats on it.

And the gatekeeper of those seats? Club President Willow Gerard, which means that every week I expect the worst from this email.

Across the classroom, people tuck their phones under their desks and scroll through the newsletter, trying to conceal chuckles at the subtle humor sprinkled into the mostly professional writing style. My heart skips a beat when Isaac glances at me before his lips curl into a smirk.

Maybe it's a coincidence, Whitney. I click on the email and feel more eyes land on me. Then, a few more chuckles and a full-blown laugh. Finally, the real killer—the comment from behind me: "If she thought she was getting a date to prom, I wouldn't count on it now."

"Unless in the last few minutes I've decided to leave my job and pursue my dreams of becoming a professional comedian, where I'll finally be able to profit off all the trauma this thankless profession has given me, there should be no laughter right now," Mr. Meyers says while still facing the board. A hush sweeps over the classroom, and he nods to himself while adjusting the lapels of his tweed jacket. "Thought so."

Bile creeps up my throat as I keep scrolling, and the tiny black font blurs before my eyes as I try to figure out where I made it into this newsletter. I scroll past the photo of me twice before I realize it *is* me, my face nearly unrecognizable.

"No," I whisper to myself, left hand concealing my face. *This can't be happening.*

Sure enough, the photo Willow took of us made it to the second page. With one eye closed, fire-red cheeks, my mouth hanging open, and my sagging tank top revealing the ugly sports bra I knew I shouldn't have worn, this photo makes every single picture of me on Mom's Facebook look like it could belong in a modeling portfolio.

But the real kicker?

The caption: *True Greene Hill values on display. Charitable senior Willow Gerard cuts her race short to help struggling fellow classmate Whitney Carmichael after she collapsed at her first-ever 5K.*

I look up, meeting silent stares. This is a joke. *Beyond* a joke. Everyone at this school knows Willow hates me, and that I despise her even more. The only reason she put this photo and caption together is for exactly the reaction she knew it would get, both from the students who'd laugh another laugh at my expense, and the naive parents who are going to read this segment and rave to her mother about what an angel her demonic daughter is.

Jaw clenched and seeing fire, I scribble in my notebook for the rest of class, ignoring the whispers around me.

By the time the bell rings, I've written *thirty-eight days* two hundred times.

CHAPTER TWO

One week into summer break, and I'm already bored.

I can't admit that to Mom and Dad, or they'll give me the typical self-righteous I-told-you-so lecture parents always give, and I can't tell that to Ava, since she's the reason I'm already bored. We've spent the past five days tanning outside by her pool, listening to music, and raiding her mother's organic smoothie stockpile. While I needed a bit of color on my milky white skin, I was hoping we'd do other things this summer besides fast-track skin cancer.

Luckily, today will be a change of routine. Poppy and Levi are finally visiting home after graduating from Columbia. They've spent nearly three weeks vacationing around the country, doing, in her words, "things Mom won't ever know about." I can't say they didn't *deserve* the break, as they're both textbook overachievers with respective plans to head to law school and medical school next, but I've missed having some life in the house.

Ava sits up on her lounge chair and pushes her long dark hair back with her Prada sunglasses. "Wait, where are you going, Whitney?" She taps her phone screen and looks up. "It's barely noon. We still have four more hours before the UV index drops below three!"

"Sorry, can't stay," I say, tugging my denim shorts up my oiled legs. They get stuck halfway up my thighs, and I give them a hard yank that nearly sends me stumbling into the pool. "The golden child and her boyfriend are coming home for lunch today."

"Poppy? Wow, I feel like I haven't seen her in ages."

"It's because you haven't. She avoids any chance to be around my mother."

"Like you do with your dad?"

"We're not rehashing that today," I mumble, not denying her claim, although she failed to mention that Dad also avoids any chance to be around *me*. "Try not to get too pretty in the meantime."

"Can't guarantee it!" she says, stretching out her lean, tan body as she waves goodbye.

When I come home, I waste nearly an hour showering and doing my hair and makeup, despite how pointless the effort is, given we're eating at home. As I restraighten the same strand of my puffy brown hair, I overhear Poppy with our dad downstairs. She's rambling on about how nice it is to be back, and every now and then I hear Dad laugh at something she says. I clamp down on my straightener harder as their laughter grows louder and only let the piece fall halfway down my back when I catch a whiff of something charred in the air.

A few minutes later when I join them, Poppy's sitting next to Dad on the couch and Levi is with Mom in the kitchen, offering her some unsolicited medical advice.

"Whit!" Poppy squeals, running over to squeeze me into a hug.

"Hey, Poppy." I squeeze her back, enjoying the sisterly

comfort. She angles her head down to look at me, while I tilt my head up, lessening the four inches that separate us in height. "Wow, you've got a really great tan."

She lets go and adjusts the strap of her floral blue sundress, probably by some organic brand I've never heard of. Paired with her blue eyes and wavy dirty-blond hair, it only adds to her effortless beauty. "I have the Florida sun to thank for that one—although it looks like you might be more tanned than I am."

"Occasionally the Connecticut sun pulls through," I laugh.

I follow her to the dining room, where everyone else has migrated. Before we eat, Dad pops open a bottle of champagne and fills everyone's flutes but mine. I hold my glass out, wanting to fit in for once and not be the baby of these gatherings.

"How have you two been?" Mom asks, bringing her flute to her lips.

Poppy smiles and wraps her arm around Levi's back. "We've been great. Neither of us has had as much of a break in years. Best of all, I even dragged this guy to his first-ever beach cleanup when we were in Florida." Levi squeezes her hand and forces a tight smile for the rest of us, clearly not as enthused by environmental protection as she is.

"We didn't expect anything less of you two." Dad takes a sip of champagne and eyes Mom. They share a puzzling smirk. "Don't you have something else to say?"

The four other people at this table look between each other knowingly, making me realize that while this lunch is about Levi and Poppy, maybe it's for *me*.

"Am I missing something?"

I lock eyes with Poppy, whose cheeks tint pink. Levi gestures for her to speak, smiling softly.

"Levi and I are engaged!"

My hand falls to the table and flings my fork into the air. It clatters against the hardwood, landing several feet away from me. Mom and I dive to the ground at the same time to pick it up and bash heads on the way up, each gripping one end of the fork. The impact feels almost concussive, duplicating both Levi and Poppy before me.

"Whitney, are you all right?" Poppy rises from her seat in a panic, but I wave her off and let go of my forehead. "Mom, are you okay?"

She winces and nods but excuses herself from the table. I stare up at the chandelier in sheer embarrassment, wondering how I always manage to ruin everything.

"I was a little taken aback." I try to laugh it off, realizing I've transformed the atmosphere from celebratory to plain awkward. "But congratulations, really. I'm so happy for you guys."

Mom returns from the kitchen with a tall glass of water, still rubbing her head. I try to utter an apology, but she brushes me off and turns to the newly engaged couple. "Let's dive into some of the details now that Whitney knows. When are you two planning on holding the wedding?"

Levi's brown eyes widen, and Poppy clears her throat, finding the hardwood floor a lot more interesting now.

"Towards the end of August," she says, her voice barely there.

Any trace of amusement vanishes from Mom's face, replaced with slight horror, and even my eyebrows furrow together. *Who plans a wedding in less than three months?*

Poppy continues. "Since we've been together for almost four years, there's no need to prolong the engagement. We never planned on an elaborate wedding anyway, so we can definitely make this work."

"But what about your future plans?" Mom asks. "You're already taking a year off before law school. Are you sure rushing your marriage won't make you want to hold off on those dreams forever?"

As much as Dad and I avoid one another, Mom and Poppy clash over *everything*. I can tell my sister knew this topic was coming because she grips her fork a little harder and closes her eyes to keep herself from making the snappy remark that's probably dancing on her tongue.

"Mom, we don't need to talk about this now," she says and forces a smile to preserve what's left of the mood. "Why don't we forget the wedding plans and enjoy the rest of the afternoon?"

Enjoy is a bit of an overstatement, as everyone goes back to shoveling in forkfuls of arugula salad. I pick at mine, my stomach rumbling as I try to pretend the wilted leaves are pasta. Dad distracts Poppy with a discussion of the stock market, which, for all my academic smarts, still makes no sense to me. When the two of them start throwing around percentages and funky acronyms all with *X*s in them, Levi sends me a bewildered look over the table, and I shrug in response.

"You know what, it's a beautiful day out," Dad says, like none of us noticed the sunlight streaming through the bay windows. "How about we finish up lunch and go play doubles?"

Poppy and Levi smile and nod, while I continue dragging an arugula leaf across my plate with my fork.

"What do you think, Whit?" Dad asks.

"Me?"

I look up and meet his ice-blue gaze, wondering if I've

entered an alternate dimension. I was sure he implied he, Mom, Poppy, and Levi would be playing, the usual lineup. A *no thanks* starts to form on my lips, before I figure there has to be a first time for everything.

"Um, sure, why not?"

What the hell did I just say?

"Great," he says and peeks at his gold-trimmed watch. "Let's head out in an hour."

I spend the better part of that next hour shoveling in the last of my arugula salad for some energy, unearthing a navy polo-style dress I bought back in eighth grade from my closet—right before those stubborn hips came in—and then nursing myself through a mild panic attack before half running, half waddling down the stairs and out the front door. I catch up with Dad, Poppy, and Levi in the driveway and make a beeline to Dad's BMW, but Poppy stops me in my tracks.

"Wait, are we taking the Range Rover?"

"We're walking to the courts on Maple Road," she says and charges forward, a pep in her step. "Our feet don't emit carbon dioxide like cars do, Whitney."

I comment that those courts are also *two and a half miles* away, but today, everyone is on the side of the climate and not me. With no choice, I drag myself behind the rest of the group and pluck at the stretchy material straining against my body every few minutes. By the time the blue tennis courts come into view, the back of my neck is slick with sweat and my calves ache from trying to keep up with Poppy's natural speed-walking pace.

Mr. Sullivan, one of our next-door neighbors, walks off the tennis court, pulling off his Ray-Bans. He flashes us a huge grin that shows off his veneers, which, paired with the Botox around his eyes, always make his smiles slightly off-putting.

"Jason, so great to see you!" he calls. He shakes hands with Dad, and his eyes land on me as I try to slink behind Poppy. "And is that Whitney? Almost forgot you had a second daughter, Jay! Happy to see you out playing with the rest of the family, kiddo."

I swallow and barely force back a nod as Dad chuckles along with him.

"I had to invite all the kids out to play for today's occasion." Dad slings an arm around Levi's shoulder and pushes him forward. "Say hello to my future son-in-law."

Mr. Sullivan grasps Levi's hand and gives it a strong shake that rattles his lanky body. "Congratulations, bud! You're marrying into a great family. Hope you love the outdoors, though."

My favorite *thing*. Dad and Poppy laugh along and continue the small talk.

Sneaking onto the court, I repeat Mr. Sullivan's remarks under my breath. Who *cares* what that senile man thinks? He should probably get his memory checked if he forgot I existed when I used to drive behind him every morning on my way to school.

Bouncing a ball up and down on the court, I wait for the conversation to end, the dull *thud, thud, thud* drowning out my bitter thoughts. Eventually, Poppy and Levi break free from Mr. Sullivan and agree to form one team, while Dad and I make the other. Before he can ask, I choose to be the returner's partner, figuring it'll be the easier position to play. I lie and tell Poppy yes when she asks if I remember the rules of the game, wanting to get this experience over with as quickly as possible.

"Ready?" she calls while bouncing the ball up and down on the court.

She makes a wide serve over to Dad, who darts to the side and returns the ball in one clean shot to Levi. Thinking he'll hit it back to Dad, I mistakenly relax my stance and barely graze the ball with the tip of my racket before it sails into the net.

"It's okay, Whitney!" Poppy says and flashes me a thumbs-up. "You got this."

The next time she serves, we manage to rally before Dad's racket misses the ball entirely. I try not to let my elation show that it's *his* fault this time that we're losing, secretly hoping he fumbles the next return as well.

As the game continues, and I manage to keep contact with the ball, I try to block out the thoughts telling me I need to beat Poppy and Levi, especially when she cheers when Dad and I finally score a point. For being better than me in all ways, she's never been cocky about it, but it doesn't mean I feel any less inferior.

Focus, Whitney, I remind myself, but when I look up, the yellow sphere is sailing towards my face, faster than my reaction time can save me. My racket clatters to the court, and I fall to my knees, cradling my throbbing eye in my hand. Dad rushes over to me and tries to peek at my eye, but I swat him away and keep my right hand pressed over my face. The pain is throbbing—no, *searing*—radiating up my temple and making my head spin.

"Goddammit, Poppy," he says, tugging his fingers through the roots of his graying hair. "Why would you hit the ball that hard?"

"I'm *sorry*, Dad!" she cries, racing to our side of the court. "I thought she could return it!"

He loops an arm around my back and helps me up. Probably thinking I can't hear him, he grumbles under his breath, *"I knew I shouldn't have invited her,"* and my already crumbling world becomes a pile of ash.

Levi shoves himself between Dad and Poppy as they begin bickering over my head. "Hey, do you feel dizzy or nauseated, Whitney? Have double vision?"

"I'm *fine.*" I pull out of his grasp and stumble into the net, clearly convincing him of my next words: "I can walk back home."

"Like hell you are," Dad says to me. "I'm getting the car."

He takes off faster than I've ever seen him run, and I watch him with my good eye as Poppy and Levi lead me over to a bench. When he's finally out of sight, hot tears drip down my cheeks. Poppy comforts me by lying that my eye won't bruise, while Levi showers me with more frantic questions, clearly preparing for his future medical career.

If only they knew that Dad's words hurt far more than a stupid tennis ball to the eye ever would.

———

I spend the next three days having a pity party in my room.

It's much less dramatic than it sounds; I come out for at least two out of the three meals of the day when no one else is in the kitchen and for my ritualistic thirty-minute showers at night, but other than that, my bedsheets are my new best friends.

Groaning, I roll off my mattress at eleven in the morning on the third day, by which even Jesus would've risen from the dead, and take my tangled sheets down with me. As I clamber to my feet, I catch sight of my face in the full-length mirror adjacent to my bed, grateful I'm seeing myself with both eyes. The injury is mostly cosmetic at this point, the reddish-purple bruise around my eyelid matching the one to my ego, partly the reason I've been unable to face anyone in my family.

I work through my embarrassment and anger by shoving my bedsheets into my hamper, followed by the pile of sweat-pants, T-shirts, and shorts practically rendering the hardwood floor invisible. Then I move on to organization, remembering the bottomless pits that are my desk drawers. It takes three yanks to even open the first one, blocked by a collection of miscellaneous awards I won in high school, mostly for academic excellence, community service, and various science and writing contests.

I stare at them until my eyes glaze over, trying to remind myself that I'm good at many things—none of which are athletic, of course.

I slam the door closed and move on to the next, finding a pile of used notebooks and a crumpled blue tote bag. It takes a moment to remember that I got this at the 5K I ran—well, tried to run—with Ava, and all those feelings of failure start suffocating me again. Exhaling some steam, I crack it open and fish out the first thing my fingers touch.

Ha.

Of course, it's the brochure for that fitness camp.

I give the blurb on the inside of the first flap a chance.

> *Discover Camp Campbell, a summer fitness boot camp for young women. Our five-week program, located at our scenic forty-acre campus in Coastal Connecticut, will leave you not only stronger and*

*fitter but challenged to your utmost capacity. With
individualized training, empowering mentorship,
and a work-hard-play-hard attitude, our camp is
right for everyone, no matter your fitness level. By
the time the program is over, our campers leave with
newfound confidence, skills, and lifetime friends.
Visit campcampbell.com today for more information
on how to change your life. Hope to meet you this
summer!*

I wince at how well basic advertising works on me, already
convinced this place could actually be somewhat life-changing,
until I flicker my eyes to the staff list. If going to a camp run
by Willow's mom wouldn't be bad enough, the namesake and
founder of the camp, Bob Campbell, is a former military officer
turned bodybuilder.

But what if this is my one chance to reinvent myself?

It would only be five weeks of my life during a summer
where I already have no plans, and if I'll finally feel like I fit into
my stupid athletic family, who cares if Willow's mom runs it?
It's not like Willow herself will be there when she could spend
her summer locked away in her dance studio or trying to salvage
what's left of her popularity now that high school is over.

"Fuck it," I mutter and pull my laptop down from my desk.

When I google the website and notice I'm only one day
away from the application deadline, I take it as a sign that I need
to apply, despite the voices in my head, which coincidentally all
sound like Willow, telling me I'll never survive a day there.

"*Whitney!* Time for dinner!" Mom calls as my cursor hovers
over the submit button. When I don't answer her, heart thumping

in my chest as I press down on my trackpad, her footsteps clatter at the bottom of the staircase. "I'm not bringing it up to your room this time, so you'd better come down."

I hit Submit at last and slam my laptop shut. "Coming, Mom!"

All the way down the stairs, my heart races like I've secretly committed a crime behind my parents' backs. I walk in a daze to the kitchen table, where Dad, Mom, and Poppy are already sitting before plates of chicken and rice.

"There you are," Mom says, handing me my plate. Her eyes land where Dad's and Poppy's do, creasing up slightly at the sides as she takes in the purple color. She manages to force out, "The bruise looks a little lighter than it was a few days ago."

"It really does," Poppy agrees. "Can hardly notice it."

We eat in silence for a few moments, broken only by the clink of cutlery against ceramic. Every few moments, I glance at Mom's and Dad's faces, debating whether to tell them. With how late into the night Dad usually works, it's a miracle I even have the two of them together for dinner, so I decide to go for it.

"I have an announcement," I say and wipe my mouth with a napkin. Poppy's eyes flicker to my face with curiosity, while Dad and Mom share an unnerved look. "I'm going to fitness camp this summer. Correction, I *applied* to a fitness camp, but if I get in, I'm going."

"A fitness camp," Dad says slowly, digesting it like a new vocabulary word. "As in a camp for . . . exercise?"

"Pretty sure that's the only definition of it," I quip, trying not to sound insolent. "The program is five weeks long, but the camp is only an hour and a half away from here, so I can come home easily if I ever need to. Plus, it's only for young women, so you don't have to worry about me getting caught up with any boys."

Dad opens his mouth to speak again, but Mom beats him to it, sending me a beaming smile. "That's a wonderful idea, honey. You were talking about wanting to find something useful to do this summer."

"But are you sure this doesn't have anything to do with what happened on the tennis court the other day?" Poppy asks. "I already told you that was my—"

"No," I say, my answer strong and firm. Despite how rash this decision seems, I've somehow never been surer of anything in my life. "I need to do this for me, Poppy."

And for everyone else who's ever doubted me, I don't say, stabbing into my piece of chicken breast and chewing the rest of my frustration away.

Week One

CHAPTER THREE

It feels almost unnatural that I'm standing in my driveway at seven in the morning, holding two bags of newly bought workout clothes (which I did try on before buying this time), with Mom and Poppy in front of me, still in their satin pajamas, ready to bid me a temporary farewell.

Poppy steps forward and draws me into a hug. "Good luck, okay? You always do everything you put your mind to, so you're not stopping now." I nod and begin to pull away, but she leans in and places her lips by my ear. "And go find yourself a hot guy."

"Highly unlikely," I say, knowing the only guaranteed male at the camp at this point is Bob. "But I'll try, Poppy."

Mom helps me load my bags into the back of my white Jeep. "Are you sure you don't want me to drive you, honey? You look a little on edge."

"No, no, I'll be fine. It might be helpful to have my car with me, anyway."

So I can get the hell out if I need to, I don't say.

"You'll have lots of fun, I'm sure of it. Keep an open mind and stay in touch with us all." Before she can turn away, I pull her into a hug and bury my face into her shoulder, inhaling her perfume like I used to when I was a kid. Mom ruffles the top of my head and sighs as she squeezes me tighter. "Now how do you expect me to ever let go?"

I laugh and pull away slowly, realizing that was my last goodbye, since Dad gave me a hurried kiss on the head an hour ago before hopping on a call with a business partner in East Asia. Maybe I could wave goodbye to Mr. Sullivan, currently watering the flowers by his mailbox, but he probably wouldn't remember me.

Exhaling, I hop into the driver's seat and configure my GPS. With my windows rolled down, I cruise down the freeway, blasting pop punk to drown out my doubts. Every now and then, I flicker my eyes to the screen of my GPS, debating whether to click Stop Navigation and floor it back home, but I can't give up before I've even seen this place.

Soon enough, I turn onto a narrow, gravelly road lined with pine trees and continue bouncing up and down in my seat as I drive for at least ten minutes before a wooden CAMP CAMPBELL sign appears. The two SUVs in front of me pull into a large chunk of asphalt paved over a clearing in the woods, and I figure this is where we should be parking.

As I turn off my car, two girls jump out of the black Lexus next to me. With long silky black hair, pouty lips, and doe-like brown eyes, they appear like extensions of each other, until I remember the proper term is "twins." Clearly, they're not too fond of one other, as the girl decked out in hot pink yanks her suitcase out of the trunk and marches off without looking back.

The other girl drops two chrome suitcases onto the ground and leans against the trunk, pulling out her phone from the pocket of her leggings. She has on the same two-piece workout set as her sister, only in black, which makes her stacked silver necklaces and earrings stand out more. As she scrolls and mind-lessly picks at one of her black acrylic nails, she seems bored and apathetic, the opposite of me.

"Hey, you," she says when I hop out of the driver's seat. "Do you know where we're supposed to go? It was in some email somewhere, but I didn't care about this shit enough to flag it."

"Uh, yeah," I say, nodding. I don't admit I've memorized the welcome message word for word last night during a panic spell over my decision to come here. "It's Room 100 of the Central Building. Which I guess should be somewhere in the center of this camp."

"Great, thanks." Without me asking, she walks over and hauls out my larger suitcase for me. "Martina, by the way."

"Whitney." I arch my neck up, asking, "Are you and the other girl—"

"Twins? Yeah. Unfortunately."

When we make it out of the parking lot, I get a better sense of this portion of the sprawling campus. There's a long paved road that must lead to the ocean, based on the tiny sliver of the horizon and the sounds of seagulls in the distance. To the left is a thick forest with trees so tall I have to crane my neck to see the tops of them. To the right lies manicured grass and various spread-out buildings, including two cabin-style dorms looming behind a glass-paneled structure, which stands in stark contrast to the rustic feel of this place.

Martina and I follow the lead of two other girls making their way to that building, and my stomach churns again with the reminder that I'm *here* and doing this. We walk through the frosted glass doors and find the inside of Room 100 mostly empty. Its endless brown hardwood floors and mirrored walls almost remind me of a dance studio, but I hope it isn't, knowing that I don't have a single graceful bone in my body. Twelve or so girls are sprawled across the room next to their bags, some engaged in lively conversation, while a few others are glued to their phones.

Martina plops down on the ground and uses her bag as a backrest. "What are you doing time here for? Parents send you away?"

I lower myself to the ground next to her, folding my legs into a pretzel. "Actually, I wanted to come." When she stares blankly at me, my cheeks tint pink. "Is that a strange answer or something?"

"Maybe for you, no. I'm only here because my sister, Adriana, wanted to be there for her friend, and my parents don't trust us to go places without each other."

"So you guys can snitch on each other?"

"Basically, yeah. Did you go to high school around here? I get the sense we're all from different parts of the state."

"No, I went to—"

Before I can answer her, someone's footsteps boom throughout the vast room, and we all snap our heads up to find a brawny man with a buzz cut and tan arms as big as some of our thighs. He sports a muscle tank and worn-out Timberland boots, and appears to be somewhere in his late forties. Although his headshot was a little more polished on the brochure, I think I can still confidently say this is Bob Campbell.

Oh, boy.

"Everyone, stand up," he barks, moving to the center of the room.

We all scramble to our feet, and we end up in a jumbled

circle, practically knocking each other over. A few girls yell at us to space out, and soon enough we form a decent line.

"That's good," he says, resting his arms behind his back. "I'm Bob Campbell, founder and owner of this camp. I'm a former military officer and certified personal trainer, and in recent years, I've won four bodybuilding competitions.

"This camp is no ordinary fitness camp. We work on a strict basis with set rules and policies. If you cannot follow them, we will personally ask you to take your sorry ass back home."

Adriana throws her bony arm up into the air. Bob looks annoyed but lets her speak.

"What are these rules?" she asks.

"One of them states 'don't ask any questions until I say so,' since you're so curious."

Her cheeks flush red, but she tries to act unbothered, shrugging her shoulders.

"Usually this is the part where I rattle off what you should be expecting over the next five weeks, but since your generation has the attention span of a housefly, I've put together a colorful slideshow presentation." He picks up a remote and points it towards the screen mounted on the wall behind him. "This morning you will complete a diagnostic fitness test. It consists of a run and a few static and dynamic exercises, designed for us to test your level of athletic ability—or lack thereof—and later to gauge your progress. Afterwards, you will meet your assigned trainer. Given our camp's small size, each of you will have access to your own personal trainer, which will permit you to complete more individualized workouts. We encourage you take advantage of this valuable opportunity."

Our own trainers? I can't tell if his tone is ominous or

encouraging, but I'm finally excited about something at this camp.

Bob continues through the slides, explaining some logistics of the camp, like what time we have to be up every day (early), how many workout sessions we will have to complete (a lot), and how much socializing we will be doing (also a lot). At least the photos of the dining hall look straight out of a five-star hotel's restaurant kitchen, making a few girls blow out a sigh of relief, me included. We also get one rest day a week on Sundays, to do whatever we want, as long as we're back on campus by nine p.m.

The door hitting the wall again cuts into the next part of Bob's speech, and in scurries a frazzled Cindy in olive green leggings and a sports bra. Trailing her by five feet, with her arms folded tightly across her front and head hanging low is . . . *Willow?*

I'd say exercise may have messed with my cognitive abilities, but I haven't even done any yet, so that is, in fact, Willow Estelle Gerard herself joining the far end of the row of girls. Of all the ways I expected her to spend her summer—dancing, shooting for some high-fashion swimsuit line, partying on a yacht on the Côte d'Azur—joining her mom and me here at Camp Campbell was very low on my list.

Is this some kind of sick joke?

"You okay?" Martina asks.

"Yeah, all good," I mumble, shaking my head.

"Sorry for the interruption," Cindy says, forcing a smile that reaches from ear to ear. "We were stuck in traffic."

Bob steps to the side so she can have the spotlight. "No, you're right on time. Go ahead, Cindy."

"All right, ladies, I'm sure Bob has already scared the living daylights out of you, but don't worry, he's just joking around."

From the grim frown on his face, Bob does not look like he was joking around.

"To start, my name is Cindy Norcross. I'm a former model and currently a Pilates instructor, wellness coach, and now camp coordinator here at Camp Campbell. I'm so honored and *delighted* to be working with Bob this summer to help you all grow as young women and unlock your hidden potential." She walks across the wooden space in front of us, her manicured fingers tented in front of her chest like she's giving a college lecture. "We know that you're all here for different reasons. Maybe some of you want to perform better in the sport you play. Maybe some of you want to finally learn how to run a mile. And maybe some of you are even hoping to find your new *besties*."

A couple girls snort at how forced the term sounds coming from her mouth, while all I can think of is how I do not plan on becoming *besties* with her diabolical daughter.

"Whatever your reasons, we all want you to make the same discovery: you are capable. Anything you put your mind to, with the right help and motivation, you can accomplish, and we are here to help you harness your inner power every step of the way."

A long pause ensues, and I figure maybe Cindy is expecting us to clap, but most of us stare ahead stone-faced, shifting awkwardly from side to side. Bob clears his throat and takes a step forward on the hardwood floor.

"Thank you, Cindy. That was very powerful." He hands her the remote, telling her, "I'll let you finish off the slides."

"Thanks, Bob. In between your personal training sessions,

you'll also be participating in team challenges once a week, which may range from running a race to completing an obstacle course."

She flips through a few slides consisting of photos from past team challenges. A couple girls currently wearing designer white sneakers wince at the mud-caked campers on the screen, their arms wrapped around each other for the photo.

They look like they became besties, at least.

"The goal behind these challenges is for you to interact with each other and develop important team-building skills, but rest assured, we will not be tracking your performance. Having fun is our primary goal here at Camp Campbell."

"Fun," Martina mumbles, shooting me a look. "Yeah, right."

I don't pay attention to the rest of the slides because I'm too focused on staring down Willow's face, half concealed by Adriana's perfect side profile. Her cheeks seem puffier than usual, like she's either been drinking or crying or both.

Wait, why do I even care?

"Now, if you have any questions, this is the time to ask," Bob says.

Adriana's hand shoots up, and I can tell Martina wants to slap her arm back down.

Bob sighs and points to her. "Before you ask anything, please tell me your name."

"Adriana. Now can I ask?"

"Of course, Adriana," he answers wryly.

"Do we get to choose our own trainers?"

Martina mutters a curse, covering her face with her palm. I stifle a laugh at her question, wondering how *that* is her biggest concern with all the torturous exercise awaiting us.

"You don't, but rest assured, Adriana, everyone who works at this camp is as pleasant as I am." Bob earns his first collective laugh from us, finally lightening up the stiff air of the room. "Any other questions? If not, go kick some ass."

Outside, we stand in a disorganized line again, and I get a better look at everyone. There are sixteen of us in total, and about four seem like they would get along perfectly with Willow, decked out in matching workout sets with styled hair and full faces of makeup at nine in the morning. Some others look like they'd get along better with me, in shorts and baggy sweat-shirts bearing those oh-gosh-what-did-we-actually-sign-up-for expressions.

"All right, girls, listen up!" Cindy calls from beside Bob, appearing about half his size from this angle. "This test will start with a simple one-mile run." *Simple?!* "Try your best to pace yourselves, as I know this might be new to some of you. We'll start with some stretches."

After a long warmup, half the girls hurry to assemble themselves at the beginning of the road, some even fighting for a specific spot. I stay towards the rear of the pack with Martina, knowing the only spot I *want* is the one as far away from the blond-haired demon as possible, hoping to avoid a repeat of the 5K race that's part of the reason I'm here in the first place.

We begin running, and I pace myself as bodies whir past me, knowing how deceptive the first couple of minutes can be. I take steady breaths in and out of my nose and keep my back straight, channeling every tried-and-true running tip I remember. For a good tenth of a mile, the strategy seems to work, allowing me to take a large stride past a petite curly-haired girl who's already huffing and puffing, but it's not long before I become her.

By the time Cindy announces that we've passed the quarter-mile mark, I am ready to pack up my belongings and head back home.

How do people run for *fun*?

"You can do it, girls! Keep going!" Cindy claps her hands above her head.

My legs shake and my heart nearly pops out of my chest as I force myself to keep running, my pace declining with every heavy stride. Martina has maintained the same rhythm as me this whole time, and I wonder if she does so out of sympathy for my glaringly unathletic self, like Ava would.

Just before the half-mile mark, my slow jog becomes a power walk, and all I need is a few judgmental old women for this experience to feel like that 5K all over again. I conceal my embarrassment with my game face as I half walk, half jog along with a few other equally inept girls. Towards the end, another wave of energy washes over me, or maybe it's frustration over how big a lead Willow has.

"Girls, the finish line is around the corner!" Cindy says, already at the end of the road.

Closing my eyes, I duck my head down and zoom ahead, despite my screaming calves and quads. I pass two other girls and cross the finish line, winded to the nth degree. I look up and lock eyes with Willow, who, for once, says nothing and turns away.

Cursing her out in my head, I shuffle away to Martina, who is busy gulping down a whole bottle of ice-cold water.

"Gosh, we actually survived." I heave a euphoric sigh of relief and bring my own bottle to my lips.

She holds up her hand for a high five, but we don't get to complete it, as Cindy's unwanted instructions come again.

"Unfortunately, there's a second half, girls, so join me back here once you've taken a moment to rest!"

Each of the rest of the exercises is more agonizing than the one before it, and when we're forced into a one-minute plank, my whole body gives out. I collapse onto the grass after twenty seconds, my arms nothing more than Jell-O. A few other girls are spent as well, and Cindy gives us her sympathies, which seem fake at this point.

If this is only the beginning, then there's no way I'm going to survive the next five weeks here.

CHAPTER FOUR

After an early lunch, Cindy and Bob herd the sixteen of us on a tour around the camp. It begins in the Central Building, which, besides housing various administrative offices, also has a yoga studio, small gym, and weight room on the first floor. Then, we trek down the sloping terrain behind the building, first to the dorms, then to the dining hall—all long cabin-style buildings—and to several multipurpose grass athletic fields overlooking a fitness and aquatic center.

"Geez, now I get why this place costs as much as a year of tuition at my Catholic school," Martina comments when we slip into the fitness center, a blast of arctic air hitting our faces.

The price tag did unnerve me when I first told Mom and Dad I wanted to come here, but then I remembered the thousands and thousands of dollars they poured into Poppy's athletic extracurricular activities growing up, and I felt a little less bad. Though . . . all I'll get out of this experience is a certificate of survival, while Poppy earned herself an Ivy League athletic career.

I'm unsure whether to laugh or cry at the contrast.

"All right, gals," Cindy says, raising her voice over the chatter like a teacher supervising recess. "After a tour of this fitness center, we're going to head back to the Central Building so you can grab your bags and move into your dorm rooms."

"I hope we can pick our roommates," I say to Martina as we walk, watching Willow in my peripheral vision. She tightens her arms over her purple tank top, eyes glued to the grass as she walks between Adriana and a model-like girl with short brown hair. "I don't want to get stuck with someone messy."

Or Willow.

"You're out of luck," she says. "I'm actually a resident slob."

"Oh no, I didn't mean—"

"Kidding, kidding," she says and makes me breathe a sigh of relief.

When we finally make it inside the trainer cabin, bags in tow, I realize the rustic wooden exterior gave no hint to the inside of this place, with gray wood floors, bright-white lighting, and eight sizable doors flanked on each end by a bathroom smelling of lemon disinfectant. Cindy alleviates my worries when she instructs us to divide ourselves into pairs and settle in.

"Let's take that room," Martina says, hurrying to the door at the end of the hallway.

I'm hit with rays of bright sunlight before I make out the two white twin beds, a large closet, and a beanbag on each side of the room. Still smelling faintly of paint, this room is nothing like the dingy triple dorm room I shared at the science camp I attended in middle school.

"Man, this is so much nicer than the dorms I toured at my college," Martina echoes my thoughts, walking to the window to check out the view. "*And* we get to ogle some shirtless hunks? Damn, maybe I should move here."

"What shirtless hunks?" I ask, whipping my head around.

"Oops, you just missed them. They headed into the other

cabin." She turns around and wiggles her eyebrows suggestively. "Think those are the trainers?"

My face pales. Embarrassing myself while exercising in front of my high school bully is one (very traumatizing) thing, but in front of someone I could potentially be attracted to?

Please, oh trainer gods, make mine an ugly woman.

We unload some of our clothes into our shared closet and fit the bedsheets we brought from home on our mattresses, hers black and red and mine baby-blue polka-dot. Right when we throw ourselves down on our beds to relax, Cindy manifests again, instructing us to meet her outside in a few minutes for a "fun" group activity. Whenever a person of authority utters that word, I know that whatever we'll be doing will be the exact opposite.

———

"Before you move on to meeting your trainers, I thought it would be great to hold an icebreaker," Cindy says, lowering herself to the grass. "Come sit, everyone."

I stare at the dirt-flecked blades, trying to angle myself in my head in a way where the grass won't touch the bare backs of my thighs, but it's impossible. Martina drops down without thinking and tugs me to the grass with her.

"Do you know that tall, skinny blond over there?" I ask.

She snorts, dropping her palms to the grass. "Do I *know* her? She is the exact reason I'm stuck here at this camp. Adriana is best friends with Willow. They've been dancing together since they were five—ballet and modern and all that girly shit." She notices the grimace on my face. "Do you know her or something?"

"From school, yeah," I say, shrugging, unsure what level of detail to divulge.

"It's okay to say you don't like her. I'm convinced no one does." She looks back at Adriana whispering something into Willow's ear that makes her chuckle. "Except for my sister, but she's never been the brightest pea in the pod."

"Before we begin," Cindy cuts into our conversation, "let's all take a few deep breaths and release some of the stress from our bodies." She closes her eyes and inhales until I can see her ribs through her tank top. "In and out, in and then out."

I fight relaxation the whole time, knowing Willow is only five feet away from me in the jagged circle we've formed. When we all open our eyes, I notice she looks away and mutters something to herself when Cindy smiles at her. In her (very rare) defense, I don't know how delighted I would feel if my mom was running this show, let alone with all that forced enthusiasm.

"Let's have everyone say their name, age, and the reason they decided to come to camp." Cindy points to a girl with dyed black hair cascading down her front in waves, sitting to the right of Adriana. "You're up first."

"Me?" she says and clears her throat. "Oh, um, I'm Noelle Rossi, I'm sixteen, and I came here because I'm trying to make varsity tennis this year." *Oh, great, another tennis player.* She pulls up her sleeve and flexes her bicep, small enough to wrap her thumb and pointer finger around it. "These babies aren't cutting it."

"We can definitely help with that," Cindy says and points to the model-like brunet sitting next to Willow.

"I'm Joanna Silva, I'm eighteen years old—just graduated high school a couple of weeks ago." A few enthusiastic nods pop up, as most of us seem to be around the same age. "Can

I be honest? I'm here because I need to get hot before sorority recruitment in the fall!"

Adriana perks up. "Oh my gosh, you want to rush? Me too!"

A lot more girls than I thought are into Greek life. Martina makes a quiet gagging noise.

Cindy visibly tenses and tries to mask her unease. "Remember, ladies, there are no wrong answers, only wrong mindsets. We'll make sure to work with all of you to deconstruct your beliefs about yourselves and work towards healthy, achievable goals." She pauses on the petite curly-haired girl I passed during our race, who freezes up when she notices every pair of eyes on her. "Go ahead."

She smiles weakly, tucking a curl behind her ear. "I'm Aspen Thomas, I'm seventeen, and I came here because I think I would look good with a six-pack." A strange silence bathes the outdoors, as I'm sure no one expected that answer from her besides Martina, who sends her a mischievous smile. "I mean, I'd like to get stronger. Yeah . . ."

"We certainly can help with that goal as well," Cindy says. Aspen nods through a wince, the light-brown skin of her cheeks tinting pink. Cindy finally pauses on her daughter, who seems more interested in the grass than this activity. "Go ahead, Willow."

"I'm Willow Gerard, I'm seventeen, and I came here because . . ." She looks up at her mother. "Well, I didn't have a choice, did I?"

Some chatter erupts around us, and I tune in to the whispered gossipy conversation from the girls to my left.

"Did you know Cindy's her mom? I bet Willow's a total nepo baby."

"Because her mom's a Pilates instructor?"

"No, dumbass, because her mom used to be a famous model. You should google her family. They're freakin' millionaires."

I know pretty much everything about the Gerard family, notably that it was her father, Alexandre Gerard, an investment banker from France, who was behind over half the family's fortune. He passed away from a heart attack the summer after freshman year, conveniently the same time Willow dialed her cruelty up to the max.

"Settle down, everyone," Cindy says to gain control of the group and avert everyone's attention from her daughter.

Miscellaneous answers ensue, some heartfelt, like breaking unhealthy habits or rebuilding strength after a sports injury. Others are more generic, like wanting to lose weight or to not waste another summer at home, which was the lie I was planning to tell before a girl named Kennedy took it.

Cindy finally gestures to me. "And last but certainly not least, Whitney."

I swallow hard, wondering if I'm reading too much into Willow's expression. Martina nudges my side, forcing me to look at everyone else.

"I'm Whitney Carmichael, I'm eighteen—also just graduated high school. And I came here because . . ." I trail off in thought, wanting my answer to be somewhat memorable. "Because what better to do the summer before college than get fit and make some nice lifelong *friends* along the way? Right, everyone?"

I send Willow the faintest smirk before turning to the rest of the crowd, wondering just how hard it would be to turn the tables.

Inside Room 100, Bob holds a tablet in one hand and a stack of papers in the other, discussing something quietly with a staff person. He looks up when we file in, chattering and laughing with each other, and his smile shoots down to a frown.

For someone who hates people so much, running a fitness camp for teenagers sure was a bright idea.

"Welcome back, everyone," he says, voice booming. We all fall silent, straightening our backs and spreading out into a straight line. "This is the moment you've all been waiting for as now is finally the time you'll meet your trainers."

"But to make things more fun," Cindy says, "you'll have to work a bit to find them."

That definitely sounds like some scam to get us to exercise more.

Cindy and Bob call out different girls' names and hand them each a sheet of paper. "These are the directions to locate your trainer anywhere on this campus. If you follow them, you should have no problem getting to the right place. Good luck, and make sure to enjoy the journey there!"

I stand outside the Central Building, reading the instructions that tell me to jog down the same road we ran earlier, but this time, to take a right at the intersection and to try to find a large wooden sign. Other girls are already speeding off in other directions, even more eager to see exactly who is going to be in charge of their physical torture for the next five weeks.

Since no one is chaperoning me, I walk the whole way, saving my energy for when I can finally spot the sign in the distance. Fifteen minutes later, it appears like my oasis in the desert, a jagged slab of wood reading, PRIVATE BEACH ENTRANCE. NO TRESPASSING. Sure enough, up a short hill, a scene of endless gray-white sand and dark rocky ocean water comes into view, and a cool breeze fans my face for me.

But who exactly am I looking for?

I trudge up the uneven ground and answer my own question a few steps later, making out a man standing a few feet from the shoreline. When I finish dragging myself up the sandy hill, I get a full view of him. His thick hair is medium brown and cropped short, which draws my attention to his eyes, which are either light brown or hazel and glint in the sunlight beating down on him. He's clearly no stranger to exercise; his arm muscles are defined, and the ripples of his abs peek through his shirt.

Yup, the trainer gods definitely didn't listen to my prayer.

"I guess I made it to the right place," I say, trying to break the thick ice.

He turns around and doesn't say anything for a moment, taking time to absorb every one of the features of my face, as if he's assessing what he has to deal with for the next five weeks. I give myself a free pass to do the same, losing myself in his angled cheekbones and smooth, full lips. While slightly awkward, when I look up, I can at least confirm that his eyes are, in fact, hazel.

"Good for you. I'm Axel Chandler. You are?"

"Whitney," I say, although I'm sure he already knows my name. I blurt the first thing that pops into my mind. "Is your name *really* Axel? Is your middle name Wheel or something?"

He doesn't seem entertained by my crappy attempt at a physics joke, a frown etched on his lips. "If humor is your style, I'm going to expect better over the next five weeks of being in each other's faces." He walks a bit closer to me, now a foot away, and I smell a perfect combination of clean salty air and cologne. "I'll start with the obvious. You hate any form of exercise but specifically, exercise in the outdoors, correct?"

"Um . . . yes?"

"Welcome to my territory, Whitney. The great outdoors. I prefer working outside with my trainees, so get used to good old-fashioned nature for now."

Also known as what I have been avoiding for the past eighteen years of my life.

I nod, trying not to display my horror. "Can I ask—can I *please* ask a question?" The more he talks, the less inviting he seems.

"Just so you know, we're not all Bob here. You can ask without asking in the future."

"Right, yeah, of course," I say. "My question: Are all our workouts going to involve running? Because to set the record straight, I'm a *bad* runner. Like maybe the worst runner you've ever encountered in your job as a trainer. Probably the slowest runner you've worked with as well." I clear my throat and rest my hands on my hips for a sense of finality. "I, quite simply, suck at everything athletic."

My rambling ends when I notice he's close to laughing.

"Then you're going to enjoy your time here," he says, the sarcasm not entirely clear, "because I *love* running."

Scratch that—it's as clear as day. Without warning, he takes off on the firmer section of the sand, calling out, "You'd better catch up!"

Tears prick the corners of my eyes—over the fact we're running or that he seems unrelenting, I don't know. All I know is that I have to force my legs from one side of the beach to the other with my body at half-charge. Actually, it's more like at one percent, and the charger is on the other side of the house, and I'm too lazy to get up from the couch to grab it.

Cursing my decision to apply to this godforsaken camp, I'm at his heels a miserable one minute later. I don't dare ask how long we'll be running, out of fear he'll double whatever he has in mind, but it turns out to be less than I thought.

"I'm impressed," he says. "Now stop."

I slow down and look up at him, squinting as the sun shines directly into my eyes. "B-but why?"

"Because you passed me. That was the point."

"The *point*? Do you believe you're supreme, and no one can surpass you?"

"It was more of a mental challenge than anything. I need to see how far you can push yourself."

"I see what you mean." (*I don't.*) "Now what?"

"We keep going."

"But I thought you said that was the challenge . . . ?"

"We're going to run through a few dynamic stretches now," he says, leading me away from the shoreline. "Let's start with ten walking lunges and ten jump squats."

I've never even heard of walking lunges, and need two different demonstrations to get it down. But by the fifth one, I understand why I never tried them before—my butt, legs, and even my *back* ache. The jump squats bring back suppressed memories from high school gym class, and by no surprise they're even worse than I remember them.

"My legs—ow, shit, they *burn*." I'm unable to complete more than seven without feeling like I'm going to tear a muscle some-where. I bend over and wince, rubbing my already sore quads.

"Can we lighten up a bit? It's only the first day." I throw in some puppy eyes to appeal to his emotions.

"They're supposed to burn," he says dryly, his thick arms folded over his chest. Eventually, the soft eyes get to him, and I realize why they're Ava's favorite trick. "You get a minute to rest, and then we'll continue the next leg of our run."

I take him by surprise when I fall to the ground, using my permitted break to its maximum. Ignoring the sand sticking to the backs of my thighs, I stretch out my legs and close my eyes, feeling the sun beat down on my face. For a moment, I forget Axel's even there.

"That's your minute," he says, after what feels more like five seconds. Towering above my head, he holds out a hand, but I don't take it and heave myself up. "Let's go."

I force my legs to keep moving down the next half of the beach, but my mind is screaming at me to stop and walk all the way home, knowing it's not *that* far from here. Axel tilts his head to the right and notices my flustered state, appearing apprehensive, as I doubt it's every day that he encounters someone breathless and drained after the most rudimentary of workouts.

He slows his pace down a notch but says nothing. My brain finds it oddly cute after the fourth time I feel his glance, but it's probably mush after all this physical activity anyway.

"You good?" he asks when we reach the end of the beach. "Need some water?"

"No, no, I'm fine. I just haven't"—I cough into my sleeve, feeling some phlegm clog my throat—"*run* at all in *years*. Apart from a 5K I tried and failed to run in April, the last voluntary run I can remember going on was sometime back in middle school." I rack my brain to be certain, recalling the innumerable times I avoided them in gym class or with Mom around the neighborhood. "Yup, definitely been that long."

"And you are now . . . ?" he asks, alluding to my age.

"Eighteen," I say, nodding once and then twice, "sadly." Even I'm realizing how tragic that sounds.

"Well, shit," he mumbles, looking away in thought. "This is going to be a lot harder than I thought, isn't it?"

"Now you're getting with the program," I joke, wishing I had a glass of champagne to toast to my impending misery and his soon-to-be perpetual annoyance. "We're not running back, are we?"

His face goes blank as he stares off at the rolling and crashing waves, making me realize I'm not the only one regretting all my life's decisions. "Give me a moment."

Dragging his fingers down the stubble on his jaw, he mumbles something indistinct and then returns with a smile that seems to pain him.

"How does walking sound instead?"

CHAPTER FIVE

The next morning at breakfast, I soothe myself with an everything bagel about the size of my head. I deserve it after making it through yesterday alive, although my calves have seen better days. Simply trying to get out of bed in the morning was an all-limb effort that resulted in me face-planting on the floor.

I look up and lock eyes with Aspen, clutching her tray and trailing her eyes across the occupied tables in the dining hall. Between blinks, I see myself any day Ava was absent in high school, my stomach sinking the way it would when I would find every table full and all eyes on me.

Once when I was a freshman, I was naive enough to take up Willow's offer to sit with her and her friends, fooled by her singsong, *Hey Whitney, come sit with us!* Still an unseasoned bully at that point, she spent the entire time poking fun at the size of my sandwich. Then she stuck her leg out and tripped me as I went to throw away the half I couldn't bring myself to eat, which I ended up wearing on my shirt for the next two class periods.

Now she sits at a table between Joanna and Adriana, swirling her spoon in a bowl of oatmeal and making eye contact with no one.

What a joke.

"Hey, Aspen!" Martina calls, waving her over. "Come sit with us."

Her brown eyes light up, and she advances towards us. I make room for her next to me at our small circular picnic table, hoping she'll become another camp friend.

"Gosh, I was so worried I was gonna be stuck sitting alone again," she says, setting down her tray with an omelet and a glass of orange juice. "How are you guys holding up after yesterday?"

Martina pushes away her empty plate and rests her fist under her chin. "Pretty good, all things considered. My guy's Ryan, and he's beyond chill. He spent half the session trying to get to know me or cracking stupid jokes. I gave him a pass on the humor because he's nice to look at." She wiggles her eyebrows.

"That's gotta be nice," Aspen sighs dreamily. "I'm stuck with this cynical blue-haired hippie who already told me not to expect to have any fun here." She looks at my face, noticing my grimace. "What about you, Whitney?"

"Let me put this out there. Is he hot? Hell yeah. Are we going to get through these next five weeks without wanting to kill each other? Hell no. I'm not sure what degree of athleticism he was expecting, but this"—I gesture from my head to my toes—"was *not* it."

"Come on, Whitney, you don't seem that bad at exercise," Martina says sympathetically. "It's not like you finished last place in our run yesterday."

"*Yeah*, because I thought that was all the *running* we were going to be doing. Are there actually people who enjoy that sport, or have I been living a lie all these years?"

We chatter for the next half hour while the dining hall slowly thins out. I offer to take our trays to the return area by the entrance, and on my way there, I pass by Willow's table. I do all I can to avoid direct eye contact with her, but I still feel the flames of her glare on my cheeks.

"Do you know that girl?" Joanna asks Willow, just loud enough for me to hear.

Willow shrugs. "Sort of, I guess."

Sort of?! I drive my teeth into my bottom lip to prevent myself from blurting out the truth, close to piercing the skin.

Before I make any bad decisions, I turn on my heel and pound the tile as I walk out of the dining hall. With Aspen trailing her, Martina catches up to me and asks what's wrong. I tell her it's nothing and begin the sloping march from the dining hall back up to the center of the camp, cursing as my thigh muscles constrict.

At this point, I'm convinced everything here is designed to make us exercise.

We make a pit stop at the Central Building, where a giant screen mounted on the wall of the hallway lists our schedule, including the where, when, and what of our workouts; the dinner specials; and the evening activities. I'm hoping this evening's game of capture the flag is optional, as I'm already dreaming of a nap, and it's only nine in the morning.

"Rope climbing," I read dryly.

"Kickboxing," Martina says, clasping her chin. She squints and adds, "That one does sound kind of cool."

Aspen stands on her toes to even see the screen. "What's *miscellaneous cardio on the beach* supposed to mean?"

"It means you try not to die," I say, giving her shoulder a comforting squeeze. "Best of luck."

I'll probably need it even more than you, I don't say as we all burst into laughter again.

Halfway through my trek across camp, I smooth out the lines in my black T-shirt and readjust the angle of my high ponytail, oddly preoccupied with my appearance for a rope climb in the middle of the woods on a humid day. Maybe I would care less about how I looked if my trainer couldn't pass for a part-time fitness model, yet another wrench thrown into this experience.

It's not like he's ever going to look at you that way, that cynical part of my subconscious tells me, and I don't disagree, knowing I'm about as inexperienced and awkward as it gets around the opposite sex.

With a little more trudging, I spot Axel on the opposite side of the road leading up to the beach, leaning against the trunk of a tree with his arms folded across his chest. I try to even out my erratic breathing before I walk up to him and shoot him a tight smile.

"Hi. Hope you're doing well."

In response, he presses his lips into a firm line and nods. "Sleep okay?" I nod, recalling my dreamless eight hours. "You're gonna need it."

He jogs up the grass without saying anything, beckoning for me to follow him. The new day brings more energy, but my strides are still heavier and far shorter than his are.

"You can do better than that!" he says as he approaches a clearing in the woods.

I force myself to his side. "Do you *really* know, though? I'm thinking these sessions will go a lot more smoothly if we share the same low standards for me, Axel."

He cracks a white-toothed smile at my remarks, finding me entertaining for once. "Whitney, while my mental perceptions of you are—well—not what comes out of my mouth, I wouldn't be your trainer if I kicked you while you were down." He pauses and stares off into the distance. "You know what, I'd get fired if I did that, but we can pretend it's because I'm nice."

I let out a belly laugh, surprised I'm not even offended. There's a certain complacency that comes when you know you're terrible at something, one that fuels the rest of our jog through the woods.

"Stop for a moment," he instructs, and I do, trying to catch my breath. "Now follow me."

We step onto a longer patch of grass, and the prickly blades tickle my ankles, sending a shiver down my spine. I have to remind myself it's just nature.

Another prick.

Ew, ew, ew.

After a few more minutes of trudging, I make out wooden poles above my head, anchoring several thick ropes looming above a padded area of ground. A few feet away from the ropes are wooden blocks, resembling seats of some sort, but I'm unsure if that's what they are.

"I don't have to climb those ropes . . . right?"

Axel walks towards me and stands about a foot away from my chest. "We could try this, and maybe you might even find it fun, or we could go on that one-mile run I had in mind. Your choice, Whitney."

"This." The reply crosses my lips in seconds, almost as fast as it takes me to get to the foot of the rope. I drag my hand down the material, noticing it's a lot smoother than I thought it would be, and then crane my neck to eye the top. "Would you catch me?"

"What?"

"If I fall," I say, running my hand down the rope again. A mischievous smile overtakes my face as I add, "I doubt your camp is in the mood for a lawsuit."

"Catch you," he muses. His eyes narrow as he continues, "Yes. You can spare me the my-dad-is-a-lawyer-and-will-sue-your-ass speech."

After this blunt reassurance, he demonstrates his technique, while I stand several feet from the rope. Axel springs up and grabs the rope, the muscles in his back visibly tightening as he pulls his knees closer to his chest. Hooking the rope around one foot, he steps on it with the other and extends his body, dragging himself upwards. He reaches the top in what feels like three steps. And then he stands in front of me again, his height and athleticism mocking my inept figure.

"What do you think now?"

"Yeah, that was great. You have impressive form—beautiful even."

"No. I meant what do you think of rope climbing. Wanna give it a shot?"

Mortification consumes me, evident in my red-hot cheeks. "I would give it a try, if you could show me how you did that"—I wave my hand in a circle in the air—"that levitating sorcery. Something's not clicking."

"Come closer to the rope," Axel commands, trailing behind me. I tilt my head up to stare at the top again, realizing it's not *that* high up, but I doubt I'll feel the same when I try to drag my feeble body up a few feet. "Grab it, one hand on top of the other, and get a good feel for the material."

I do as he says. "Now what?"

"Let go, jump, and try to hold yourself up. No need to climb up yet."

I back up about a foot and spring upwards. I latch onto the rope with one hand, while the other misses entirely. I'm too weak to bear my weight with one hand and stumble forward, catching myself before I fall on my face.

"Try again."

Cheeks even hotter now, I give it another shot and manage to hold on with both hands. He instructs me to stay up there for several seconds, likely trying to get a feel for my upper body strength, but the joke's on him. This might be the easiest exercise here so far, as my arm strength is stellar after four years of carrying around twenty-pound textbooks all day.

"Tired yet?"

"Nope," I say, swinging my legs a little for entertainment. I quicken my rhythm. "Wow, this is almost fun."

"Come down then," he says, allergic to my amusement. He gestures for me to stand at the base of the rope again and pulls the wooden cube forward. "Sit down here."

Damn, finally an exercise I can get with. Without hesitation, I slide to the middle of the seat and dangle my legs, relatively comfortable if not for the hard surface under my butt. Looking up, we lock eyes, and I notice his are a mesmerizing olive green in the sun. I can't stop staring until he speaks.

"All good?"

"Yeah, yeah. Wait, why am I sitting down again?"

"It's easier to practice the proper footing from this angle," he says and stands by my side, about half a foot away. "Grab on to the rope again and push your knees up a bit."

I hesitate, realizing how oddly suggestive this form sounds, but I remind myself he's been appropriate with me this whole time. Doing as he says, I watch him bend down a little and grab the rope by my feet.

"May I?" he asks. I nod, despite my growing discomfort—not even because of this position, but because one wrong move could make this scenario either oddly sensual or awkward as hell. Axel remains professional. "Now, I'm going to show you how you should wrap the rope around your feet for maximum stability when you climb."

He runs the rope down the outside of my right shin and lets it slide under my shoe before threading it over my left shoe. His thumbs brush my ankles as he pushes my feet together, and a shiver runs down my spine.

"Try lifting yourself up now, and keep your feet together." I begin to pull myself up a little but stop, worrying that I'll lose my footing and tumble down again. "I'm still going to be down here, by the way."

Slightly reassured, I force out a breath and yank myself up from my sitting position. With my legs fully extended, I keep the rope between my legs and feet, noticing how it creates a flimsy base.

"All right, good. Lower yourself down by spacing out your feet a little." Although there's barely any distance between me and the ground, he lets his hands float protectively in the air and gently grasps my legs as I return to my sitting position. "Let's try it again and see if you can complete one pull."

While climbing now sounds less abstract in theory, I'm not surprised when it takes multiple tries for me to even move a couple feet up the rope. Axel tries to offer some words of encouragement, even complimenting my arm strength from before, but

I underestimated the energy and willpower it takes to do more than just hang in the air motionless.

"Oh crap, oh *shit*." I lose my grip and sail to the ground after trying another pull.

Axel grabs my waist, adopting a tight and protective stance that stabilizes me on my feet, and leaves his hands there until the hold becomes awkward—to him. On the inside, my heart flutters. I can't help but swoon at how invested he is in my well-being, even if he is paid to do exactly that.

We take a break, and I sit down on one of the wooden cubes, propping up my leg. I take my hair out of my sagging ponytail, letting it flow down my back. For a second, it feels like Axel gets lost in the thick locks before he blinks and looks away.

Maybe I made that up.

"I'm sorry if I'm taking way too long to get all of this," I say, breaking the quiet after a moment. "At this point, it's not you; it's *me*." I wince, sounding like a character in a '90s rom-com.

"Whitney, come on, you don't have to keep justifying yourself," he says. "I'm not one for the sappy stuff, but the journey of a thousand miles does begin with a one-mile run."

"Isn't it 'a single step'?"

"To you," he says.

He stands before me, holding out a welcoming hand. I take it for once and realize that there might be some light at the end of the tunnel: the long and winding one-mile tunnel, that is.

CHAPTER SIX

My eyes open and take in the dim sunlight streaming through the window behind my bed. To my right, Martina is still fast asleep, the covers yanked up past her chin.

I sit up and fish for my phone on my side table. *Six thirty in the morning?* The earliest I've ever gotten up without the blare of my alarm in the summer is around eight. Since I'm awake, and there is no way I can sleep with all this sunlight shining in my face, I get up and head to the bathroom to get ready.

On my way there, I make out two figures through the window in the door leading out of the building. Drawing closer, I find Axel and a female trainer holding a gym bag walking towards the back entrance of the Central Building. I can't see her face from here, only her long shapely legs in her athletic shorts. They leave enough space between each other that I question whether she's a friend, a girlfriend, or just a coworker.

They disappear into the building, prompting me to push open the door and step outside. When I consider following them and finding out for myself what's going on, I try to snap myself out of it, reminding myself the personal life of the trainer I've known for only a couple days *should* be none of my business, but that's not a strong enough conviction to keep me inside.

I sneak through the back entrance of the building and make out a steady series of *boom*s in the distance, like someone punching something repeatedly. I walk in the direction of the sound and press myself up against the wall before peeking through the half-open gym door.

Axel pounds the life out of a punching bag, using blows that could knock someone out cold in an instant, and I hold my breath in awe. His gray cutoff shirt is soaked in sweat, and a heavy beat blares in the background, fueling the force in every punch. Leaning against the padded wall across from him is that same female trainer, her blue-streaked hair now down and framing her face. She tips her head up, and I get a good look at her angled cheekbones and narrowed eyes. I realize she's not just the cynical blue-haired hippie Aspen described as her trainer.

She's also the girl who practically shoved the camp brochure down my throat back at that 5K.

"Damn," she says, "you've definitely still got it in you, Axel."

He stops and slides off his gloves, chest heaving up and down as he tries to catch his breath. Taking a few steps forward, he dips his head down and leans a hand against the wall beside her head, that domineering aura of his making my stomach erupt with some very unwelcome butterflies.

"*Still* got it in me? I never lost it, Isla."

There's this odd tension between them as they look into each other's eyes, his heavy breaths a contrast to her tight-lipped smirk. It almost feels like I've stumbled into an intimate moment, even if it's far from it, and a pang of jealousy grips my heart, as delusional as the thoughts telling me that should be *me* against that wall.

When Isla leans her face in, I dash to the exit, unsure if Axel finding out I was stalking his workout or that I saw him kissing his supposed girlfriend would be more embarrassing.

"There you are!" Martina exclaims as I walk back into our room, still spooked. She's already made her bed and gotten dressed, having donned black shorts and a sports bra. "Where were you?"

"Took an early-morning stroll."

Who uses the word stroll, *Whitney?*

"Wow, look at you being all healthy," she laughs. "Breakfast is being served soon. Then it's off to our first *team challenge*."

I almost forgot about those, still not fully understanding what they'll entail. At the very least, competing in a group sounds better than doing so individually, as I'll have other people to rely on to pick up the slack. So far this week, I've had my fair share of embarrassment trying a plethora of new workouts, including trail running, hill sprints, and the stair climber during yesterday's rainy-afternoon session—which is apparently *not* the same thing as the elliptical.

Sue me for not knowing, I guess.

I'll need an extra shot of energy to get through the team challenge today, so I pick up a heaping bowl of oatmeal and a cup of coffee for breakfast. While I'm on my way to the table where Martina and Aspen are waiting for me, a comment pops up from behind my shoulder.

"Isn't that, like, a really huge bowl of that stuff?"

I turn on the heel of my high-top sneaker, finding Noelle wrinkling her nose at my breakfast. I don't remember when she migrated over to Willow, Joanna, and Adriana's table, but she doesn't seem particularly welcome, given the three inches of her leg hanging off the bench.

"The oatmeal here looks pretty gross," Joanna says, picking up her slice of avocado toast with long delicate fingers. Through a mouthful, she adds, "But I don't see why her breakfast is literally any of your business."

"Yeah," Adriana says, bumping Noelle another inch off the bench. "If anything, you should be more worried about not dragging your team down at the challenge today. Some of us care about winning."

Noelle's eyes widen, like she expected Joanna and Adriana to concur with her. Surprisingly, Willow, the queen of remarks like Noelle's, doesn't utter a word to me and continues chomping down on her piece of toast, not even bothering to wipe the crumbs off her lap. It's a funny contrast to her comment back in sophomore year, still ingrained in my head like she yelled it out to me yesterday.

Guys, maybe if Whitney stopped eating everything offered in the cafeteria, she could actually run. Have fun taking last place in gym class today, Whit! We're rooting for you!

"Guess we'll see how we perform in the team challenge today when your stomach is grumbling and mine is not," I snap back, surprised the remark even escapes my mouth so easily. "See you later."

Rage fuels my steps back to my table, but I try to plaster a neutral expression on my face when I approach Martina and Aspen.

"Was my sister bothering you?"

"No; Noelle," I say, dropping my tray down and letting it clatter. "She made some dumb comment."

"I should still go tell her off. Her sixteen-year-old ass needs to be put in its place."

"No, don't." My palm floats into the air to tell her to stop, an almost defensive reaction. "Honestly . . . I'm used to her kind from high school. That was hardly a scratch." I down a gulp of my coffee to drown out my emotions before nearly spitting it out in Martina's face at the bitter diesel taste that hits my tongue.

"I hated high school," Aspen says, head slumping against her hand. Dark ringlets fall over her face, concealing her doe-like brown eyes, and as she brushes them away, Martina tracks every one of her movements. "I was always known as 'the quiet one,' but I didn't like anyone enough to talk to them. It got so bad that one time one of my teachers pulled me aside after class and asked if I needed special accommodations for my 'selective mutism.'"

"Quiet isn't even a bad thing," I say, lifting a spoon of my cinnamon oatmeal to my lips. Tuning out the gossipy conversation coming from Willow and friends' table, I force it into my mouth. "Shutting up could actually serve a lot of people well in this world."

"Like that godforsaken woman behind you," Martina grumbles.

"GOOD *MORNING*, LADIES!"

Cindy's natural tone, enough to drive all microphone manufacturers out of business, erupts behind us. She climbs up onto one of the empty tables, looking like a glow stick in a highlighter-yellow sports bra and matching pair of biker shorts.

"I hope you're all eating well and excited to take on a new day. Today we'll be meeting outside the Central Building at nine thirty sharp for your first team challenge. Who's excited to get moving and make some new besties?"

A disproportionate degree of amusement overtakes me from the way Willow sinks down into her chair and covers her entire face as snickers break out from the table behind her.

Feels kind of nasty, doesn't it, bitch?

Cindy hops down to the ground and picks up a tote bag. "When I call out the members of your team, come up here, grab a T-shirt, and then sit down at a table together and try to get to know each other better." She sets out the stack of T-shirts on the table behind her, four different neon colors of the rainbow. "Up first is Team Green: Martina, Aspen, Whitney, and Willow!"

When I hear the dreaded two syllables of Willow's name, I consider staying seated in an act of protest, but Martina and Aspen are already up and walking. Biting down on the insides of my cheeks, I drag myself to Cindy's table and reach for a neon-green Camp Campbell T-shirt. Willow holds her hand out at the same time and pulls back for me to grab one first, and I notice the way her mother's eyes light up with a hopeful twinkle.

She may be the poster woman for oblivious parenting, but even she must have gathered that Willow and I can barely stand each other. But if she placed me and her on the same team hoping the forced proximity would finally prompt Willow to apologize to me—or better yet, me to forgive *her*—then she needs to rip those rose-colored glasses right off her face.

"Green is definitely your color, Whitney," Cindy says as I hold up the T-shirt to my front. "Brings out those beautiful eyes of yours."

"Thank you." I fidget when I feel the heat of Willow's gaze

on the side of my face. "I usually go for blue, but this is a nice change of routine."

Aspen and Martina grab their T-shirts and turn to Willow and me, standing three feet apart. "Do you guys want to sit—"

"Mom, I'm not feeling well," Willow cuts in. "Can I go back to my room and lie down before the challenge starts?"

Cindy forces a tight smile, placing a hand on Willow's shoulder, and lowers her voice a notch as she tells her, "Willow, honey, you can't use that excuse every time."

"Do you *want* me to throw up everywhere? I feel *sick*, Mom."

I press my lips together, eyes widening in shock, but Cindy doesn't chastise her, and I have a feeling it's not because they're in public. When Willow stalks away, Adriana breaks away from her table and chases after her, with Joanna following a few seconds after. The dining hall erupts with confused chatter and gossip.

"Damn, all that because she didn't want to sit at a table with us." Martina looks between me and Aspen. "Are we really such bad company?"

I shake my head, releasing the inside of my cheek from the snare of my teeth. "We're not the bad company, Martina. *She* is."

—

The sixteen of us stand outside in an uneven circle by the main road, with no Bob around to police our formation, some girls laughing and others looking disgruntled, like they'd rather be in a six-hour math class than here.

Something much closer to a scowl than a smile crosses my face as Isla jogs to the front of the group, Cindy's helper for the day. She jumps onto a tree stump, her tanned and defined legs appearing a mile long in her elevated position. Finally, I get a close look at her face, realizing that the streaks in her hair are the same color as her eyes, the kind of blue that turns nearly translucent in the sun.

Begrudgingly, I admit she's kind of pretty.

"Aren't you guys an enthusiastic group," she says, dragging her eyes down a line of frowning campers and pausing on my face. "Our challenge today is a simple one-mile run down this road, like you completed in the diagnostic test." There's that damn word *simple* again. "Only this time, each team will be running as a group, and we'll be tracking your mile times. The team with the lowest average mile time wins the challenge."

"What do we win?" a voice asks from behind me. *Adriana.*

"Kind of a bummer," Isla says, eyes creasing up with a tight, wry smile, "but there's no prize this time. Bragging rights only." She looks down at her tablet and calls out, "Team Green! You're up first."

It takes several minutes for the four of us to warm up and situate ourselves behind the spray-painted starting line, me on one end of the row and Willow on the other. Surprisingly, I have no qualms about running, considering the near-marathon I ran this week with Axel. I *am* worried about another repeat of last race, knowing Willow could've only improved this past week with her own trainer.

"On your marks, get set, *go!*" Isla says.

We dash from the starting point, each zeroed in on the road ahead of us. I overtake Aspen easily with the four or five inches I have on her in height, keeping me level with Martina. Knowing just how long a mile can feel when running, I remind myself there's no point in expending all my energy now, but

I can't tamp down on the resentment bubbling in my chest when Willow strides ahead of me, a whir of wispy hair and lean dancer legs.

"Okay, guys," Martina says, her long black ponytail slapping her back as she runs, "who's going to take one for the team and put in some effort?"

"Wouldn't it be better if we all picked up the pace a little?" Aspen asks, already huffing through her words.

"Sure, but two fast runners and two slow runners averages out the same as four medium-paced runners." We arch our necks and squint, all trying to make out a familiar blond head. "And one really, *really* fast runner makes up for all of us." She cups her hands around her mouth and calls out, *"Go Willow!"*

"What the hell, Martina?" I hiss, momentarily forgetting the cramping in my thighs.

"She's on our team, Whitney. I know we're not supposed to like her, but let's at least use her skills to our advantage."

As much as I don't want to admit it, Martina is right. This is the only time where praying on Willow's downfall will do me more harm than good, so, fighting every logical bone in my body, I cheer Willow on with Martina and Aspen—only this once, though.

The thought of inflating her ego again riles me up so much I clench my teeth and press forward. The world blurs together, green, then blue, then blond, and soon enough, Willow is mere paces ahead of me. Some supernormal strength builds in my legs, absent whenever Axel and I run, and I use my momentary abilities to overtake her by several feet, not even looking back once.

For the next leg of the race, I enjoy my lead, even staring off at the greenery while I run. But right as we hit the halfway point, I can barely breathe, and I know I'll have to half walk, half jog my way to the end. In a blink, Willow is a dot in the distance, and I curse to myself.

Towards the end of the race, I regain some strength and manage to sprint the last few paces to the finish line. I look up and lock eyes with Axel, who, based on the stopwatch in his hand, has been charged with tracking our mile times.

"Not bad, Carmichael," he says, nodding tightly. My heart flutters at his approval, even if his words are hardly a compliment. He jerks his head to the side. "Water's where Willow is."

I'm breathing too hard to even form a complete sentence back, so I nod and follow Martina across the grass to where Willow stands by a maple tree, chugging a whole bottle of water. Out of sight from Axel, who apparently may believe I'm somewhat competent, I drop down to the grass and lean back on my hands, grimacing as the strain of the race catches up to me.

"Here, take this."

When I open my eyes, Willow hands me a cold plastic water bottle.

"What?"

"What do you mean *what?*" When she notices me still eyeing her outstretched arm with suspicion, she huffs and drops her hand. "I don't know how to poison water in case that's what you're worried about. You looked like you were about to pass out, so I figured I'd offer you some H_2O."

I freeze. Is she just being . . . *nice?* It seems almost impossible after the spectacle she made of me at that 5K race, but when I give her a few more moments, and a nasty remark doesn't roll off her lips, I push myself up to my feet and take the bottle from her.

"Thanks," I say and pause before adding, "for not poisoning my water, that is."

She cracks the smallest smile before stalking away, and for some stupid reason, I take that as a win.

Week Two

CHAPTER SEVEN

Sunday is our rest day, and I take advantage of the change in the routine, snoozing my alarm until eleven in the morning. Wincing as my eyes adjust to the brilliant sunshine streaming through the open curtains, I turn to Martina's bed and find it empty with the covers pulled taut.

My phone vibrates on my side table, and I pick it up.

Martina: At the beach with Aspen, feel free to join whenever.
Whitney: Meet you there in an hour.

Scrolling through the remainder of my notifications, I find a check-in text from Ava, followed by a rant about the three Persian weddings she's had to attend in the past week, and then a missed phone call and FaceTime call from Poppy. Realizing I've neglected almost everyone in my personal life over this past busy week, I call Poppy back first, needing a taste of home.

Her face appears on the screen, and her normally bright eyes droop slightly at the corners. "Whitney!" She waves at me through the camera. "I'm so happy you answered. I've been dying to talk to you."

"Hey! What's going on? Wedding plans?"

"You bet. Levi's parents are visiting from New York to help with those."

"Gosh, that bad?"

She exhales and drags her fingers through the roots of her dirty-blond hair. "Let's just say if we were living in *The Purge*, our mom and Levi's would have already killed each other without question. You know, as if I needed *more* problems with Mom."

"What do they act like around each other?"

"Let's see. Indirectly insulting each other's looks, claiming each wedding idea the other comes up with sucks—even if both would've liked it otherwise—and then waging a war over whose child is more perfect? Did neither of them get the memo that we're twenty-two, not twelve?"

"Maybe they're the ones acting like twelve-year-olds," I say, cringing at the mental picture. "What about Levi's dad?"

"Dave? He and Dad act like they're long-lost friends. Dad showed him the golf course the other day, and they've spent nearly every afternoon there. It's either that, or they're trying to avoid their wives. Don't blame them at this point."

"That's good, at least," I mumble and decide to change the subject from Dad. "You know what, I feel bad I'm not home to help with any of the planning. This is such an important point in your life."

"And in your life, Whitney," she says, taking me aback. My sister has always been levelheaded, but I'm surprised she doesn't draw the line at her wedding. "Do you really think I'd keep you from finally achieving your fitness dreams to help plan the elaborate wedding I don't even want? If it were up to me, I'd hold it in a damn barn with twenty guests."

"Then do that. It's your wedding, isn't it?"

"Sure, yeah," she mumbles, almost like she can't believe it. "But Mom would never go for it, so I should stick to something traditional."

"Don't even try to talk to me about traditional." Finally mustering up the energy to roll out of bed, I stagger a couple steps forward and rub my sore calf. "I'm here at a fitness camp run by a WWE-wrestler-slash-military-officer and a wellness freak who also happens to be Willow Gerard's mom. Running on a treadmill? Who needs to do that when you can climb a rope in the middle of the woods while your Instagram model of a trainer makes sure you don't die? Oh, and don't forget, not only do I have to deal with the same type of people who made my life a living hell in high school, I also can't go home every afternoon to escape them."

"Whitney, this is kind of a lot to unpack."

"Tell me about it," I say, turning the camera around so she can catch a look at me in the mirror. My hair sticks up in three directions, my shorts have ridden so far up my thighs they look like underwear, and the sunburn on my nose from that rope climbing session is finally starting to peel. "Go plan your barn wedding. It can't be harder than this."

"Wow. The *last* thing I expected after only one week at this place was for you to become my life coach." She leans into the camera. "Do elaborate more on the hot trainer, please."

"If you're hoping there's a chance he becomes my boyfriend, please lower your expectations."

"Weren't *you* just being the optimistic one?"

"Yeah," I scoff, "for you. Still working on me." I adjust my hold on my phone and make out the tiniest indent in my triceps in the mirror that I could swear wasn't there last week. "But to answer your question, he's tall and broad, definitely over six feet. A perfectly angled face and hazel eyes that turn an entirely different color in the sun."

"Aren't those all eyes?"

"Maybe," I mumble, "but his are prettier."

"Aw, Whitney, you're falling already." She flutters her eyelashes, and I resist the urge to punch her through the screen. "Don't worry, I have room for you to bring a plus-one to the wedding."

"*Goodbye*, Poppy," I say, not feeling bad when I hang up on her, especially when I recall how much laundry I've put off.

I don't even bother changing out of my satin shorts and old high school T-shirt as I lug my hamper down the hallway to the laundry room. I mull over my conversation with Poppy as I walk, about her faith in me finding a boyfriend. Whenever I'd start agonizing over my single status in high school, I'd remind myself that I was too busy for a boyfriend, between all my AP classes, running multiple clubs in the afternoons, and volunteering on the weekends.

But the truth was no guy ever, from my innocent kindergarten days to my dateless senior prom, expressed an interest in me. If only I knew if it was my looks, personality, or something else that explained my nonexistent love life. I'm not sure which would be an easier pill to swallow, but I usually lean to the mysterious "something else." I'm not particularly terrible to look at, maybe a little plain with my medium-brown hair, average height and weight, and just-about-average everything else, but that doesn't mean ugly. I also like to believe my rock star sense of humor makes up for some of my worst qualities, like my nosiness and unwavering fixation on all the bad, and not good, that happens to me, most of which can be traced back to a certain blond-haired demon.

It's almost disgusting how far Willow has buried herself into my psyche all these years. And any hope that I could pry her out sometime during this camp experience clearly disappeared the moment I discovered she followed me here.

After a few more distracted steps, my musing seems to manifest in human form.

Clothes spring out of my hamper and onto the ground at the impact. "What the—" Willow tries to pull herself up from the tiled floor of the laundry room. I hurry to collect my underwear and bras before she criticizes those too. And just like that, I'm transported back to the winter of sophomore year.

~

I hurried down the winding hallways between classes, trying to avoid the Luddite of a hall monitor, who would've confiscated my phone or reported me to my homeroom teacher. At least I was texting for a semijustifiable purpose: to distract Ava from her pain, as she had been out sick with the stomach flu for the past week.

As I rounded the corner, my heart almost popped out of my chest, thinking I'd run into my doom. In a way I had, because Willow Gerard materialized before me, Gucci sunglasses resting atop her slicked-back hair. Both our phones landed on the tiled floor in the collision, and we reached for them at the same time.

"You want this?" she asked, holding one in each hand. I reached my hand out to snatch my phone from hers, but she snuck it behind her back. "Hm, not yet."

To my utter horror and that of the pesky hall monitor, who decided not to interfere the one time it was actually called for, Willow scrolled through my phone, having picked it up while the screen was still on.

"Willow, give it back," I said, using my words at first. My fingers were itching to sock her in the eye, curling into a fist by my side. "Come on, it's not funny."

"Ooh, maybe it is, though. Were you really texting Ava about William King? Wait, lemme see." With zero shame, she scrolled further up in our texts, her burgundy nails clacking against my screen. "Oh my god, you were. A *senior*, Whitney? Come on, you can barely get a sophomore to like you—aim a little lower."

By then, a small crowd had assembled around Willow, consisting of Naomi Bernstein, a freshman who worshipped the ground Willow walked on; Willow's boyfriend of the month, Carter Forbes, a senior himself; and a few of Ava's tennis teammates.

"Come on, Willow, knock it off," Carter said, stepping between us. "You're invading her privacy, which is pretty low, even for you."

"Yeah, plus, has Whitney ever done anything to you?" Naomi chimed in. "It's not like she was the one who spread your nudes around last year."

Willow whirled around, eyes ablaze. "Shut the fuck up, Naomi—you weren't even here last year."

If she were anyone else, the tears forming in the corners of my eyes would've started flowing, but I held them back and swallowed that hard lump in my throat. Carter handed me my phone and offered me an apology on his depraved girlfriend's behalf, but I just snatched it from his hands and ran away, like I always did.

———

I look around, remembering that the washing machines aren't lockers and the pile of clothes on the ground aren't textbooks. My phone lies untouched too.

But the girl in front of me is still the same person.

I scoop up my clothes and dump them back into my hamper, not looking up. With little apology, I grumble, "Sorry for bumping into you."

"Definitely done worse to you," Willow mutters back. I freeze and trail my eyes upwards, taking in the first time I've witnessed any self-awareness from her. She slams the door to the washing machine shut behind her and heads to the hallway. "Don't bother with that one, by the way. It's broken."

———

In the evening after a day at the beach, Martina, Aspen, and I load into my Jeep and head to a local Italian restaurant on the outskirts of camp. With how far away we are from the nearest urban area, I'm surprised the restaurant is teeming with people. The three of us squeeze behind the couples huddled around the bar as the hostess leads us to a table towards the back of the dimly lit place.

"What are the odds we get carded if I order us all cocktails?" Martina asks once we settle in. "I lost my fake ID at a bar in New Jersey."

I look between Aspen to my right and Martina across from

me. "That's not the question you should be asking. It's what are the odds *Aspen* gets carded?"

"Hey, no need to point it out," Aspen says, narrowing her big brown eyes. "I know I look thirteen, maybe fourteen on a good day."

Compared to some of the scantily clad women sipping cocktails on the barstools, we all look like middle schoolers. I hadn't expected to leave the campus at all during these five weeks—well, apart from home if I needed to escape—so I'm making do makeup-less in the sole pair of jeans I packed and a white T-shirt I knotted at the front to make it somewhat pass for a crop top. Aspen went for the same look, while Martina sports a black band T-shirt and frayed denim shorts with a ponytail high enough to give her a tension headache.

"Coke it is, then," Martina declares and flips to the next page of the menu. After a solid three seconds of reading, she slams it closed and looks up at both of us with a pensive smile. "You know what, guys, this whole camp thing isn't turning out to be as bad as I thought."

"You're only saying that because we haven't exercised in over twenty-four hours," I say.

"And your trainer doesn't take their job as seriously as an assistant professor gunning for tenure at an Ivy League institution," Aspen says. When Martina and I stare at her blankly for the oddly specific analogy, she clears her throat and adds quietly, "Both my parents are professors at Yale . . ."

"*Speaking* of trainers, we seem to have summoned them, guys." Martina leans back in her chair with a mischievous grin, lifting her glass of water. "Twelve o'clock at the bar."

I whip my head to the left and struggle to find any familiar faces in a crowd of similarly dressed twentysomethings all brushing up against each other. Then I see him—Axel—resting on one arm on the counter, looking as casual as ever in a white cotton shirt and dark jeans that hug his hips exactly right. The girlish grin that appears on my lips shoots down to a frown when Isla pops out from behind a stocky male trainer Martina tells me is Ryan. She slings an arm around Axel's shoulder and tips his face down towards her.

"How much do you want to bet Axel and Isla are dating?" I ask, gripping my menu harder.

"And why do *you* care?" Martina leans over the table, eyes darkening with mischief. "Someone's got a little crush?"

"No," I snap, quick enough to pass a lie detector test.

In some ways, it isn't a lie at all. I can't have a crush on someone I've only known for a week, who's also my personal trainer and quite literally *paid* to be around me every day.

I have more dignity than that . . . right?

"Sure, sure," Martina hums, and I avert my attention to our server circling back around. "Whatever you say."

Our food arrives almost as quickly as we order it—three Neapolitan pizzas and an order of parmesan fries for the table—and our conversation jumps from mindless anecdotes to embarrassing childhood stories and finally to our future plans. When I learn we're going to college in three different states, a sinking feeling hits my full stomach, maybe a reminder that this experience, including the people I'm meeting during it, is transient. The thought almost makes me want to take more risks, which is exactly why, when we begin a game of Truth or Dare to kill more time after splitting the bill, I answer "dare" and not my usual "truth."

"Oh no," I say when Martina grins like the Joker. "I shouldn't have said that, right? I take it back."

"No takebacks in Truth or Dare," Aspen says, on Martina's side. "We play by the rules or not at all."

I roll out my shoulders before plastering on my game face, secretly hoping Martina will at least give me a socially acceptable dare. Three families with toddlers surround our table, and I'd rather not traumatize their poor children for life.

"I dare you . . ." Martina trails off and takes the last swig from her bottle of Coke. She turns back to me, and I suck in a breath. "I dare you to walk right in between Axel and Isla when we leave the restaurant."

"Martina—"

"And then ask them if they're dating or just friends."

"No way am I doing the second half of that dare," I say, crossing my arms over my chest. Before Martina can open her mouth and object, I hold up my index finger and assert, "I agreed to a *dare*, not *dares*."

"Fine," she huffs. She pushes herself off the table and starts walking. "I'll do it myself, then."

"Martina, wait—"

I clamber out of my seat and catch up to her as she confidently strides towards the bar. Aspen is at my heels, also hissing for Martina to slow down, but she stops walking halfway to the gathering of trainers.

"I only did that so you'd actually get up," she says. Stepping to the side, she gestures to the chipped dark wood floor below like it's the red carpet. "Your time to shine, Whitney."

The longer I stay standing there in the middle of the restaurant, knocking into servers trying to scurry by, the more

I'll attract attention, defeating my goal of nonchalance. So, brushing my hair out my face and standing tall, I keep walking ahead, each step closer to Axel and Isla deep in conversation making me pound the floor a little harder.

I'm barely thinking when I cut right in between them. And I certainly don't think when I brush my arm against Axel's, too caught up in the cloud of citrus and sandalwood cologne wafting off him, something Tom Ford or Chanel if Axel's taste is as good as I hope it is.

"Well, well, well. Who do we have here?" Isla asks.

I slowly turn around at her playful tone, finding her glaring between me and Martina and Aspen a few steps behind us like we're children sneaking out of school. The teal silk tank top she has on makes her blue gaze appear even more electric, and I hate that she intimidates me enough to look away.

"Looks like the little campers found our secret spot, Axel."

"It took me three seconds to find it on Google Maps, so calling it that is a bit of a stretch," Aspen says. After a silent moment, she shrugs and holds up her hands, muttering, "Just saying."

I laugh, but the noise gets garbled in my throat when I realize Axel hasn't stopped looking at me this whole time, assessing my face with his soft hazel eyes like he's trying to find something there. He doesn't have a drink in his hand, which makes me wonder if he's even old enough *to* drink, which then makes me realize I know close to nothing about this gorgeous man.

When he takes a step towards me, my knees practically give way.

"You got something there," he says, gesturing to the corner of his lip with his thumb. I slowly bring my fingers to my lips, unsure what I'm looking for, but I figure if I scrub hard enough, I'll get rid of it. He nods and pulls back slowly, murmuring, "All good now."

Isla clears her throat and flattens her palm across Axel's abdomen. He doesn't lean into her touch but doesn't object to it either, which maybe says something about their relationship.

"Anyway, you guys should hop on back to camp and get some rest before another week of torture—I mean exercise—starts. Axel and I just finished making the schedules, and they're *bru*-tal."

With one last glance at Axel, I pull Martina and Aspen towards the door.

"You *definitely* have a crush," Martina says when we tumble out of the restaurant. The soupy evening air hits my face, doing nothing to alleviate my blush. "You looked like you were about to pass out when he got close to you."

"Isla might've beaten her to him, though," Aspen says. "Not that I understand how he'd like her back. She's *insufferable*."

She might be, but she has the body of a fitness model and exudes a certain kind of cocky confidence that lets me know she always gets what she wants, reminding me of Willow in high school.

Stop it, Whitney. You can't start thinking about her again on your one day off.

"You know what, guys, since I'm driving, I make the rules," I say, sliding into the driver's seat. "We're not talking about Axel for the rest of the night."

"Could we at least discuss his abs, though?" Martina asks from the back seat after a moment. "Isla was definitely feeling them up through his shirt."

"*No*. No Axel. No abs." After a moment, I throw in for good measure, "And no exercise."

"Until tomorrow," Aspen says from beside me, and I wish I had a drink just from that.

CHAPTER EIGHT

With July approaching, it's hot enough that the beach in the morning feels no cooler than the anywhere else on this sprawling campus. Thankfully, I packed a lifetime supply of shorts and white T-shirts.

Axel winces in the blinding sun and shrugs off his camp-issued hoodie. Underneath he also wears a white shirt, emphasizing his tan bulky arms and the faint ridges of abs through the thin material. The bronze of his skin seems less natural and more like the aftermath of working out in the sun too many times, so I only pray the same will happen to me by the end of this experience.

"Today we're going to focus on the upper body and abs," he says, beginning to walk down the sand. "Follow me." He leads me close to the shoreline, where the sand is firmer and darker, and rolls out an exercise mat.

He says something, but I get distracted by the water again, entranced by the low tide.

"Wait, what?"

"Get down into a plank position," he says, looking down at his phone where I can faintly make out a clock app. Noticing I don't budge even after he repeats his instructions, he smirks.

"You haven't told me if you're as bad at planks as you are at running."

I don't explain that I've only attempted a plank two times before as I struggle to position my body correctly, realizing how much harder this exercise is on unstable ground. My body strains in seconds, my arms and abdomen vibrating like my phone would if I were popular.

Axel crouches down next to me. "Lessen the distance between your arms, that'll make it easier."

I do as he says but still feel shaky, maybe because my body has barely recovered from this past week.

"Can I help a bit?"

I tilt my head up. "What?"

"Show you how it's done. Only if you're comfortable, that is."

A murmured yes leaves my mouth, and he draws closer, his fingers dangling in the air. I nod, and he connects one hand with my lower stomach, while the other rests on my back. He pushes upwards gently and fixes my curved form. He lets his fingers linger for a second or two longer than needed—or maybe I imagine that he does—and I burn holes into the sand with my eyes, trying not to let him notice I'm affected.

After another twenty seconds, my hair sticks to the back of my neck, and my face is hot enough to fry an egg. All the muscles in my lower and upper body struggle to keep me up, crying out to me to spare them. They give up on me not long after, ignoring my wish to make it to a full minute.

"Thirty-six seconds," he says, his tone low and equivocal. "What do you think?"

"I was aiming for a minute, but thirty-six seconds is pretty good. If you round it up by four seconds, I made it forty seconds.

And then if you round that number to the nearest minute, *technically*, I reached my goal."

"That's the spirit," he chuckles and holds out his hand, as always.

He leads me through a series of upper-body exercises without weights, equipment I once thought was necessary for building arm strength. I breeze through most of them and send a small mental shoutout to all academic textbook publishers on the last set.

"Let's try a plank again now."

I groan at his usage of "let's," given it's always *me* doing all these exercises. I crawl back onto the mat and get into position, remembering to straighten my back and keep my elbows parallel to my shoulders. I change my strategy this time, trying not to focus on time and instead on what it would feel like to kiss him.

Wait, what?

"Tired yet?" he teases.

His voice pulls me out of my reverie, and I shake my head, feeling my cheeks grow hotter than they already are from exhaustion. I can't even guess how much time has passed when I finally crumple to the mat.

"Fifty-eight seconds."

"Seriously?"

"Look for yourself, if you want to," he says, showing me his phone. Sure enough, the number is what he said, and that boosts my nearly nonexistent ego.

I hand it back to him, beaming. "Now what?"

I should've already expected his answer: "Now we run."

Halfway down the beach, I grow bored of the quiet, wondering how his thoughts keep him so entertained. I normally try to escape mine, diving into TV series or sappy novels about people with lives ten times more interesting than my own.

Maybe I've craved them less this week because my life finally is interesting.

"Axel," I say, less breathless than usual, "are we ever gonna—you know—get to know each other a little? We can't keep going on like this for four more weeks."

He waits a beat before answering, "Whitney, the purpose of this experience isn't to become friends."

It's to become lovers, I finish for him in my head, joking. Okay, *half* joking.

"Okay, cool." I shrug, looking down at the sand. "Forget I asked."

"I'm just messing with you. What are you dying to know?"

I perk up and blurt the first thing that comes to my mind. "You could start by confirming you're not thirty. Your age is still a little muddy in my mind."

"Subtract a decade from that," he chuckles. "Just finished my sophomore year of college, actually."

"Are you an exercise science major?" It has to be something similar, given that he *willingly* works at a fitness camp.

"Close, kinesiology. I plan to become a physical therapist and hopefully open my own gym." We make it to the end of the beach, and for once, he doesn't demand we run back right away. "What about you? Any big life aspirations?"

"I want to be premed in college, but it feels so unoriginal. Everybody's parents at my school were either doctors, bankers, or lawyers, and it makes people think I'm into the career for the wrong reasons."

"From someone who's about two years ahead of you in life, I

say if you're passionate about medicine, fuck what people think."
His blunt reply feels like some ice water to the face, refreshing
and sobering at the same time. I wonder what it would be like to
naturally think like him. "Where's home for you?"

"Greenwich. Although I did spend the first six years of my
life in Manhattan. I don't have a ton of notable memories, but I
do remember life being a lot more vibrant than the Connecticut
suburbs."

"I'm from Brooklyn," he says. I suddenly feel odd for talking
about the city like he doesn't know it through and through. "Not
sure if I enjoyed the place that much growing up. My mom
worked a lot of the time, so I took on most of the responsibility
for my younger brother." A tight crease forms between his eyebrows. "Never betrayed the city for Hedge Fund Land, though,
so I guess we can't entirely relate."

"I was just a kid," I mumble, although I know he's joking. I
fail to mention my dad left New York to work *at* a hedge fund.
"Is your brother a lot younger than you?"

"Yeah, he's a baby. Fifteen next month," he says, and I laugh.
"Got any siblings yourself?"

"One sister, a couple years older than you. So, *not* a baby."

We continue talking, sharing a few more details about our
lives and ourselves, before beginning the run back down the
beach. Each time he says something, I let him talk as much as
he wants, realizing that no matter what he shares, I'm interested.

So damn interested.

———

After dinner, Cindy and a few other female trainers gather the
sixteen of us in the yoga studio for a "relax and recharge" session,

as if I will be doing any *relaxing* with Willow breathing the same air as me.

"Gather in a circle so we can begin today's session." Cindy summons us with a circular hand motion. Reluctantly, I head over to the middle of the room, finding a spot between Martina and Joanna, one step up from Willow. "We talk a lot about empowerment when it comes to working out, but we tend to forget about the word nestled in it: *power*. All of you, whether you realize it or not, hold a tremendous amount of power. But if you're not careful, you can let other people, bad circumstances, or even your own lack of self-confidence take it away from you and keep you from reaching your highest potential."

As Cindy speaks, the room stays silent. Some girls point their heads down towards the wooden floor while others seem a step away from whipping out a notebook and jotting down her every word. I lean back on my hands and blind myself with the spotlights on the ceiling, wondering where she's going with all these buzzwords.

"I'll have May continue this session for us."

"Thanks, Cindy," May says. She's pretty in that cute way, with noticeable dimples in her cheeks and short black hair that flows like water with the movements of her head.

Martina leans into my ear. "That's Ryan's girlfriend—I think. Still holding out hope he's single."

I glance down at the rock on her left ring finger, visible as she wraps her hands around her knees. "Are you sure she's just his girlfriend?"

"Oh, *shit*. You're more observant than I am."

"When I was in high school," May begins with the classic

dramatic phrase, "I was a lot bigger than I am now. It wasn't that big a deal, and I wasn't even that insecure about it, since I'd always looked that way. But there were a few girls in my grade who always made me feel otherwise.

"They invited me to go prom dress shopping with them senior year, and we hit up store after store, and at every one, I failed to find a dress that fit me. I still forced myself to smile and tell them how *beautiful* they looked in their dresses, but by the end of the day, instead of trying to find a store that would work for me, those same girls looked me in the eyes, and do you know what they said? 'You know what, May, maybe if you lost some weight, you could shop like the rest of us do.'" A few girls suck in a breath, like someone had insulted them the same way. "I let that comment get to me so much, I skipped prom and missed out on that once-in-a-lifetime event. Now I realize I didn't have to give them that kind of power over my own joy and self-worth. They weren't worth it."

"Has anyone given someone else power they don't deserve?" Cindy asks, her eyes gliding over the room. I swear they rest a second longer on my downturned face before moving to her daughter. "Or has anyone ever used their power in a way they weren't supposed to?"

Hands pop up in the air, and I kind of like that I can't tell whether these girls are saying yes to the first or second question. It emboldens me enough to raise my own hand, and soon enough Martina's and Aspen's follow. Willow's hand stays glued to the floor, along with her eyes.

"Does anyone want to share?" May asks. "This is a judgment-free zone."

Thirty seconds pass, and no one has spoken up. I make

sure to stare intently at my white sneakers in case May or Cindy start calling on people, but to my relief, a raspy voice behind me speaks up.

"I'll go," Kennedy says, and I shoot her a smile for sparing us all. "I'm dyslexic. It wasn't something that was a big deal to people until my parents transferred me to a supercompetitive high school during my sophomore year. After everyone found out, there was this group of assholes that would always try to get me to read out loud in class so they could laugh at how it'd take me twice as long as everyone else to get through one damn paragraph. One day, I saw this guy I really liked leaving a note on my desk, and for a second, I thought maybe he was asking me out or complimenting me or something cute like that. But that note . . . I honestly don't even want to repeat what he said out loud here, but none of you guys would want to find that on your desk first thing Monday morning."

I grimace as she talks, unsure how her classmates derived any entertainment from something as common as dyslexia, until I remember exactly how the brain of a bully works.

Oh, wait—it doesn't.

"When I picked it up and read it, I could hear that same guy from the back of the class telling his friends, 'Don't worry, guys, Kennedy can't read that.'" A couple of girls gasp, but she shrugs and pushes her waist-length blond hair away from her blue eyes, clearly having grown thick enough skin. "Gosh, I just wanted to *scream* at that moment, 'I'm dyslexic, not freakin' *illiterate*, you morons,' but what could I do? Maybe there was *something* I could've done, but instead, I made my parents transfer me from that school, and I missed out on what could've been a great education. Or gave away my academic power, to be metaphorical."

A couple of girls follow Kennedy's lead, displaying a kind of vulnerability that's almost admirable as they share intimate stories from their lives. Moments from high school float through my head, all the years of ducking my head down and trying to slink down the hallways to avoid being the victim of another one of Willow's schemes. My fingernails dig deeper into my palms as I think about what a shell of a person she made me, but I wonder if it was all her. I recall that moment at the restaurant yesterday, walking between Axel and Isla with no shame, and I wonder if that could've been me all along.

"Thank you, all, that was very brave of you to share," Cindy says, sliding a box of tissues forward. While some girls dab at their eyes with theirs, I pluck a tissue to wipe away the tiny droplets of blood on my palm and then crush it into a ball in my fist. "Before this session ends, I want you all to realize that even if other people have taken your power from you, you can still reclaim it. You can grow stronger, you can forgive, and maybe if you're lucky, you can even forget. And if you've taken someone else's power from them, you can always redeem yourself. Try to make amends and start anew. Because it's never too late."

Willow and I look at each other for a fleeting moment when her mother finishes talking, and there's some soft emotion creasing up her eyes on the sides, but it's gone in a blink.

And we're back to two enemies sitting on opposite sides of the yoga studio.

Business as usual.

CHAPTER NINE

Axel and I meet at the rope climbing fixture in the woods again, which somehow seems smaller now that I've spent a week away from it.

"Need a demonstration?" he asks, cracking his knuckles.

The muggy weather today is insect-bite heaven, and he's sporting a sleeveless shirt. I don't complain, admiring the veins bulging down the insides of his arms when he grasps the rope, practically a phlebotomist's dream.

"Sure," I say, snapping out of it, "why not?"

Like every other athletic feat, Axel performs it like it's nothing, effortlessly gliding to the top of the unrelenting rope. He explains how I should approach each pull, and more excitement than apprehension fills my mind.

Deciding not to overthink it, I jump as high as I can into the air. My grip viselike, I pull myself up while fumbling with the end of the rope at my feet. Axel hovers below me, arms outstretched, ready to catch my struggling body. His presence motivates me to impress him for once, and with all my little might, I drag myself up the first third of the rope.

"Nice job, keep up that form," Axel comments from below, moving out of the way. "You think you can keep going?"

The coarse rope bites my soft palms and my core aches from

how hard I'm clenching it, but I still yell back a yes. As I walk my hands up about a foot, I draw my knees closer to my chest, squinting as the cloud-covered sun shines in my face. As I push my feet together and extend my body, the top is almost reachable. But the pain in my hands is unbearable; I'm still unused to the strain climbing puts on them.

"If you can't keep going, slowly walk yourself down," he says, tilting his head up. I look down at his warm expression and feel less bad about myself. "Come on, Whit, you've got this."

Whit? That nickname is forever associated with family members or close friends, too casual for everyday life. But I've always loved it, and I like it even more coming from his mouth.

In my distraction, I let my sweaty palms drag down the rest of the rope, sending me careening to the dirt ground. Axel's hands lock onto either side of my hips to keep me on my feet. A jolt of electricity hits my body when his rough fingers meet the skin peeking out of the hem of my shirt, and I stumble backwards, my back to his chest, my heavy breaths matching his.

"You good?" he asks, taking a step back. I nod, noticing the one hand still on my body. His fingers dance across my skin as he removes it, and I shiver. "You had the descent at first."

"Sorry, I got a little distracted. Can I try again?"

As I give the rope climb another go, I filter any thoughts from my brain, laser focused on the top. As I complete pull after pull, I can only hope my grunts and groans aren't nearly as loud as I think they are, exaggerated by my building aggravation.

"Almost there!" Axel calls right as my hand hits the fixture of the rope.

When I finally make it to the top, I may as well be at the peak of Mount Everest from all the endorphins rushing through my body. I look down at a smiling Axel as I catch my breath before making my way down with caution, ignoring the pain in my arms and focusing on the shock in my mind. By the time I'm standing on my own two feet, I almost can't believe I was just *at* the top, because all I see is that moment two years ago, when I experienced the same shock—not over my success, but over the fact the rope had snapped in half just from me attempting to climb it.

~

"Come on, Whit!" Ava called from below, clapping her hands. "You can do it!"

A couple of other girls cheered with her as I hauled my shaking body up another inch of the rope, blinded by the fluorescent ceiling lights of the gym. I'd volunteered to go last, mostly because I already knew it would take me nearly twice as long as every other girl to make it up a few feet. I caught sight of a fraying portion of the rope and lifted one wary hand to assess the material.

"Don't worry, Whitney!" Willow said, and I squeezed my eyes shut as I prepared for the blow. "You're not heavy enough to snap it—yet, at least."

The cackles from below overpowered a failed attempt from Ava to defend me, and I opened my eyes. Seeing red, I clawed and fought my way up another few inches of the rope, ignoring all the warning signs flashing in my head when I latched onto the thinning material.

"Whitney, I think you need to—"

I blocked out my gym teacher's voice and completed one more pull, adrenaline pumping with each inch closer to the top.

Right when I thought I might make it, a creak blended into the sound of my own yelp, and in seconds, I lay flat on my backside on the mat. Groaning in pain, I stared up through bright white lights at the sports banners lining the walls of the gym, wondering if I'd died and made it to athletic heaven.

Above my unmoving body—from embarrassment and not paralysis—frazzled voices blended into each other.

And none of them were St. Peter.

"Oh my god, Whit, are you okay?"

"You should totally sue the school for this, girl. My dad's a personal injury lawyer, and he'd take your case in a second."

"Hey, you guys, back off. She might have a concussion. Whitney, can you see how many fingers I'm holding up?"

"I don't think she hit her head when she landed. Do you think her tailbone's broken, though? My sister broke hers giving birth, and she said it hurt like a bitch."

But one voice was clear among the rest.

"Oh, this is going to make some great content for the newsletter this week."

~

Axel halts my drifting thoughts by handing me a bottle of water.

"I don't get it," I breathe, cracking the cap open with extra force. "I spent the past four years of my life getting humiliated for my shitty athletic skills—among other things—and you're telling me after less than two weeks here, I can do *that*? Where was this willpower *during* high school?"

"Maybe it exists only because you know what it's like to not have had it." I stay silent for a few moments, and he notices my downturned lips and heavy eyes. "Look, I don't know your reason for hating high school—because trust me, we all have one—but you're still young, and you can only keep improving from here. School matters way less than you think it does right now."

"That sounds like advice the former captain of the varsity football team would give me."

"I was more of a wannabe Eminem than the next Tom Brady growing up, if that helps paint a picture."

For the duration of our winding jog back to the center of the camp, I grill him on his former rapper dreams, forced to stop every few moments to contain my laughter. All I could picture were oversized light denim jeans and a bag of burned CDs on hand, with a few Eminem posters on a bedroom wall as the cherry on top. That was enough for me to thank my lucky stars that I never had that idea myself, knowing that I did not possess any musical ability to counteract my missing athletic gene.

"Feeling better now?" he asks when I start wheezing between laughs. "Very glad to be your entertainment for the day."

"Y-yes, I-I think s-so." I bend over and cough my lungs out, questioning whether an asthma diagnosis is in my future. When I straighten up again, I do everything in my power to wipe the smile off my face, even physically dragging my hand across it. "Sorry. I needed that laugh today."

"I'll let it slide this time, Whitney." His voice drops a notch when he dips his head down and says, "Only because I like you better when you're happy."

I smile even harder.

—

Most nights at camp, I've had the communal bathroom to myself as I get ready for bed, at some sweet spot between eleven p.m.

and midnight. This time, as I brush my teeth with drooping eyelids, Willow steps out of a stall and ducks her head down as she walks to the sink.

I work my toothbrush over my molars with a little more vigor, watching her wash her hands in my peripheral vision. She lets water run over the soapy foam for at least a minute, arms frozen in place, and curiosity starts to eat at my brain.

"Willow . . . why are you *really* here?"

She pulls her hands away from the sink. The sensors detect the lack of movement and shut the water off at last, and from miles away, my environmentalist sister cheers. "Like I told everyone during that icebreaker, I had no choice." She scoffs. "Does it look like *I* needed to go to a fitness camp, Whitney?"

"Does it look like *I* needed to go to one?"

"That's not what I'm saying," she snaps and rips off a paper towel from the dispenser. "All I'm saying is you're not being held hostage in this place. So, I don't know—maybe try to have some more fun while you're here instead of frowning all the time and giving yourself premature wrinkles?"

"And how can I do that when you're here with me?"

For the first time in my life, I've managed to say something that hurts her, and I watch her suck in her cheeks and wipe at her hands like she's trying to peel off a layer of skin. Instinctually, I cringe and wait for the blow: the remark, the insult, the promise of humiliation to come.

Instead, she puffs up her shoulders and scrunches her face into her signature scowl, crumpling the paper towel in her hands into a ball. "I guess you'll have to take that one up with my mother."

She aims for the trash can from afar, and when she misses, I refrain from commenting, even though I want to.

I want to be just as fucking mean as she was to me.

"But to answer your question, Whitney, I don't think you needed to go to a fitness camp. And definitely not this hellhole."

She's gone before I can say anything, and I curse softly, dropping my hands to the counter. My fingers curling into the granite, I stare at myself in the mirror, watching the lines in my forehead and cheeks flatten and my anger fade to confusion. I always thought if I had the chance to crawl into her head, I'd find only air, but it turns out her mind is a complex web.

I hate that I understand nothing in there.

I pick up her crumpled paper towel and chuck it into the trash before marching back to my room. When I push open the door, I almost trip over Martina, who's set up camp between our two beds. She hunches over with her headphones on, blasting something by The Killers, and saws away her thumbnail with a nail file. Registering my presence, she drops her headphones to her neck and cracks a smile.

"What's gotten into you?" she asks, noticing the scowl on my face.

"Ran into Willow in the bathroom," I answer, throwing myself face down onto my bed.

"Oh, wait, never mind. That explains everything."

I sit up on my elbows. "She basically all but implied her mother is holding her hostage here. Honestly, did Adriana ever mention why Cindy made Willow come here in the first place? It sure as hell wasn't to get fit."

She shrugs. "Not sure if she even told Adriana the truth, but from what I heard, it had something to do with not wanting her to dance this summer. I don't think Cindy's ever been very supportive of her dancing."

I figured Cindy would love anything that involved movement and grace, especially since that art form may be the only thing Willow has a natural aptitude for besides ruining lives. Every other photo on her Instagram is her holding a medal after winning yet another competition.

"You know, what *is* your deal with her?" Martina asks after a moment. "Look, I don't like any of the airheads Adriana is friends with either, but I'm gathering you and Willow go way back, and not in a good way."

I rise to a sitting position and lean back on my hands, staring off at the opposite wall. "I wish it was just one thing that happened, not years of continuous hell. But do you wanna know the funniest thing?" Martina nods. "When I first started high school, we were friends. We used to spend our lonely lunches or free periods together and bond over dumb stuff, like indie bands or our hatred of world history class. And then second semester, she returned to school with an expensive wardrobe, a colorful vocabulary, and a brand-new set of friends. It was all downhill from there, especially after her dad died that summer."

Martina sits down next to me on my bed. "Sounds like you became the victim of her sudden popularity."

"Yeah. In an instant, she'd transformed me from neutral outsider to a complete social pariah. There was always something to make fun of: my boring clothes, my dedication to school, my nonexistent boyfriends . . . and her favorite, how bad I was at sports. I'm thankful I always had my friend Ava by my side, but there was only so much she could do to defend me."

Martina ignores everything but the last point. "Wait—you're friends with *Ava?*"

"You know her?"

"Hell yeah, I do. We used to bond over our desire to jump off a cliff whenever we'd be dragged to those brunches Willow's mom would host."

Groaning, I fall back to my mattress, hands fanned out on opposite sides of my head. At this point, it seems like all roads in my life lead to Willow, and with my luck, she's probably also Axel's secret ex-girlfriend and my second cousin once removed.

Martina follows my lead, and we both lie the wrong way across my bed, taking in a different corner of the ceiling.

"You know just a couple more weeks and you'll be free of her, right?" she says, turning to look at me. "I won't be, for the record."

I chuckle softly with her, not telling her I also thought that before I graduated, and yet here we are. At this point, it seems easier to accept Willow as some semipermanent fixture in my life than a parasite I keep trying and failing to kill.

"Sure," I mumble in return, closing my eyes as sleep consumes me, "only a couple more weeks."

CHAPTER TEN

With each day full of intense workouts, exercise starts to have an opposite, almost invigorating effect on me.

Instead of napping after dinner, I somehow want to move even more, so I shove my hands into the pockets of my blue hoodie and stroll down the sidewalk overlooking the athletic fields. As my sneakers crunch against gravel, I look up at the angry gray color of the accumulating clouds above me. A droplet of rain plops onto my nose, then one on my cheek.

When I make it back up the hill, I search for an open seat to rest my sore legs, but the two stone benches behind the dorm are occupied by Adriana, Willow, Joanna, and Noelle. Noelle lays her hands daintily on top of her pink shorts, laughing with a little too much amusement at whatever Willow says. Her mascara-framed eyes fall on me as I walk by, and she whispers something to the group. Adriana's pointed glare intimidates Noelle enough to shyly look away.

I wonder if Martina threatened her into being nice to me, but she hasn't seemed that bad this whole time. Weirdly competitive and a little vain, yes, but nowhere near as terrible as Willow is—well, I guess *was*.

Feeling another droplet paint my face, I turn around and

spot Axel standing outside the trainer dorm. When he catches my gaze, he beckons to me and mouths something unintelligible. My brow furrowing, I point my thumb towards my chest, and he nods.

The words on his lips grow clear.

Come here.

I force myself to casually stroll to him, even though my heart is fluttering like a lovestruck idiot at the fact he's giving *me* attention, not any of the four girls behind me I'd have surely lost to in high school. I stop in front of his waiting form, propped up against the back entrance. He's traded in his typical T-shirt for a gray hoodie and smells like a fresh shower.

"What's up?"

"It's gonna start pouring any second now," he says, stating the obvious. He glances up at the clouds then back at me and drops his mouth to my ear. "Get a head start on those airheads over there and go back inside."

The sky responds no more than five seconds later, sending the first wave of heavy rain. Moments later, a standard summer storm morphs into a biblical deluge, rumbling thunder and all.

"Oh crap, oh shit, oh crap." I duck down and safeguard my hair with my hands as I try to figure out the quickest route back to my room that won't destroy my crisp white sneakers.

I begin to sprint away, but for once, Axel doesn't care about how fast I can run. He grabs my arm and pulls me through the rear entrance of the building, pushing me into the dry indoors with the kind of strength I almost forgot he possessed.

"I should check the weather more often," I say, watching him peel off his damp hoodie. His T-shirt underneath lifts and offers me a glimpse of the V of his hard abdomen. I avert my eyes to the lining of glass on the door, blurred by droplets of rain. "I'll just wait out here until the storm calms down a bit. Thanks."

"You'll probably be here for two hours." He checks his phone to be sure. "But if that's okay with you, I'll get going." He pulls out what looks like a key card and heads to the door about five feet down the hall.

I stay in place, wondering if he's going to go in. Sure enough, he unlocks the door and holds it open with his elbow, turning his head to the left to observe my expression.

"This isn't an invitation to your room, is it?" I keep my voice down in case anyone is listening.

He smirks and leans against the wooden door. Rocking from one leg to another, I try to evade his curious gaze trailing from my wide eyes to my folded hands. At this point, it'd probably be easier to whip out a sign reading INEXPERIENCED LOSER than explain myself.

"I'll leave my door open."

He disappears into his room, leaving me even more conflicted. Sighing, I slide down to the floor and pull my phone out of my back pocket, hoping to find a few notifications, but my empty home screen mocks me. I rest the back of my head on the hard wall, staring at the spotlights on the ceiling. After two minutes of thinking about nothing, I fight the urge to fall asleep, somehow soothed by the intermittent cracks of thunder. When my heavy eyelids finally start to give in, I shoot up to my feet, terrified of someone—Bob, to be specific—finding me here.

I creep down the hall, wincing at the squeak of my sneakers on the polished linoleum. I peek into Axel's doorway and find an organized room with a mostly dark-blue interior, aside from the white walls. He's crouching by his side table, thumbing through a stack of papers.

"Hi."

He rises to his feet at the sound of my voice, a small smile tugging on the edges of his lips. "Giving in already?"

"I'm kind of terrified of someone finding me. Isn't this—you know—against the rules?"

"Sheltering you from a violent thunderstorm?" He cocks his head to the side, clucking his tongue. "Nah, I don't think even Bob would be mad about that."

"You could've told me to stay out there."

"And you could've done that," he says, walking towards me and leaning forward so that I feel just shy of trapped. "Yet you're here, Whitney. Door's still open, by the way."

Once again, his teasing muddles my thinking, but I don't want to concede just yet. I duck into the foot of space between his desk and the wall to conceal myself from any passersby.

"Your room is . . ." I trail my eyes from the wrinkle-free double bed to the aligned notebooks on his desk. ". . . neat. I like it."

"Thanks," Axel says, crumpling a piece of paper into a ball. "Bob assigns twenty push-ups for each unmade bed found on random room checks, so there's no messing around."

"Wait, really? That's wild."

"God no. He never even enters this building." He chucks the ball of paper into the small recycling bin and takes a seat on the edge of his bed. "The true story is my roommate my first semester of college was an absolute fucking pig and put me off dirty laundry and trash that's not *in* a can for good."

"That makes much more sense," I laugh. "Is Bob as intimidating as we all think he is? Or was that persona on the first day just an act?"

"It's hard to say. Once he gets to know you better, he lightens up, but some part of him thrives on destroying the enthusiasm of the new campers, so the introductory speech is probably never going to change. But he is a lot more lenient on the female trainers than he is on us guys."

"Because he thinks they're less competent?"

He gives me a half-assed answer, and I end the conversation. To pass the time, I glance at the mementos on his desk, hoping to find the answers to the questions I still can't find the time and place to ask, about his family, his upbringing, about Isla . . .

Decorating the corner of the wooden surface are two picture frames and a couple of plaques that appear to be awards from college or high school. I'm interested only in the photos, one of which is of him in a cap and gown standing next to a woman with his same eyes. *His mother?* Probably. The other picture is much older, slightly wrinkled in the frame, featuring a baby-faced version of him with a younger boy who I'm guessing is his brother, and a kind-eyed man wrapping his arms around them both. *Maybe his father?* They sit on a bench in a public park, in front of buildings that remind me more of those in Boston than the skyscrapers of New York.

"Is that the Common?" I ask, trying to subtly introduce my interest in this photo.

"It is," he says, standing up. He places his hands on his hips and eyes the photo from a distance, something he looks like he's done a hundred times before. "Kid on the left is my brother, Jake. The man in between us is my dad. He . . ." Axel pauses and squints, like he's restraining some emotion, which becomes clearer when he finishes the sentence. "He passed away when I was twelve."

His words sink in for a moment. "I'm so sorry," I whisper and bring my hand to his forearm. It's a soft, almost instinctual touch I use whenever I comfort someone, but I forgot this *someone* is my personal trainer, and he's looking at where we're connected with parted lips and a slightly furrowed brow.

I yank my hand away, cheeks warming. "That, uh, that must have been difficult to go through at that age. Not that losing your parent is easy at any age, of course, but it would've been especially hard in middle school. I can't say I speak from experience, but I do know a couple of people who lost their parents, and it's something—"

"Whitney," he says, taking a step forward, "it's okay." He ducks his head down, and at the sudden proximity, my breath gets stuck in my throat, which would have been great ten seconds ago when I was rambling like an idiot. "That's definitely a more creative response than I'm used to. Refreshing, almost."

"Most people who know me would probably use the word *awkward.*"

He laughs. "You must have some very boring people in your life then."

When he takes another step towards me, I fall back into the wall, flattening my hand across the cold surface to keep myself upright. The rain pounds outside, pelleting against the windows, and thumps almost as strongly as my heart with him this close to me. Between flashes of lightning, I don't know if I tilt my head up first or he lowers his, but in my fantasies, this would be the part where we kiss and then roll onto his bed and cuddle until the storm ends.

The next crack of thunder seems to knock him to his senses, and he pulls back right as the room plunges into darkness. Every few seconds, we can make each other out with the help of the intermittent flashes outside, doing the job of the now-useless ceiling lights.

"Can you stay here for a couple of minutes?" Axel asks. He grabs his phone and room key, grumbling, "I'm gonna go see what to do about the power."

"Sure," I say, slowly sinking down into his desk chair in the dark.

When he leaves and shuts the door behind him, I remind myself that at end of the day, this is his job and I'm just a part of it—the only way it should be.

CHAPTER ELEVEN

Unlike Willow's mother, my mom has pretty much left me to my own devices at camp. She's called me only twice since I left, saying she wanted to give me a sense of independence, but with the number of conflicting experiences I'm having—my undeniable attraction to Axel, my quickly dwindling aversion to exercise, and my encounters with a semitolerable Willow—I need some reassurance from my mother. (A hug would be nice too, but I'll take what I can get.)

"All right, Whit, spill the beans. Is this camp worth all the moolah we shelled out?"

Ten minutes later, sitting on one of the benches behind the dorm, I've poured out my thoughts on the workouts, the people, and the food. I've mentioned almost everything except my trainer being a guy named Axel.

"All that in less than two weeks?" She chuckles. "I wouldn't be surprised if you came back home an Olympic athlete."

"Let's not get too ahead of ourselves," I laugh. "How are *you*, Mom? I talked to Poppy a little while ago, and I'm not sure what to think about the situation."

She shuffles and then there's a click of a door on the other end of the line. "Sorry, your dad just hopped on a video call. Alice and Dave—Levi's parents—left a couple of days ago, so the house is remarkably quiet. Empty without you, of course."

We're not on a video call so she can't see my wide smile. "Is Alice as bad as Poppy says?"

"I thought I was controlling, but damn, does that woman take the cake. To be honest, I'm not sure where Levi got his personality from with those two for parents. Dave isn't so bad; he's practically a clone of your father, apart from the righteous profession." She refers to the long line of doctors on Levi's dad's side. "Sorry, I'm ranting to you like one of my Pilates friends."

"I miss home," I say dreamily, shading my eyes from the sun. I hate that Dad is on another call, secretly having hoped he would've asked to talk to me himself. "Hey, Mom, could you ask Dad if . . ."

I swallow tightly, unsure how I even want to finish that question. *He's around later? He could call me back? He's proud of me?*

I shut myself up before I blurt out a variation that'll keep me up at night, regretting it ever rolled off my tongue.

"Could you tell Dad I say hi?" I ask meekly.

"Of course, honey," Mom murmurs after a moment, and I wonder if she even knows that's not what I wanted to ask. "If you ever feel like this experience is too much, you can always come back home."

"Oh no, I can't look like a quitter, Mom."

"That's my Whitney," she says.

———

After breakfast, we gather in the large gym of the fitness center down the hill from the dorms. It looks like an elevated version of my high school's gymnasium, minus the blinding fluorescent lights and hopefully the asbestos in the wall paint. When I spot the rope climbing station on the other side and Willow behind me, I may as well be reliving that embarrassing day all over again.

"Welcome to your second team challenge," says Danielle, another trainer. Her curly hair is piled up in a bun, and her petite frame is draped in baby pink from head to toe. "Today we have four stations planned, each testing different skills you've learned over the past couple of weeks. For two of them, you will be facing off against a member of another team, while the other two are team-based. Remember, while competition is healthy, collaboration is also key."

Cindy and Danielle shepherd us across the gym, explaining we'll first have to climb up the ropes and then jump over a series of hurdles, one member of each team against the other. I crane my neck and realize the ropes are at least a little shorter than the ones in the middle of the woods and even the one I fell from in gym class, putting my racing mind at ease.

"You should have each tried out rope climbing before with your trainers, but remember, we're judging on completion, not perfection." Cindy walks towards one of the ropes, getting a feel for it, before turning to us again. "For a little bit of fun, the faster climber in each round will win a special-edition camp sweatshirt."

"Does it have Bob's face on it or something?" Martina asks in my ear, and we giggle.

"Everything okay, girls?" Cindy asks.

"All good," I mumble.

Willow and Adriana walk up to the two ropes and get a hold of the material. Adriana swallows a gulp as she cranes her neck, while Willow feigns confidence, her long arm extended in an elegant line.

"Three, two, one, *go!*" Danielle says, and they shuffle up their ropes.

Their strategies differ; Adriana climbs like a young child, pinching the rope with her feet, while Willow mirrors Axel's perfect form, giving her a clear advantage over her struggling friend. As I watch them, that stupid memory from high school resurfaces, making me wish Adriana would speed up and overtake Willow for my sake. But, of course, the latter reaches the top in seconds and then lowers herself down, dainty hand by dainty hand.

Martina is nudging my side, beckoning me to go next. I snap out of my thoughts and notice Cindy gesturing to me and Joanna. Her neutral expression and spindly legs, almost half the length of the rope, unnerve me even more. Once my sweaty hands latch onto the rope, the only way I can drag myself even an inch up is by pretending I'm back outside with Axel.

You know how to do this, Whitney, my inner voice screams. As I climb, Axel's smooth, deep voice overpowers my own mental words of encouragement, telling me I can keep going and that I'm almost there.

In what feels like seconds—because maybe it's been only that long—my hand hits the rope's fixture.

"Nice job, Whitney!" Cindy cheers when I descend, holding up her hand to give me a high five.

Willow shoots lasers at the side of my head when I return her mother's high five, and for a moment, I wonder if I shouldn't have done that. Then, I remember I couldn't care less how she feels and march past her to the next station.

The hurdles that follow don't go as smoothly, mostly because my average height becomes my downfall when my sneaker gets caught under one and knocks it over, and Joanna speeds past me to the finish line. I hold more hopes for the weightlifting challenge, considering we're scored based on how many combined pounds our team can lift.

"Martina, that one might be too—"

Martina ignores Cindy's warning and swings a fifty-pound kettlebell like it's nothing, leading our team to victory. I lift my arm up for a high five, and she slams it back hard enough to almost knock me off my feet.

"This last activity is usually one of the toughest on our beginners, but it's a great chance to gauge your arm strength," Danielle explains, stopping in front of a set of pull-up bars. Facing away from us, she steps onto a stool and latches onto the bar, allowing us a view of all the indents and curves of the muscles in her back. She hops back down after a few seconds. "This is known as a dead hang. Your task is to hold on for forty seconds. If you fall off before forty seconds are up, your team earns zero points. If you make it forty seconds or more, your team earns one point. The team with the higher number of points wins another piece of camp merchandise."

"And what if there's a tie?" Adriana asks.

"We'll cross that bridge if we get there," Cindy says.

I step under the bar to the far right, hoping it's the lucky one. Before climbing onto the stool, I send a mini prayer to the universe that my arms won't fall off.

That's impossible, right?

"Go!"

I squeeze my fingers around the bar, feeling the metal bite

down on my soft palms. Martina seems relaxed as she holds on, while Willow stares down at her purple Golden Goose sneakers, sparing her neck.

"Ten seconds in, girls!"

Danielle yells that meager amount of time, and my arms are already aching. I bite down on the inside of my cheek and wiggle my legs a bit, trying to spread the pain out all over my body, even though I know it defeats the purpose of a dead hang.

Martina's arms start shaking, while Aspen, on the other side of her, already fell down a few seconds ago, looking like she was holding back tears. In seconds, Martina follows her lead and hisses out a curse.

"Twenty seconds in, and two are already down. Keep going, Whitney and Willow!"

"You tired yet?" I ask her, glancing to my right.

"No. You?"

"No," I lie.

Exhaling loudly, I adjust my grip. Willow's hands slip a few inches, probably covered in as much sweat as mine. Seconds later, one of my arms begins to give out. I half let go of the bar to shake out my left arm but almost send my whole body careening to the floor when I try to regain my grip, only saving myself at the last minute.

"*And* . . . forty seconds are up!" Danielle says after what feels like three hours.

Willow and I fall to a heap on the ground, red-faced and breathing heavily. Cindy pats me on the shoulder and then smooths down Willow's hair, who yanks herself away and glares at her mother like she just slapped her across the face.

Cindy blinks some emotion away before forcing out, "Great job, girls. You gave it your all today."

I climb up to my feet, while Willow stays there on the ground, hands clenched into fists, staring off at the blue padded wall across from us. I can't tell if she's lost in a trance or about to faint, but when I open my mouth to ask if she's okay, Martina's hand lands on my shoulder.

"Come on, Whitney, let's go enjoy our freedom," she says and tugs me away.

Week Three

CHAPTER TWELVE

"Ready for a hike?" Axel asks, stretching his arms behind his head.

"Is now a bad time to mention I've never actually completed a hike before?"

He laughs. "Whitney, at this point, I don't expect you've done *anything* remotely athletic before. But you can try humoring me."

I brush past him and begin the climb up the trail, realizing the terrain is far steeper than it looks, challenging the limits of my perpetually sore leg muscles. Between bouts of fanning the heat away from my face as the hot July sun peeks out of the clouds, I have to swat a fly or a bee or whatever other buzzing flying creature jumps into my line of vision every few seconds. I don't feel bad for laughing in his face when a wasp lands on Axel's forearm and he lets out something closer to a squeal than a yelp.

"A-are we any closer to the top?" I ask through a couple of huffs, unable to catch my breath. I press my hands to my cheeks, which feel hotter than a stovetop burner after cooking a long meal. I use the outside of my water bottle as an ice pack to temper my skin before guzzling down half of it.

"Impatient today, aren't we?" he hums without even turning around.

I can hardly make out a droplet of sweat on the back of his neck, while I look like I dunked my entire head under the sink. Twice.

"I've been wanting to ask you something, Axel." He turns around. "How did you get into fitness?"

He nods before taking a huge swig of water, finally convincing me he's human. "I boxed in middle school through an after-school program and then joined a gym instead of trying out for a sports team in high school. I used to sneak out there most nights with my friends." I giggle at the mental picture of him sneaking out to go to the gym of all places, and he rolls his eyes. "Very badass of me, I know. But it was a great escape from all the pressures of home."

"I guess I'm escaping home too." He perks up, and I explain, "My family is made up of a bunch of Ivy League college athletes, and being in that atmosphere all the time was suffocating. So, I signed up for a fitness camp, and here I am"—I toss my arms up in the air, laughing—"*still* barely able to run a mile."

He doesn't laugh along, which sucks all the humor out of me. "Why didn't you try working out from before, then? Wouldn't your family have motivated you?"

"Not exactly," I say, hating myself for bringing up this topic. Because now he deserves an answer. I leap over a rock and continue. "Sports has always been my sister's thing. School was, too, so I guess in all ways, she's better than me."

"Says who?" he scoffs.

My dad, probably.

"No one," I mutter and shake my head. "I'm being insecure and stupid."

At my answer, he stops in his tracks, and there's a tight crease of disapproval between his eyebrows, like me insulting myself insulted him.

"Whitney." My name comes out of his mouth like a warning, so I force myself to make eye contact with him. Despite his harsh tone, his eyes soften, pure olive green in the bright sunlight, and it makes my heart flutter in that weird way again. "I don't know why you really feel inferior to your sister, but you're not in competition with her. Or anyone else for that matter. In fact, nothing you accomplish here at this camp should be to prove a point to anyone but yourself."

"But what if I like proving myself to you?"

I know I'm deflecting, mostly because my throat was starting to close up, and I was one more hypercritical thought away from a tear rolling down my cheek in front of him, but I didn't expect the words to leave my lips in that drawn-out, flirty way. Hell, I don't even know *how* to flirt.

Axel presses his lips together in thought, and with each passing second, my stomach twists with the realization that just like that evening in his room, I did it again.

I made everything awkward.

He turns around and forces out, "Let's keep going."

Lagging behind him by five feet, I drag myself up the rest of the trail, swatting my thoughts away like the bees that keep whirring by my ears. I wish I could've opened up to him instead, told him why I'll never feel good enough, but the topic of fathers is already a sore spot for him. It's not like Dad's favoritism towards Poppy has ever felt like a real enough reason to tell anyone else either.

What if it's all in my head, anyway?

Maybe the bitterness I've been harboring all these years is

a symptom of an untreated case of younger sister syndrome, or perhaps it's just plain jealousy.

With that sinking realization, I don't notice the jagged rock inches from the tip of my sneaker and stumble to my hands and knees, sprinkling dirt onto my face and lips. Tasting the earth's elements, I begin to clamber up to my feet, but a hand around my bicep spares me the rest of the effort and hauls me up in one go.

Face-to-face, Axel and I are still for a moment, breathing heavily as we look into each other's eyes. Slowly, he lifts his other hand and cups my face, and I can't breathe as his thumb slides down my cheek in a slow, torturous line. The rattle of my heart against my rib cage drowns out all the sounds of nature around me—the chirping, the buzzing, the rustle of leaves in the breeze that's fanning the heat away from my face.

I close my eyes in bliss, thinking this is it.

I'm finally going to have my first kiss.

"There. That was bothering me."

His hand falls away, and he lets me go. Heart sinking, I open my eyes to see the dusting of dirt on his thumb that he wipes away on the corner of his T-shirt, and I come crashing back down to earth.

———

Martina and I are five minutes late to tonight's "relax and recharge" session when we slip into the entrance of the yoga studio, but we go unnoticed among all the buzz and chatter.

Cindy stands before a table in the center of the room, adjusting the tarp that covers its surface, like a magician setting up before a show. Before I can even begin to guess what's behind it, she quiets us down and pulls off the tarp in one stroke, revealing a puzzle and a pile of missing pieces next to it.

"You all might be *puzzled* at what you're looking at right now—good pun there—but I promise it will make sense in a bit." Girls exchange skeptical looks across the room, and a few even laugh. "Any volunteers to try to finish this puzzle?"

By no surprise, Adriana flings her arm up into the air and heads over to the table before Cindy can even call on her. For the next five minutes, we watch the back of her pink-clad body as she shuffles through the pieces, pressing in and removing ten different ones. Her leg bobs up and down faster with each failed attempt, until eventually she snaps and drops her hands to the table.

"I-I don't get it," she breathes, looking up. "Why can't I solve it?"

Cindy places a hand on her forearm, a soft motherly touch. "How about we let someone else give it a go?"

She doesn't budge until Martina grumbles something in Spanish to her that I imagine would translate to *Move your ass right now or else.*

A girl named Neha takes a stab at it next, and unlike Adriana, she tests out three pieces at random before tossing her long hair over her shoulder and passing off the torch to her friend Kennedy, who allows herself a solid minute to stare at the twenty or so options lying on the table.

"It has to be this one," she says and presses it into a hole in the puzzle with a crack. She freezes and holds up the two broken pieces for us to see. "Okay, never mind—*not* this one."

The competitive straight-A student in me awakens watching each girl try and fail, and I volunteer next. Somehow, I'm convinced I'll be the one to finish this mysterious puzzle, which is starting to feel more like one of those unsolved problems in mathematics that my calculus teacher would assign us as extra credit we could never actually earn.

All eyes are on me as I stand before the low table, making my heart thump slightly as I survey the puzzle itself, a portrait of a bouquet of roses missing a single petal. With my hands by my sides, I dart my eyes between the empty center of the puzzle and the pile of pieces and twist, flip, and turn over each one in my head. My brow furrows more with each piece that isn't a match, until I realize that's exactly the point.

"None of these pieces fits," I say when I've exhausted all my options, looking up at Cindy. "There's no solution here."

"That's right, Whitney," she says. In my head, there's a tiny version of me pumping my fist and hissing out a *yes*, but I simply grin as I hurry back over to my spot between Aspen and Martina. "Now, how do you all propose we solve this puzzle?"

A voice pops up from the back of the room. "What if we bought another version of it and found the missing piece?"

"That would be a great idea, but this puzzle is a one-of-a-kind antique I bought at a yard sale. As far as I know, there are no other versions of it out on the market." I can't tell whether Cindy's bluffing or being serious, especially when no one else questions her response. "What else?"

"Couldn't you cut out a piece of cardboard in the same shape and just paint a petal on it?" Joanna suggests.

"That's not a bad idea, Joanna. But it might be quite a bit of work finding the right materials and painting a design as intricate as this one." Cindy turns to the group. "Does anyone have any other suggestions, or should we stick with that one?"

Martina, Aspen, and I look between each other, shrugging. Muted chatter erupts around us, and I make out snippets of ideas, but no one offers anything concrete.

"What if you just accepted it the way it is?"

We all turn our heads in the direction of that dry, disinterested voice, and I do a double take when I register it's Willow who posed that question to Cindy. She tips down the hood of her black sweatshirt with the name of some dance company on the back, shooting her mother a sharp, irreverent look.

"Correct," Cindy murmurs, nodding slowly. "That's exactly the answer I was looking for."

Willow snorts in laughter, but the sound drowns in the thud of the tarp covering the table again.

Cindy sits down on the wooden floor before us, wrapping her arms around her knees. "This exercise isn't about the puzzle at all. It's about all of us, living in a society that tries to convince us that perfection is more attainable than acceptance, until we spend our whole lives chasing that missing one percent and losing the ninety-nine percent already there. Back when I was a model—gosh, over twenty years ago at this point—perfection was the exact reason I'd spend weeks depriving myself of food and fun and my own sanity, only to still get asked why my waist wasn't an inch smaller or my jawline a little slimmer, or what would be so hard about working out for five hours a day instead of four."

Her words are profound, and it makes me shift uncomfortably. I hope she goes back to the buzzwords so I can zone out in peace again. I may have skated by without discovering or revealing much about myself at the last session, but I'm not holding out hope that I can be as invisible for this one if Cindy starts poking at the root of the insecurities eating me alive all day. I bet I haven't even crossed Dad's mind since I left, while I can't imagine all the tennis matches he's enjoyed with Poppy in the meantime.

If you were perfect like her, my subconscious tells me as Cindy drones on about her modeling career, *maybe he'd love you just the same.*

"Even years after leaving the industry, I can't stand the damn word. Because if you pay close enough attention, it's everywhere, even in the sayings that are supposed to make us feel better. *You're perfect the way you are. Practice makes perfect. Your imperfections are beautiful.*"

"What word should we use instead?" Adriana asks, with more accusation than curiosity. "It clearly serves a purpose."

"It's not the word we need to let go of, Adriana. Clearly, neither you nor I can change the English language. It's the *concept*. Everyone, try something with me for a minute." Cindy folds her legs into a pretzel and rests her palms on her knees. "Close your eyes and picture your own idea of perfection. Although you might be tempted, I don't want you to think too hard. Lean into whatever image pops up in your mind instead."

Reluctantly, I flutter my eyelids closed, my fingers curling into the wooden floor below me. All I see is pixelated darkness, even after squeezing my eyes shut, and after twenty seconds of nothingness passes, I wonder if maybe I'm discovering I'm one of those unlucky people with aphantasia, unable to visualize a person that's not there. That would be easier to accept than the blond locks and blue eyes that start to color the darkness, followed by a bright white smile that could light up any room she walks into.

"Now I want you to imagine that image *slowly* getting smaller," Cindy says, "before letting it fade away."

I squeeze my eyes shut again and try to shrink this version of Poppy down to nothing, but she only gets bigger, and the sound of her airy laughter with Dad starts clouding my brain. Soon enough she's expanded into every open crevice in my brain and ignites a slew of conflicting feelings—anger, love, jealousy, longing—some of which I've never even felt in her presence.

My chest starts heaving up and down as I become defenseless against my own imagination, and I snap my eyes open, breathing like I just ran a mile.

"How was that, everyone?" Cindy asks when the activity draws to a close. "Did that help at all?"

Heart still thudding, I look around the room and realize I'm the only one who shakes my head no.

CHAPTER THIRTEEN

"Happy Friday, all you half-asleep young ladies!" Cindy calls, clapping her hands together. I jolt out of my standing nap, knocking into Aspen, who's saved by Martina's fast reflexes. "Today's challenge will surely wake you all up. Get ready to tackle an obstacle course, where you can, and probably *will*, get messy."

Please don't let it be mud. Please don't let it be mud. Please don't let it—

"That's right, I'm talking about mud." Cindy reads my mind, a bright smile appearing on her face.

Cold silence replaces the buzzing chatter.

"Mud?" Noelle says. Her lips part in disgust. "We're not *boys*. That's revolting."

Surprisingly, I'm on her side.

"Yeah, like, I don't wanna be that person, but is there any way I can change my shoes?" Joanna sticks her leg up, letting us see her white Nike sneakers in mint condition. "I just got these babies for my birthday."

"Sorry, girls, but we have to get things going," Cindy says with little apology and continues guiding our trek down the sloping grass behind the dorms.

We make it past the fitness center, then the athletic fields, and through a clearing in the woods all the way on the other side of campus, an area I didn't even think was also owned by Camp Campbell. One step in, and it becomes clear why Cindy gave us a warning. Murky green water from last night's thunderstorm has pooled in the small valleys in the grass and dirt, rendering the terrain a spongy, miry mess. Noelle and Joanna practically play a game of hopscotch to avoid soiling their white shoes, while I've already declared my busted gray Converse a lost cause.

"Is that your knight in shining black Nike I see in the distance?" Martina asks, craning her neck.

"My knight in—"

I don't finish the question before I spot Axel weaving his way between two trees, appearing like a dark cloud in a sea of neon-clad campers. He walks to Cindy and dips his head down to tell her something, somehow dwarfing her five-foot-nine figure with his broad shoulders and bulky arms and stony aura. For a fleeting second, I wonder if I look that tiny next to him.

"All right, everyone." He doesn't even have to clap his hands, his booming voice alone prompting the chattering around us to come to a halt. "Behind me you'll find an obstacle course. Unlike other challenges you've completed, which have included individual components, this is a team effort. None of you are going to get through this unless you can work together."

He glances between me and Willow, and I wonder if he's gathered that we don't like each other. *Is it that obvious?*

"The first portion of this obstacle course involves a basic sprint down a narrow path, then through a series of tires, which will then lead you to a raised wooden bar you'll have to hoist yourself over. Tall people, help the vertically challenged people out here." Aspen looks up at Martina and me with puppy eyes, and Martina pats her bun lovingly. "This will then take you to a set of monkey bars and a rope swing over a mass of mud. There you will encounter your most challenging obstacle: a twelve-foot wall, which is about"—he hops up onto a tree stump and lifts his hand high into the air—"this tall. You'll have to come up with a clever strategy to climb over it."

"Damn, the only thing I'd like to climb is him," a voice comes from behind me.

"What was that?" Axel jumps down from the stump and walks towards us. Silence follows, so sharp it cuts through the thick, muggy air. "Did someone say something?"

The same girl mumbles a curse, and the green-eyed monster in me screaming *he's mine* wants Axel to put her in her place. She doesn't win this time.

"No one said anything," I say, tilting my head up and locking my eyes with his. "You're hearing things."

He cocks his head to the side, his eyebrows lifting in some combination of surprise and tempered offense, and then walks back to his makeshift podium.

"On the other side of the wall, you'll find a platform, which will lead you to a fixture made up of a series of logs, spaced about a foot apart. If you managed not to soil your white Nikes before, you'll have the perfect chance to do so if you fall down crossing them." Joanna cringes, and Axel smiles wickedly, drawing some sort of satisfaction from her horror. Maybe he doesn't fall too far from the Bob tree after all. "After that, you're done, and before one of you asks, your only prize is surviving. Any other questions?"

A voice from the back of the group asks, "Did Bob design this course by any chance?"

Axel lets out a low laugh. "It was actually partly inspired by his military training, which means you guys will need all the luck you can get." *How delightfully reassuring.* "Does a team want to volunteer to go first, or should I choose?"

Cindy gives him the go-ahead to wait for volunteers, and he trails his eyes across the group of girls, searching for any desperate hands to shoot up in the air.

"We'll go first."

I whip my head to the side to match the voice to the person before I realize it was Martina, her arm still raised in the air.

"Why would you suggest going *first?*" Aspen hisses, tugging Martina's arm down.

"Come on, guys, would you rather sit here and die of antic- ipation as we wait our turn?" she says. "Let's get this shit over with."

No one argues with Martina as we walk to the beginning of the obstacle course, not even Willow—not that she has even engaged with our group this whole time. Her mother doesn't seem to have any better luck. Cindy grabs Willow's arm and tries to whisper something into her ear, but she pulls away and rolls her eyes, an act I would never dare try with my mother.

"Team Green, the course starts in three, two, one—*go!*"

Willow no longer matters to me as a burst of energy sends me breezing through the first part of the course, a simple sprint down a dirt path. The next obstacle seems right up a football player's alley, but too bad I only watch the Super Bowl. My thighs burn as I navigate my way in and out of each tire. My foot gets tangled up in the second to last one, but I catch myself before kissing the ground.

This course is seeming too easy and then I get a good look at the height of the wooden log ahead of me, almost tall enough that I can walk right under it. I turn around and wait for Martina and Aspen to catch up. After some deliberation, I agree to let Aspen climb up onto my back and hoist her over the log while Martina holds her arms out on the other side in case she falls. Aspen cheers as she clambers up to her feet while Martina and I look at each other warily. We're tall enough that we can haul ourselves over the log without help, but clearly not clever enough to figure out how. As we bounce ideas off each other, Willow slips past us. She jumps up, drives her palms down into the wood, and manages to hook a leg over the log, then another. She sits up there for a few moments, swinging her legs, before elegantly jumping down to the dirt.

Show-off.

Mirroring her form, I jump up and try to latch onto the log, but the wooden material is smoother than I thought. I slip and land flat on my back on the ground.

"It's easier if you get your elbows up top," Willow says from the other side. When I don't answer her, she shrugs and mutters, "But you can try it your way again."

Gritting my teeth, I take her advice and give the obstacle a go again, and in an instant, I'm on my own two feet on the other side of the log. Willow smiles when I brush past her, but I can't tell if it's out of self-satisfaction or genuine encouragement.

Even though I haven't attempted monkey bars since elementary school, some combination of muscle memory and elbow grease allows me to get through them unscathed and even have a little fun on my way across. I jump down and freeze midsquat when I get a good look at the length of the mass of mud ahead of the rope swing, realizing this obstacle won't be nearly as forgiving as the last two.

Martina plants a hand on my shoulder from behind as the four of us glance between the rope and the thick sticky mud. "Hope you're not too attached to your clothes, guys. We're not making it through this unscathed."

"Any volunteers?" I ask, sounding like Axel.

A moment of silence passes, interspersed with the calls of birds and leaves rustling in the breeze, before Willow steps forward.

"I'll go." She stretches out her arms and then tightens her high ponytail. "I've done this before."

"Where the hell have you done this before?" Aspen asks her. "*Gym* class?"

"Summer camp. When your parents didn't have the time of day for you growing up, you get pretty used to these kinds of activities. All those damn camps are the same, anyway."

Willow says everything like she doesn't care, but the way her voice falls a notch on the last few words gives her away, and for a second, she feels human. It makes me want to wrap my arms around her and give her a hug and tell her it's okay before I have to slap myself back to reality.

Sucking in her breath, she pulls back, latches onto the rope, and then soars over the pool of mud, letting go just inches away from the edge of the soupy brown liquid. She lands in a squat and topples forward as she tries to extend her legs but still saves herself at the last minute.

"Nice job, Willow!" Axel calls, and I nearly jump back.

I didn't realize he's been following us this whole time through the trees lining the sides of this course, but I shouldn't be surprised, knowing at least one staff member needs to make sure we're actually getting through this course and not finding a way to sneak around it.

Not that I'd ever try to do that.

"Whitney, you're up next."

I snap my head up, finding him smirking at me. "I thought you said we were supposed to figure out our strategy as a group?"

"Well, I'm not hearing any deliberating, so you'll do as I say, Carmichael."

Goddamn. Authoritative language shouldn't make my stomach flutter the way it does, but there's just something so sexy about him giving me commands. It's almost like he knows I'd listen to him even if he ordered me to go run to the grocery store and buy him a bag of apples.

I grip the rope and give myself a little mental pep talk, reminding myself how many more strenuous activities I've tried at this camp. With a small grunt, I soar across the pool of mud and land on my butt, my arms stretched behind me. There's no mistaking the goopy liquid trailing down my palms is mud, and I wince as I wipe them off on the front of my T-shirt, having no other choice.

"Watch out!"

I dart to the side at Martina's voice but do a double take when I find Aspen on her back. The two sail across the mud together and land in a heap on their hands and knees on the edge of the pool, splattering brown liquid across their faces and hair.

"Extra points for creativity!" Axel calls from the sidelines, fanning his hands over his mouth. "Zero points for the execution."

"I'll take it!" Martina yells, shooting up to her feet and wiping flecks of brown from her hair.

Willow and I glance between each other and burst into

laughter, and she tries to conceal the noise into her hands while I use the crook of my elbow. We lock eyes for a moment, and it's the first time I realize how pretty they are, a honey brown in the sun that contrasts so naturally with her bright-blond hair, even if the color is partly bleach.

"Here comes the hard part!" Axel calls out, egging us on.

The four of us stand in a Bob-approved row and gawk at the wall ahead of us, having to crane our necks to take it all in. There are some grooves in the surface towards the top few feet, but they won't be any use until we figure out a way to reach them.

"Any chance you've done this before too, Willow?" Aspen asks, looking unnerved.

"Unfortunately, no." She extends her arm to run her finger-tips down the wall's surface. "Ideas, Whitney?"

I touch the wall as well, realizing it's more textured than I thought, but nowhere near enough to climb alone. "The smart-est strategy is to have the two tallest people go first. One can hoist the other up until the other can latch onto those grooves at the top and pull themselves over the wall onto the platform. Everything will be easier once we have someone up there."

"Okay," Martina concurs after a moment, nodding. "The two tallest people would be you and Willow, then."

I whip my head around. "You're, like, half an inch shorter than me, Martina."

"Yeah, and every inch counts here," she says, and her eyes twinkle as she adds, "just like in some other circumstances."

I elbow her so hard she nearly chokes, but the connotations of her remark don't pass over Willow, who drives her teeth into her bottom lip to keep from laughing when she registers Axel is now standing behind us.

"What are you doing here?" I ask, heart skipping a beat with him this close.

"Spotting you all." He clears his throat. "And sparing Bob a lawsuit."

"Damn, is this a bad time to mention my dad owns a law firm, then?" Martina asks cheekily. "Sandoval and Baker, experts in class-action litigation . . ."

"Don't push my buttons, Martina," Axel says, tone darkening. "I'm not in the mood."

"Yes, sir." She mock-salutes him as she darts out of the way.

"Do you want to be the base or should I?"

I snap my head up. There's no way Willow is being serious with that question, when I weigh at least thirty pounds more than she does. For a moment, I think she's waiting for me to slip and say her just so she can snap some backhanded comment about my body, but she stands still, waiting for me to answer.

"I'll be the base," I say. "You just get up there."

Knitting my fingers together, I form a stand for the mud-caked sole of her sneaker in my palms and wince when my arms give out with just a light step. She may be lithe, but it doesn't change the fact that I'm the furthest thing from a cheerleader.

"We can change—"

"*No.* Keep going, Willow."

Her body tenses as she presses her full weight into my hands and extends one of her long, bony arms. My quads scream as I extend from a squat to a full standing position, but I forget the pain when Willow latches a hand around one of the grooves in the wall. As I give her another forceful shove upwards, she manages to curl her fingers over the edge of the wall, her grip loose but there.

"There you go, Willow," Axel calls from next to me, and I duck my head down, hating how much I loathe the sound of him praising her. "Almost got it."

Willow swings one leg over the wall and nearly tumbles headfirst to the other side. Only when I see her standing tall on the platform do I let out that breath I've been holding this whole time. With it, all the blood surges back to my aching palms, my natural skin color nearly invisible under all the cakey mud at this point.

With another person at the top, hauling Martina takes half as much work, yanked up by Willow's surprisingly strong arm. Aspen makes it over after a short struggle to grip Martina's hand, and when I'm standing alone at the foot of the wall, I realize I never factored myself into the strategy. I stand frozen, drowning out Martina and Willow dangling their arms down the edge, yelling out to grab on to each of them. Between two blinks, I'm back in gym class again, and the arms reaching out are broken ropes, the cheers mocking laughter.

"Breathe, Whitney," a voice says into my ear. "I've got you."

The fog in my mind clears when I register that voice is Axel's, and his two strong hands are gripping my waist. He lifts me into the air in one fluid motion and holds me up until my sweaty hands lock around Willow's and Martina's. They yank me over and I land on my back on the platform, my chest heaving up and down—from anxiety or exhaustion, I don't even know.

"He *definitely* likes you," Martina says as she pulls me up to my feet.

I don't say anything, but I can't hide the pink crawling across my cheeks, only grateful it can be mistaken for sunburn.

Willow tackles the series of logs that follows first, and by no surprise doesn't look fazed, probably confident in her balance from years of dancing, or maybe she's done this at another summer camp. When Martina and Aspen have taken their turns, both somehow making it through unscathed as well, I try a different approach and crawl up onto the long beam lining the perimeter of the fixture, using my hands for support.

When I feel stable enough, I extend my body and take the first few baby steps, my arms fanned out on either side of my hips. I swallow and continue down the unnerving beam, and with each step, my mind drifts, first to the feeling of Axel's strong hands against my waist, then that smooth sultry voice in my ear. I wonder if he'd help any camper like that, or if he acts this way only around me.

A war between insecurity and attraction starts waging in my brain, one voice telling me I really am that special and the other trying to snap me out of my delusion. I don't even realize I've made it across nearly half the beam with my eyes closed. Opening them and feeling mistakenly confident, I pick up the pace and zoom down the rest of the narrow wood. On my last step, my ankle rolls, and I waver in the air like a gymnast fighting for her Olympic career before I come crashing down to the mud. My hands brace my fall, but I'm knee-deep into the sticky brown liquid before I can regain my balance.

When Willow notices, she turns around and runs towards me. She grabs my arm and helps pull me up to my feet, her eyes growing wide with concern.

"Hey, are you okay? I didn't even notice you fell."

I pull my arm out of her grasp, shaking the mud off my hands and sending flecks of brown into the air. Maybe it's because my clothes are ruined or my hands are aching or because I'm a sweaty, overstimulated mess, but I find myself unable to bite my tongue, especially around Willow of all people.

"Did you really think I'd expect *you* to notice? You can cut the act now, Willow."

She draws back and purses her lips in return, and it's funny how such a heartless person can be so easily offended. A tinge of sympathy grips my heart when she blinks a few times, like she's about to cry, but she seems to come to her usual senses and scowls.

"You know, you don't have to act like such a bitch all the time, Whitney."

"Me?" I slap a mud-caked palm against my chest. "*I'm* the bitch?"

"Uh-huh. The least you can do is say thank you when someone offers to help you."

I throw my head back and howl in laughter. "Oh, *that's* rich. I never thought I'd be here getting schooled on manners from *you* of all people."

She takes a menacing step forward, ducking her head down until we're eye to eye. "You should watch what you say to me, you know. My mom runs this place in case you forgot."

"Really now?" I close the distance between us. "That's why you've spent this whole time pretending like you're not related to her, right?"

She presses her palms into my front and shoves me back a foot. "Don't make assumptions when you know *nothing* about my life, Whitney."

I push her back, underestimating how much brute force I possess—and harbored rage I want to unleash. She stumbles into the pool of mud but catches herself before she meets my same muddy fate. Eyes ablaze, she grips my forearm, nails digging into my skin, and yanks me down to the ground, but if she's taking me down, I'm bringing her with me.

I roll onto my back and kick her in the back of the knees, and she doubles forward into the mud with a whimper. Crawling army-style, she latches onto the ends of my hair. I shriek when she yanks hard enough to rip out a few hairs, sending a searing pain to my scalp. Pouncing on her, I manage to grab the sleeve of her shirt and tug hard enough to rip a line up to her collar. I reveal the strap of her cupcake-patterned sports bra, and I can't help but throw my head back and cackle in laugher.

"You stupid *bitch*," Willow seethes, throwing me off her. "You're gonna pay for this!"

With our hands grabbing any limb in sight, we start rolling around in the mud and screaming profanities into each other's faces, flecks of mud flying in the air and painting our cheeks and noses. Eventually, while she flails like a dying cockroach, I pin her down to the ground by her shoulders and spit out the hairs in my mouth that were probably supposed to be on my head.

"That's enough!"

Like he's picking up a toddler throwing a hissy fit, Axel grabs me under the armpits and hauls me to my feet. I shimmy out of his hold, but he lunges forward and presses me against his hard body. If I wasn't still seeing red, maybe I'd find the position somewhat romantic. Before Willow can try to throw a fit of her own, Cindy loops two arms around her waist and yanks her off the ground. Her legs helplessly beat the air, trying to hit anything in sight, while I eventually stop fighting Axel and slump down in defeat.

With no one around to supervise them, the rest of the girls encircle us, some even cheering us on. Martina yells at them to scram, but the gossipy chatter continues even as Axel and Cindy drag us away and end the spectacle.

CHAPTER FOURTEEN

When I was in high school, I never got sent to the principal's office. But sitting in Bob's office on the second floor of the Central Building, a seat away from Willow, with Axel standing by my side and Cindy hovering over her daughter's head, I imagine it would've gone a lot like this.

Bob exhales and pinches the bridge of his nose, glancing up from the surface of his desk. Apart from a mug with the letter *B* on it and two picture frames, the photos in which I can't make out from my angle, it's not a very personal space.

"Is this really worth ruining my very expensive white club chairs?"

His initial reaction makes me laugh, but Axel's hard expression forces me to clamp my mouth shut and wipe away the mud stain on the cushion of my seat with the heel of my hand.

Cindy sighs, gripping the back of Willow's chair until her knuckles turn white. "I don't want to be here any more than you do, Bob. But we do have a strict no-violence policy at this camp, and we must set a precedent for the rest of the campers."

Bob leans back in his swivel chair, bending it almost past its limit, his beefy arms folded across his chest. His fingertips dance under his graying stubble as he looks between me and Willow, who, like me, has done everything to avoid direct eye contact with him, probably because she's sitting here in a cupcake-themed sports bra. Thankfully, I had on a black tank top underneath the T-shirt now crumpled into a muddy ball in the trash.

"I'm afraid you're not really in a place to adjudicate this matter," Bob says to Cindy, clearly alluding to her blood relation with the girl sitting next to me. "And I don't have the brain space for this now. Axel, you'll decide their fate."

"Come on, Bob," Cindy says. "You know I only have him here so these two won't start tearing each other's hair apart again."

"I said what I said." Bob tents his fingers under his chin and nods at Axel. "Any ideas?"

My stomach roils as I wait for Axel to speak, and I wonder if Bob realizes my trainer isn't an unbiased party either. But from the dangerous twinkle in his eyes, I have a feeling he's not going to let us off easy.

"Their fight may have been justified"—my hopes reignite before he crushes them, almost delightedly—"but they both need to learn a lesson. How about dining hall duty tomorrow morning? I've been hearing the cleaning staff is a little short-staffed this summer."

"You can't be serious," Willow breathes. "I'm already forced to be here, and now I have to be the camp's *maid* too?"

"Washing a couple of dishes won't kill you, Gerard," Axel says wryly and looks up. "Your thoughts, Bob?"

He rises to his feet, sliding his hands into the pockets of his cargo shorts. "Works for me. Frankly, I would've suggested taking their phones away, but I have a feeling these two would take cleaning toilets over going a day without Wi-Fi."

He's right, but I don't dare say a word.

"But," he continues, flattening his palms and leaning over his desk, "if I catch you two fighting again, damaging camp property, coming back to campus late on Sundays—whatever it is, Willow and Whitney, you can kiss those phones goodbye, if not your spots at this camp. I don't like people who waste my time."

I gasp softly when I notice the grim frown etched onto Bob's mouth, realizing he's not joking around. To my right, Willow's fists unfurl and her eyes gleam, almost with elation, like getting expelled would be her dream come true.

Just how bad is this place for her?

Bob juts his thumb towards the door. "Go yell at your kid in peace, Cindy. Whitney, you're free—until tomorrow morning, that is."

With his send-off, I make a beeline to the door, but I don't get far when Axel blocks my path down the hallway. I want to cuss him out and shove him to the side, in need of nothing more than a shower and some peace and quiet, but I've already racked up enough camp transgressions today.

"What do you want now? Didn't you already dish out my punishment?"

"Whitney, come on. That was nothing. Usually, we would call your parents in these scenarios."

"I'm *eighteen*," I bite back, arms akimbo. Real mature of me, I know. "Not a kid."

"You sure as hell were acting like one outside. You know this reflects badly on me as your trainer, too, right?"

"Oh, you're *definitely* not going to make this about you right now. You have no idea the things that girl has done to me, and how patient I've been. Ruining her shirt has nothing on destroying my self-esteem every fucking day of high school."

The tears I've been holding back this whole time prick my eyes, but I blink them away when I realize even Axel doesn't deserve my vulnerability. "Besides, if you wanted a trainee with no baggage, maybe you should've asked Bob to include a sob story essay in the application to weed out all the losers like me. I would've gone to town on that."

I do what I do best and try to run away, but Axel catches my hand and pulls me back. An uncharacteristic yelp leaves my mouth as his grip sends a surge of pain down my palm, and he lets me go in a panic.

"What's wrong?" he asks. "Did I hurt you?"

"N-no," I stammer, lifting my hand. I notice a hot red patch on the edge of my palm and a pinprick-sized hole in the middle of it. "I must've hurt my hand on one of the obstacles."

He takes it in his, touch featherlight this time, and runs his thumb over the red spot. "You have a splinter. I can take it out for you."

I pull my hand out of his grasp. "No, I don't need—"

"Just listen to me for once, Whitney."

I don't argue with him—not that I don't want to—because with how low my sense of adventure has always been, I've never even gotten a splinter before, let alone learned how to safely remove one. I follow him down the hallway to a small room that resembles my high school nurse's office, a cramped white place with a few motivational posters on the walls.

I sit below the one telling me to be myself because everyone else is taken. Super original.

"Are you sure you know what you're doing?" I ask after he washes his hands and pulls out a first aid kit.

"Do you not trust me?"

I stay quiet, knowing I do trust him, probably with my life, but that's too embarrassing to admit after knowing each other for only a few weeks. He sets his supplies on the small table next to my chair and crouches down in front of me.

"First aid is Camp Campbell 101, for the record," he reassures me. "Breaking up a catfight? Yeah, that still hasn't made its way into the curriculum."

"You should probably suggest adding that for next year," I say dryly, looking away as he disinfects my palm. "I'd be happy to provide a demonstration at orientation."

"Think you'll feel the same way a year from now, huh?"

"I don't know," I grumble, fingers curling inwards. "Maybe I might."

I mull over my anger as he works and takes caution not to press too hard on my sensitive skin. Something about being cared for makes my heart feel all warm and fuzzy, and I hate that with one look at his gorgeous eyes, I'll probably forget that I'm mad at him. And mad at Willow. And mad at myself for reacting the way I did, because of course the one time I give her a taste of her own medicine, I have to pay for it too.

"This might hurt a bit," he warns, but I can barely suck in my next breath before I feel a pinch and a rush of relief. He holds the tweezers up to the fluorescent light above my head, and there's the splinter, barely thicker than a few hairs twisted together. "Wanna keep it for good luck?"

"Is that actually a thing?"

"Nah, I'm messing with you." I hide my face in my shoulder as I giggle, and the smile on his face grows wider. "There. Got you to laugh."

"Now I'm going to frown to piss you off, Axel."

"And I'll make you laugh again," he says, like it's a threat, and everything in me twists and tightens.

"Hey, Axel, I wanted to ask if you're down to go out—" Blue-tinted hair pops into my peripheral vision before Isla pokes her head into the room. Her body goes rigid as she stands in the doorway, and she clears her throat. "Oh, um, is something going on?"

"I'll explain later," Axel tells Isla and then turns to me. He shoots me a tight smile and gestures to the door, and all the warm feelings from this moment with him vanish. "You should be all good, Whitney."

I take that as my cue to leave, but I don't want to come out from behind him and reveal myself to the Lululemon model standing in the doorway. Isla shoots me a look of pity as I slink away with my head down, and I bite the inside of my cheek to keep from scowling at her like the petulant teenager I actually am.

—

"Come *on*, Whitney, wake up. It's almost eight in the morning."

Martina says that like it's past noon already, ripping open the curtains behind my bed. Unfortunately, nothing can motivate me to crawl out from under these covers this morning, not when I have a cleaning session with Willow ahead while trying not to think about what might have happened if Axel and Isla went out last night.

"Ten more minutes," I grumble, tugging my sheets over my head as sunlight streams through my stinging eyes. "Can't do this shit today."

"Five more minutes, and I'll be back if you're not up."

"Are you my mom now?"

"No, but I can yell as loud as one, so you might want to haul your ass out of bed."

I shoot up ramrod straight. "I'm up now."

Ten minutes later, I've pulled on a pair of baggy shorts and one of Poppy's tattered Columbia Golf hoodies, not even bothering to take my hair out of the messy sleep bun on top of my head. Even with the low-profile look, heads turn as Martina, Aspen, and I file into the dining hall. I ignore the stares, but that icky feeling that eyes are on my face lingers even as I duck my head down and shovel in spoonful after spoonful of cereal.

"Whitney, right?"

I glance up, finding Kennedy and Neha standing before our table.

"Uh, yes?"

"That was so badass yesterday," Kennedy says, placing her tray of food down on the tabletop. She takes a seat next to me while Neha plops down next to her. This circular picnic table is already cramped without them, making me shift closer to Aspen. "Gosh, you have no idea how much I wish I beat up someone like that when I was high school."

"Um, thanks," I chuckle, glancing at Martina. She shrugs, leaving it up to me to continue or end this interaction. "But I'm paying for it today."

"Oh my god, *stop*." Neha flattens a hand against her front, leaning in. She's pretty in the same way Ava is, with black hair that tumbles to her waist and siren-like dark-brown eyes. "Are they kicking you out?"

"If they were kicking her out, do you think she'd be here eating with us, dumbass?" Kennedy says to her.

"Sorry," Neha mumbles. "Rumor has it you and Willow got sent to Bob's office. I'd be shitting myself if I were in your place yesterday. The man's so intimidating."

"*Beyond* intimidating," I laugh. "But don't worry, I'm not going anywhere."

We launch into a full-blown conversation, and I can feel eyes on us from Willow and Adriana's table. The five of us now overpower their four, and they sense it, huddling together and whispering in each other's ears.

"Okay, you guys," Kennedy says, leaning back and looking between Martina and Aspen. "Have you heard about all the couples here?"

"Like who?" Aspen asks.

"Like the engaged trainers," Neha says. "May's my trainer, and she's accidentally whacked me in the face with her ring twice, and it felt like a meteor hitting me, I swear."

"Wait . . ." Martina cocks her head to the side, eyebrows lifting. "Ryan's my trainer. Do you know when they got engaged?"

"Yeah, last summer. May told me the whole story when I was trying to stall a workout the other day, and turns out it was kind of a hot mess because that blue-haired girl—"

"Isla," I correct, pinching a loose thread in my shorts.

"Right, her," Neha says. "She and Axel were supposed to help orchestrate the proposal—it was somewhere public on a boat or whatever—but they got in a huge fight before, and the whole thing fell apart, so Ryan proposed in the backyard of her parents' house. Which is still romantic and all, but I don't know . . . I'd be kind of mad."

"Totally," I murmur, and Martina and Aspen shoot me funny looks at my forced nonchalance. "Were they dating?"

Kennedy scoffs, "Probably. I'm guessing that was the breakup."

"Yeah, 'cause he can do way better than her," Neha says, and Kennedy nods in agreement. "The guy's literally sex on legs. Everyone at this camp thinks that."

Martina snorts, and I kick her under the table to keep her from exposing me. No one needs to know about my big fat crush on my personal trainer, who's apparently way out of my league as well.

Kennedy and Neha head out with Martina and Aspen, who squeeze me into a hug before my morning from hell truly begins. While I wait for the dining hall to thin out, I remain in my seat and finish texting back a three-paragraph life update to Ava, notably leaving out my adventures of the past day. A couple of minutes later, only Willow and her squad remain, eyeing me from afar.

When I look up, Adriana, Noelle, and Joanna are walking towards me.

"Can I help you?" I ask, putting my phone down.

"Look, Whitney," Adriana says, the spokesperson for the trio. She flattens her hands on the tabletop, her chipped hot-pink manicure distracting me for a moment. "I don't usually go looking for drama. But since it seems like you do, just know something: you mess with Willow, you mess with us."

"And what are you gonna do?" I slowly stand up. "Beat me up?"

"No," Noelle answers me from behind her. "Unlike both you and Willow, we don't prefer violence."

The smirk on her lips grows more devious as she lifts her hand holding a blueberry smoothie into the air. It all occurs in slow motion, or maybe it's the fastest five seconds of my life, because between two blinks, she's dumped the contents of the glass onto the floor, splattering blue all over the canvas of my sneakers.

"Have fun cleaning!" Adriana calls over her shoulder as she heads out with Noelle and Joanna.

Halfway down the hallway, Joanna scurries back and ducks her head down, out of breath. "Look, I don't know about the floor, but for your shoes, some baking soda and water should do the trick." When Adriana waves her over, she mouths a *sorry* before leaping over the blue puddle and hurrying out of sight.

"Teenage girls," someone says, startling me. A member of the dining hall staff pops out of the kitchen with a pile of rags in one hand and a mop in the other. "Been forty years since I graduated high school, and they're still the same."

"How reassuring," I say back, barely audibly. I walk towards her and reach for a rag. "I'll get going on this."

"No, don't worry about this mess, hon." Her brown eyes crease up with sympathy, and my chest tightens. Finally, someone gets it. "Just wipe off the tables for me. Paper towels and disinfectant are in the kitchen. The name's Brandy, by the way."

"Whitney," I say and stay still for a moment, waiting for the catch, but she shoos me away to the kitchen. Maybe this isn't going to be as bad as I thought, especially when I realize Willow's all the way on the other side of the dining hall, sweeping the floor with choppy, aggressive strokes.

For the next fifteen minutes, we work on opposite sides of the room, and I throw all my power into wiping these tables down, realizing the more I zero in on every nook and cranny, the more my unwanted thoughts begin to flee from me. By table five, I've pretty much forgotten yesterday's fight, and my bitterness over Axel and Isla has faded to mild annoyance at best.

With another wide stroke across the table that shoots a searing pain up my arm, my elbow knocks into someone, and I whip my head around, finding Willow sweeping the floor around my feet.

"Sorry," I say, stepping out of the way.

"It's fine," she mutters, bending down to drag her broom under the table. The wispy hairs by her ears are damp, and her lip is stuck in the snare of her teeth, making me wonder if she's ever actually cleaned before.

"Do you want to trade places?"

"Like you sweep, and I wipe the tables down?"

"Pretty much," I say, unsure if she seems suspicious because I'm willingly talking to her or because she doesn't want to switch tasks. "Unless you don't know how to wipe a table down or something."

She snatches the paper towel roll from my hands. "Excuse me, I definitely do. I worked as a waitress at a country club for a month when I was fifteen."

"Why only a month?"

"Because I got fired." She sprays down the bench of the table and begins rubbing vigorously, her ponytail swinging from side to side. Quietly, she says, "I sucked at sweeping floors."

I try to hold back the loud laugh that follows but don't bother when Willow cracks a smile herself. "I didn't expect you to say that."

"Well, surprisingly I have a sense of humor that doesn't come at the expense of other people. Not that anyone appreciates it, though."

"Hey, if you need any tips, I'm willing to drop a few. Self-deprecating humor is kind of my thing."

We work in silence around each other, but some of the heavy tension lifts from the air. Every few moments, we sneak a glance at each other, like a rabbit would in the vicinity of a fox, waiting for our façades to crumble and for one of us to pounce on the other again.

"All right, girls," Brandy announces, her voice echoing off the walls of the empty dining hall, "follow me back to the kitchen for your next task."

Willow and I keep our heads down as we trail behind Brandy, perhaps knowing deep down that we both deserve what's coming to us. But when we slip through the double doors of the kitchen, Brandy doesn't thrust any cleaning supplies into our hands.

"I appreciate both of your help today, and *especially* your civility around each other. Feel free to take one before you leave."

She cracks open the plastic lid to a container of cookies and pushes it towards us. My hand gravitates on instinct to the largest chocolate-chunk cookie, but my fingers freeze midair when I notice Willow's lips purse and her eyes dart across the platter. I half expect her to make some comment on how I don't need a cookie, but instead, she asks, "What's your favorite flavor? I'm so bad at decisions like these."

Oh.

"Probably a tie between chocolate chunk and snickerdoodle."

I push the platter towards her. "But you should pick whatever you like."

She surprises me by taking one of each, motivating me to grab a second chocolate-chunk cookie and finally sort out my nagging craving. We thank Brandy and head out the back entrance of the dining hall, alternating bites from each cookie. The chocolate chunk in the last bite melts under the heat of Willow's fingertips and dribbles down her bottom lip. I fish out a tissue from my sweatshirt pocket and hand it to her before the chocolate stains her white shirt, and she giggles as she dabs at her mouth and makes an even bigger mess.

"About our fight yesterday," I say, swallowing the last bite of my cookie. "Do we talk about it, or do we move on and pretend like it never happened?"

"I'd choose the second option, but I've showered three times since yesterday, and I'm still finding dirt in places I didn't think dirt could be."

The sound of our laughter cuts through the thick, muggy air, and it's the first time Willow is laughing with me and not *at* me.

"I'm sorry, you know." My eyes widen in shock, but then Willow continues. "For ripping your hair out, that is. You have beautiful thick hair, but you deserved to keep those five strands on your head."

I laugh again, covering my chocolatey mouth with my knuckles. "I'm also sorry for destroying your shirt. But then again, if I hadn't, I wouldn't have known I need to add a pink cupcake-themed sports bra to my collection."

"Oh my god, please stop. All the ones that give me boobs were in my hamper."

After the events of the past twenty-four hours, feeling any sort of lighthearted emotion while eating cookies on a walk with my mortal enemy sure seems like one hell of a plot twist. But I don't try to end the moment, and we continue our banter the entire way back to our dorm.

CHAPTER FIFTEEN

As I trek from my dorm to the Central Building with my hood tugged over my head, I'm dreading my workout session with Axel, for multiple reasons. One, it started raining, so he's forced to hold it in the gym, which means more equipment for me to mix up. Two, now that most of the rageful feelings from my fight with Willow have faded to some reluctant acceptance, I'm almost embarrassed that he had to witness such a low point in my life.

"Sorry I'm late."

A voice from behind startles me, and I turn around, finding Axel ducking into the building in a gray hoodie and shorts to match, his damp hair sticking to his forehead. The lid of his coffee cup is speckled with rain droplets, and he strategically tries to drink around them as he brings the cup to his lips.

"It's fine," I say, pulling down my hood and revealing my dry brown locks. "Rain get you?"

He holds open the gym door for me, and I slip inside. "My fault for not checking my weather app this morning. How was dining hall duty, by the way?"

"Fine," I grumble. "Not as bad as I thought." He smirks, as if knowing I'd find it that way. As I make eye contact with him, I can't miss the slight puffiness to his normally angled face and the dull sheen around his eyes, like he only got a few hours of sleep. "How was your night?"

"Why do you ask . . . ?"

"No reason," I say and shrug, forcing that nonchalance again. "You look tired, that's all."

"Maybe I was up all night coming up with your workout today. It's tough work being a trainer after all."

"It's *way* tougher on this side. At least you know what you're doing."

"I don't always," he grumbles before changing the subject. "Let's warm up. A hundred jumping jacks, and actually count this time."

He drinks coffee and messes around on his phone as I start moving, and my jealousy compounds as my sneakers pound the gym floor and my heavy breaths cut into the air. From my angle, I can't make out what he's typing, only the contact name at the top of his screen—Isla S. My curiosity piques, and with a second glance, I confirm there are no emojis or embellishments or even a nickname. She might as well be some contact he added for a group project and forgot to remove from his phone, but then he grins, deep satisfaction etched into the lines of his face, and I give up playing detective.

At the ninety-eighth jumping jack, I fall into a heap on the floor on my face and can barely lift my head up when I hear his footsteps again.

"Today, Whitney," he says, holding out a pair of boxing gloves, "we're going to try my favorite sport: boxing. We'll begin by learning to throw a jab."

Slightly unnerved, I slide on the gloves and ignore those

thoughts telling me how out of place I look when I catch sight of myself in the mirror. If anything, I should be excited I'll be coming out of this session with a new skill, one that not even one of my family members possesses.

"To assume the proper stance, move this hand closer to your face," he says, bringing my right arm level with my jawline. "Hold the other out in front of you and keep your chin towards your chest. Make sure your feet are around shoulder width apart, knees slightly bent."

"Okay," I say and shuffle my feet around. I accidentally bump back into his chest and mutter an apology, but he doesn't say anything.

"Punch with your left hand, turning your wrist as you do so that your knuckles are up, palm down, when you connect." He demonstrates for me, punching the air instead. "After, you want to snap back and bring your arm back into the starting position to protect your face."

He holds up a strike pad and waits for me to get into the proper position again. My heart thumps faster as I try to remember his instructions, as if this is an exam and he'll be grading me on my first try.

"Deep breaths," he says, snapping me out of my trance. "Give it a go."

I do and laugh when he barely budges at the weak tap that grazes the pad.

"Now pretend like the person you hate the most is standing in front of you and give it another go."

I still and look up at him, my hands still in position by my face. "You're doing this on purpose, aren't you?"

"I'm doing this because I'd rather you learn how to channel

your anger in safer ways." He draws closer, dipping his head down in a warning. "*Not* beat someone up."

"I didn't *beat* Willow up, Axel." Okay, maybe I kind of did. "If anything, she started the fight."

"But you continued it. Violence is never the solution to violence."

"You know, that sounds like advice from either a failing peace activist or someone who's never been bullied before. But that could just be me."

"You're right." My eyebrows lift at the easy concession. *Axel admitting I'm right?* Then he continues, "But I have been wronged before, and acting like a fucking idiot in response cost me my peace and sanity. Now try again; I'm not going to ask twice."

Mustering up all my strength, I step forward, assume the correct position, and punch the strike pad again. I look up at his reaction. To my surprise, there's a hint of approval in those slightly upturned lips, so I continue punching, channeling my pent-up anger in every movement. Soon my heart drums in my chest to the rhythm created by the pounding of my fist. My energy levels seem to increase each time my boxing glove meets the strike pad, but Axel stops me before I can get too ahead of myself.

"Let's take a short break," he says, taking the gloves from me. "I have too much planned for today to tire you out already."

Not having to be told twice, I drop to the padded floor with my legs in front of me and palms pressed flat behind me. He throws me a water bottle and takes one for himself.

After a silent moment passes, he observes, "Willow really did a number on you in high school, didn't she?"

"You could say that." I scoff and roll the cold water bottle over my aching shoulder, close to moaning in relief. "But I'm mostly over it by now."

"No, you're not." Axel reads right through my glass exterior, but I'm still determined to defy him, opening my mouth with a rebuttal. "Lying doesn't make you seem stronger to me."

"Then what does, huh?"

"Owning the ugly in life. The hurt. The anger. The pain." He leans back against the mirror across from me, trailing his eyes up my arm. "Your shoulder's hurting you right now, isn't it?"

It's not like I'm being particularly discreet about it, but maybe he's testing how vulnerable I'm willing to be. "Yeah, it is," I mumble, letting the hand trying and failing to get that knot out fall to the floor. "Can you fix it?"

He waits a beat before offering, "I can try."

He calls me over to what I think is the bench press machine, and I sit sideways on the seat, glad I don't have to use it for its real purpose. I watch in the mirror as he lifts his hand, and before it makes contact with my exposed shoulder in my tank top, he moves my ponytail out of the way, his fingers brushing the back of my neck and making me shiver.

"Let me know if this hurts," he says, his fingers forming a C-shape around my shoulder.

When his thumb presses into my trapezius muscle, a gasp escapes my mouth, and Axel stills, but I shake my head and tell him to keep going. He remains rigid the whole time, massaging my shoulder with calculated strokes, probably using me as practice for his future physical therapy career. I close my eyes as relief sinks into my perpetually sore muscles and don't even notice my head start to roll back. The base of my ponytail brushes against his hard abdomen, and I jolt forward. Axel doesn't seem to notice, his eyebrows still drawn together in concentration in the mirror in front of me. I duck my head down before my overheating face gives me away and let him finish working his magic.

When he lifts his hand, and I think he's going to let go, he tucks a few loose strands of hair sticking out of my ponytail behind my ear, his gaze transfixed on my parted lips in the mirror. That knot of desire tightens in my stomach, and I look up at him almost in awe, at the way he towers over me with his broad shoulders and tall stature, our height difference even more pronounced with me closer to the ground.

Somehow, I've never felt safer in my life.

Axel drops his hand and steps back. "Do you want to finish this session, or should we call it a day?"

I can't believe he's giving me the choice, usually one to push me far past my limits, but to the utter shock of the Whitney of three weeks ago and perhaps even Axel himself, I choose the former.

"Can't have you out of a job today, can we?" I joke, rising to my feet. I run my fingers down my shoulder, trying to sweep the feeling of him off me, or else I won't focus on anything else the rest of this session. "Honestly, I don't even know what else you'd do with your free time besides annoy the hell out of me."

"I can think of many things." He hands me back my boxing gloves, and our fingers brush as I take them, making my heart flutter in that weird way again. He turns around, murmuring, "But none quite as entertaining as you, Whitney."

—

In the evening, with no therapy sessions à la Cindy on the schedule, Martina, Aspen, and I decide to treat ourselves to an outing at the camp's pool and hot tub.

"Is that what you're gonna wear?" Martina asks me. Usually not one to judge, she stares blankly at the blue athletic one-piece in my hands, her nostrils flared.

"Is it that bad?" I gesture to Aspen in the doorway of our room, donning a sleek black one-piece swimsuit. "*She's* wearing a one-piece."

Okay, I know mine isn't trendy like Aspen's, which dips into a low V at the front with slits all up the sides, but at least it's snug and practical, almost guaranteed to not accidentally come undone and flash everyone in sight. And, unlike a bikini, it covers that third roll in my stomach that appears whenever I sit down.

"It has a hole in it," Martina says. "*Two* holes, actually."

I think she's trying to rile me up until I look down and catch sight of the two dime-sized holes, one around the armpit and the other a couple of inches above the crotch-line. Before I can insist it'll be fine, she stands up and yanks out a white basket from the closet. She rifles through piles of tank tops and shorts and finally pulls out a collection of green strings from the bottom.

She thrusts it into my hand. "You can wear this."

I hold it up into the air and grimace. I'm not exactly well-endowed up there, but even this bikini top will barely cover the necessities. "What about the bottom?"

"I don't have a spare one, unfortunately. I'm sure you can just wear your underwear or something."

"Yeah, that's pretty much what a bikini bottom is," Aspen says, but it doesn't alleviate the tight ball in my chest. "The difference is just a social construct."

Not to me.

"Wait." Martina looks up while tightening the strings on her black top. "Is this some modesty thing? Because last I recall, you weren't religious or anything."

"Modesty isn't only a religious thing, though. We shouldn't assume, Martina."

I don't know if I should be relieved or annoyed that they don't understand my hesitation. Maybe my insecurities really are all in my head, a thought which motivates me to turn around and peel my shirt over my head in one go. I ignore the mirror as I fiddle with the top and try to spread the cups to cover more than just my nipples.

I spin around, and before Martina can open her mouth, I say, "I'm keeping the shorts on, though."

"Finally," Aspen breathes, yanking open the door.

A cloud of muggy air settles into our pores as we head down the sloping grass behind the dorms, and I try not to think about how many insects can feast on my bare legs. Between swatting at my ankles and thighs, I catch a mischievous twinkle in Martina's eyes, and I brace myself.

"Tomorrow is Sunday." Aspen and I look at her, waiting for the catch. "Our free day, guys."

"And?" Aspen says.

"We should do something exciting."

"Like find a new restaurant that none of the trainers frequent?" Aspen suggests.

"Like go to New York."

"New York?" I repeat. "You want to go all the way to New *York?*"

Martina rolls her eyes. "Don't look at me like I suggested we hitchhike to Disney World. We're a state away, guys. The city is the only reason people can stand to live here, anyway."

She's not wrong on that point, but maybe I've gotten so used to the confines of this camp and the small town encasing it that I've forgotten how big the world actually is, and how many things I can do besides go on one-mile runs and fantasize about my off-limits personal trainer.

"Then let's go to New York," I say after a moment of contemplation, for once not putting up a fight. "But no way in hell am I driving there."

Three mosquito bites later, we make it to the aquatic center, and the scent of chlorine hits my nostrils, a strange sense of nostalgia washing over me from my childhood swimming lessons. When I catch sight of the pool, long and rectangular and surrounded by marbled tiles and floor-to-ceiling windows overlooking dense forest, I realize, once again, exactly where all the money our parents paid for this experience goes. Although the water is clear and inviting, I have my eyes set on the hot tub, knowing nothing else will soothe my sore muscles.

As I slide into the tub and the jets pound against my back, I'm back in that moment in the gym with Axel this morning. It felt like I got a taste of him beyond my fantasies, but maybe it was only a teaser at best, like something I could experience in full if only I wasn't his trainee and he didn't have someone else competing for his heart. My own heart tightening, I sink even lower, so the jets massage my sore shoulder, and close my eyes to will those thoughts away. The ones that tell me how pathetic I am for even believing someone like him could be into me, and how I should move on before anything has even happened between us. College is only a month and a half away at this point, and there has to be some desperate freshman willing to take his chances with me.

I open my eyes at the sound of a door clicking shut.

Joanna and Willow stand at the edge of the pool, looking between each other and the three of us already in the water—me in the hot tub while Martina and Aspen are in the pool.

"*Okaaay*, I wasn't expecting anyone to be here," Joanna says, taking a huge step back. She glances at Willow. "Should we leave?"

"Do you guys want us to leave?" Willow asks us instead.

An instinctual *yes* forms on my tongue, but it doesn't roll off it, an invisible force holding it back. I wonder if that fleeting moment eating cookies together was enough to change my subconscious opinion of her.

No way is it *that* simple. Just yesterday we were rolling around in the mud tearing at each other's hair, and today I can't even bring myself to tell her to get the hell out?

"Honestly, yeah," Martina answers them for me, not mincing her words. "But this place is yours as much as it's ours, so knock yourselves out."

I keep my head low as I observe them in my peripheral vision, sinking an inch every time Joanna strips off another article of clothing and reveals more of her lean, sculpted body. Briefly, I wonder if she hangs around Willow all the time hoping to score a modeling contract from one of Cindy's connections in the industry. By the time the two of them climb down the ladder into the hot tub, I'm down to my chin, and I wish either Martina and Aspen were here. I steal a glance their way and find them taking turns holding each other down in the water, their airy laughter echoing off the walls.

The jets start working again and muffle the sounds around me. I look anywhere but Willow's eyes as I bob lightly in the water, arms crossed tightly over my skimpy top.

"Is it too hot?" Joanna asks, and it takes a second for me to register she's talking to me.

"No, it's fine," I say.

"Good." She nods and leans back, draping her long arms over the deck of the hot tub. "God, this was just what I needed."

"Tell me about it," Willow breathes, sinking lower.

No one says anything for at least a couple of minutes, and I feel that awkwardness that always comes with silence.

"Where are Adriana and Noelle?" I ask.

"Adriana's on her period, and Noelle's boyfriend broke up with her," Willow says. "She was losing it earlier."

"Yeah, but I don't know why she was that shocked, though," Joanna scoffs. "Her boyfriend was at least a nine, and she's like a . . . five?"

Willow laughs. "Oh, come on, at least a six. Negative ten in personality, though."

Willow's comment makes me flinch, because that was probably how she spoke about me behind my back in high school. But this situation feels almost worse because it's not like I ever wanted to be a part of her friend group. Noelle has done nothing but suck up to Willow and Joanna this whole time—maybe too naively—and this is the thanks she gets.

I open my mouth to come to her defense, but then Joanna turns to me, her eyes gleaming with curiosity, and my mind goes blank.

"Do you have a boyfriend, Whitney?" she asks.

"No, I don't. I, uh, didn't really have time to date and stuff in high school."

Before Joanna can continue, Willow speaks up. "Whitney's really smart, Jo. She was valedictorian of our high school."

"Wait, really?" I nod slowly at Joanna. "Where are you going to college?"

"Yale," I say. Willow looks down at the water in response, shoulders slumping an inch. I don't know why I feel the need to downplay my accomplishment to make her feel better, but I do. "But my grandpa went to college there, so I'm one of those annoying legacies."

"Damn, I wish," Joanna sighs dreamily. "I was in the bottom third of my class, so I'm going to the same college as, like, two hundred other people in my grade. Gonna be a freakin' high school reunion at sorority recruitment in the fall, I swear."

"Are you going to college, Willow?" I ask her. She skipped College T-shirt Day in May, but I didn't think much of it.

"I am. But I'm deferring my admission to the spring. Or maybe next fall . . . I don't know. I'm still figuring things out."

"But aren't you already young for your grade, anyway? You don't want to go to college before you can even buy a lottery ticket." Joanna tries to make her feel better by alluding to her November birthday, but Willow barely forces a smile.

"At this point I don't even think winning the lottery would solve all my problems. And not just because my parents—well, *parent*—is loaded."

Willow's voice falls a notch, and another shard of ice encasing her chips away and shatters. Just like that moment on the obstacle course, I want to pull her into a hug, but that would be far too awkward in my nearly half-naked state, and maybe, too, because we're still only a day removed from wanting to kill each other.

"I'm sorry," I tell her instead. "About your dad. That must've been really hard."

Her lips part before she swallows tightly and shakes her head. "Oh, um, it's fine, Whitney. It's not like it was your fault."

Joanna looks between us, allowing the awkward moment to pass, before changing the subject. "What do you want to do after college, Whitney?"

"Med school's the plan." I've never thought about what kind of doctor I want to be, but the answer that slips out of my mouth as I glance at Willow seems to make sense. "Then maybe become a psychiatrist."

"Wow, your parents must be so proud of you," Joanna says, and I want to answer, *Oh, if only it was that simple*. "I'm planning on majoring in marketing. Maybe I'll do social media or work in PR after I graduate, but honestly? I want to model."

Willow snorts. "You don't want to be a model. *Trust* me."

"Come on, you're just saying that because you don't like your mom," Joanna says and Willow bites her lip. "I need to finally use being five-ten to my advantage. I swear being called 'Joanna the Giraffe' all my life has messed with my head."

"Who called you that?" I ask.

"Literally everyone. My family, friends, even my teachers sometimes. And that was the cute nickname. In middle school, a bunch of boys used to call me Bigfoot when they found out I wore a bigger shoe size than they did, as if someone my height was gonna have these cute, tiny feet." She looks away and starts grumbling to herself, and I try not to let the shock show in my eyes.

If *she's* insecure, then what the hell should I be?

"Wanna join me and Aspen, Whitney?"

I turn around and lock eyes with Martina, who angles her chin towards the pool behind us. I wish I could explain that I'm not actually having as bad a time as I thought I would around Willow and Joanna, but I know that would sound absurd to her, so I pull myself out of the hot tub. I keep my arms folded over my stomach, my fingernails digging into the skin on my rib cage as I feel two searing gazes on every inch of my body.

Right when I think it's over, Joanna speaks again. "That's a really cute top, Whitney."

I turn around slowly, my arms still cradling my front. "Oh, it's not actually—"

"It is, isn't it?" Martina slings an arm over my shoulder and pulls me into her side. "It makes her boobs look *so* good. And her eyes too. Green is really your color, Whitney."

I'm gonna kill you, I mouth when I turn around.

Love you too, she mouths back and gives me a shove to start walking.

Week Four

CHAPTER SIXTEEN

"Ah, at *last*, the smell of freedom and adventure."

Martina, Aspen, and I walk out of the doors of Penn Station, and my head spins trying to take in the sensory overload of New York City. All around us, the blare of car horns blends into the sound of a jackhammer and construction workers yelling down the street, a foreign melody to my ears after weeks of listening to sounds only nature can produce.

"You mean diesel and cigarette smoke," Aspen corrects Martina, wrinkling her nose. "And that's festering garbage."

"And *freedom*, baby," Martina says, like an overzealous patriot. She slings an arm around each of our shoulders and gives us both a healthy slap on the back. "I've already got the whole day planned, my friends. Follow my lead."

We first stop at a bagel shop about ten blocks away, and I take back any regret over going on this trip when I sink my teeth into a lox bagel with extra cream cheese worth all sixteen dollars it cost. I wash it down with an iced vanilla latte that burns another hole in my wallet, but at least the taste of espresso finally spares my tastebuds from suffering through another cup of dining hall coffee.

"Apart from shoving food in our faces, what's on the agenda? I'd totally be down to eat some more, for the record," Aspen says as she collects the plastic cups littering the cramped table for two we've turned into a table for three. We weave our way through a group of tourists in I Love NY T-shirts extending the line at this coffee shop out the door.

"We're gonna take a pause on the eating because we're going to the Met," Martina says. "But first we gotta buy some new clothes."

Aspen looks between our mostly black athletic attire. "New *clothes*? Are we going to the Met or the Met Gala?"

"Yeah," I say, "I was just there a couple of months ago on a school trip, and I don't remember them having a dress code or anything. I'm sure we look fine."

Martina snorts, turning around at the crosswalk. "If we were running the New York City Marathon, then sure—we look *great*. I'm not going to that museum in my sweaty gym clothes, and neither are you guys."

That's how we end up dragging ourselves over a mile up Fifth Avenue in the sticky July weather, which I'm convinced was a ploy by Martina to drench us in enough sweat that Aspen and I would have no choice but to buy new outfits. By the time we set foot in some high-end boutique with gold signage, my skin is covered in a layer of moisture thick enough to freeze into an icy shell from the air-conditioning blasting into our faces.

A store associate standing towards the front, a short redhead with her hair pulled into a bun so tight her eyes crease, barely forces out a greeting before grimacing at her coworker on the other side of the store.

"Bitch about us all you want," Martina mutters under her breath, striding right past her. "We're not going anywhere."

To spite the woman even more, I walk over to what appears

to be the most expensive section of the boutique, full of silken fabrics and colorful suits fitting for a political debate. I trail my fingers across the smooth, buttery material of the blouses, watching them ripple and sway, and then stop when my hand hits a much thicker linen material, belonging to an olive green blazer.

The first and last time I ever wore a suit was to a scholarship interview last year. I'd borrowed the navy pinstripe set from my mother's size-zero closet and spent half the interview hoping no one could tell my arms were about to bust out of the blazer or that I had half my lung capacity while rattling off my rehearsed answers. I've sworn off suits since then, yet here I am, oddly entranced by the light summery fabric under my fingertips, the same color as my eyes in dim lighting.

"Oh my gosh, you should totally try this."

I can barely blink before Martina jumps up towards the rack and plucks the blazer and matching slacks off the hanger and throws them at me.

"Martina," I say, angling my head so that I can see her over the clothing in my hands, "I can't wear a suit to a *museum*."

"You can when we're in New York, Whitney." There's that justification for everything we've done today again. "A suit is the least weird thing people wear here."

Once again, I can't argue with her on that, so I find a pair of brown block heels in my size to top off the look. Reluctantly, the store associate, Lilian—far too pretty a name for such a bitter person—opens a fitting room for me and practically slams it back into my face as I try to enter, trying to balance my uneven pile of clothing in my hands. I flip her the bird from behind the door and start peeling off my sweaty leggings and then my tank top, knowing there's no way I'm going to willingly put them back on my body.

Here goes nothing, I think and start with the suit pants, bracing myself for a struggle with the zipper. To my surprise, it slides up like butter, and there's even room to spare when I finally button the pants. I tug on the cowl neck silk tank and then the blazer with no issues either. When I finally face the mirror, I don't just like what I see.

I *love* it.

I look like I'm stopping by for brunch at a five-star hotel before heading off to present my research at a conference, the picture of a woman who has places to be and no time for people to mess with her. With an extra three inches in height, I strut out of the fitting room, each click of my heels against the polished marble floor firing me up more. Martina and Aspen are on either side of me, in opposite but complementary styles—a black high-neck minidress and long platform sock boots and a white satin blouse and black leather shorts—and the three of us march towards the counter like we own the place.

"Everyone got a parent-issued credit card?" I ask over my shoulder, holding my matte-black card up in the air. "Ours aren't going to cut it for this one."

Martina fishes hers out of her wallet and blows some imaginary dust off it. "Right here, baby. Been an authorized user on it since I was thirteen." She then turns to Aspen. "Got yours?"

"My parents make me work for my money, guys. It's apparently supposed to build character."

Martina doubles over and clutches her heart in agony. "Oh, dear god, you poor thing." Winking, she adds, "I've got you, don't worry."

Before Aspen can protest, we pay for our new outfits and a tote-style purse to throw our old clothing in, and we all smile cheekily at Lilian on our way out.

Take that, bitch.

———

After hours of circling the many exhibitions of the Met, admiring Egyptian artifacts over five thousand years old and poking our heads into the American Wing period rooms and squinting at the odd European depictions of Jesus, we end up more drained than after a day of workouts with our trainers.

Sighing in relief, I kick my feet up onto the fourth chair at our table, trying not to think about my pinky toes' blisters after all that walking in those heels. Martina somehow found us dinner reservations at a swanky rooftop restaurant with a skyline view, where we've eaten our body weight and then some in bread and pasta over the past two hours.

"Guys, I have some bad news," Martina says, looking up from her phone. She sets her third mocktail down on the glass table with a clink, which means she means business. "Our train is running late."

"How late?" Aspen asks through a mouthful of tiramisu.

"Two hours late? But we'll get back to camp at ten thirty at the max."

"But aren't we supposed to be back at camp at *nine* on Sundays?" I ask. "I can't mess up again. Bob warned me I'll be toast."

Martina sighs. "I'm sure we'll be fine. And if we get busted, we can be honest and say our train was late. It's not like that's our fault." She flickers her eyes to my face contorting in horror and huffs. "Come on, Whitney, you don't have to make a big deal out of *everything*. It's getting old."

I snort before tipping back the rest of my virgin Moscow mule, like it'll ease any of my anxiety. "Some of us just don't know how to chill out, okay? This is what happens after burying your nose in a textbook all your life so you can get straight As."

"Okay, but at least that got you into Yale," Aspen says. "My parents work there, and I'm still on the wait list."

"Damn, your life just gets sadder and sadder, Aspen," Martina says, and we all burst into laughter.

———

With our luck, the train back is two and a half hours late after some delay in Philly, and it's well past eleven by the time we pull into the parking lot buried in the woods after a short drive from the station.

"What the hell was that?" Aspen hisses when Martina beeps the horn trying to back into a parking spot.

"*Sorry,*" she hisses back, jerking the steering wheel to the right. I knock my head into the window and add a concussion to my list of novel camp experiences. "I have a pointy-ass elbow, and it gets in the way sometimes."

The car is parked at a forty-five-degree angle when we vacate it, but none of us bothers to fix it, instead trying to figure out the most inconspicuous path back to the dorms. Aspen's vote is a trek through the woods, during which the two of them spend the entire time whisper-yelling at me to stop slapping mosquitoes away from my face and arms, as if *I'm* the weird one for not wanting to contract West Nile virus. While mosquitoes are a nonissue for Aspen, she apparently draws the line at a twig snapping in half under her shoe and shrieks as she falls over onto her face into a pile of dried-up leaves.

"Wait, did you hear that, guys?" a voice calls in the distance. "One of us should go check."

Martina and I gape at each other, our eyes growing wide.

"Yeah, I did hear that," someone responds, voice low and raspy. "It sounded like the last two hours of my freedom before I go to bed and relive the same day all over again for the fourth week in a row. I'm not getting up for shit."

Aspen ducks her head down sheepishly as she scrambles up to her feet, and the three of us stand frozen, realizing we're not alone in the woods. And based on that comment and the scent of alcohol wafting into the air, there must be a gathering of trainers ahead of us.

"Only one way out of this, guys," Martina whispers, hiking the tote bag up her shoulder. "We're going in."

She charges towards the clearing in the woods, and Aspen and I reluctantly drag ourselves behind her. With our cover soon to be blown, I go back to slapping my mosquitoes freely and even manage to flick a tick off Aspen's bare forearm, which is enough of a win for me.

"I *knew* it! We caught some trespassers."

I don't have to look up to know it's Isla hissing that statement, jumping up from her seat in the center of the trainer gathering. Some of them are lying across the ground, and others have set up beach chairs around a small bonfire, which can barely mask the stench of alcohol and stale weed in the air. Scattered across the grass are cans of beer and discarded bags of chips and enough plastic waste to make my environmentalist sister scream.

I lock eyes with Axel reclining in a beach chair, with a half-empty bottle of beer in his loose grip. He trails his gaze from my sweaty hair in a top knot to my wrinkled suit and my ankles awkwardly bent in those heels I'm one step away from tossing into the bonfire. Instead of looking confused or looking away, he *smiles*. His lips curl up, revealing his white teeth and a tiny dimple in his cheek I swear I've never seen before, and the sight makes my heart swell to twice its size.

"Do you guys want to explain yourselves?" Isla barks, folding her arms over her oversized Camp Campbell hoodie. It looks big enough to be Axel's, but I ignore the thought.

"Yeah, Mar-*tina*, wanna explain yourself?" Ryan slurs before tossing his head back and laughing, seemingly at the sight of a pine tree. Apart from the lighter hair and blue-green eyes, he's a clone of Axel, with the same muscular build and cheeky smile—but probably not the same level of intoxication.

"Oh, he's *definitely* zooted," Aspen whispers into my ear.

Martina takes several confident strides towards the bonfire, and a couple of male trainers sitting off to the side trail their eyes up her tan, shapely legs in her minidress. "You know what, should *we* be explaining ourselves, or should *you* all be doing just that? Because if my teenage nostrils aren't mistaken, that's the smell of weed and alcohol in the air." She sniffs again for good measure, her eyes landing on the beer bottle in Axel's hand, the label hidden behind his thumb. "Show of hands: Who here is over twenty-one?"

Surprisingly, the trainers bow to her authority, and half the arms present rise into the air, Axel's and Isla's notably excluded.

"Thought so," I hum, playing along with Martina's game.

I walk—or more like wobble—towards Axel and pluck the

bottle of beer out of his hands, sniffing its contents just to make sure. When I give it back to him, I shake my hand hard enough to sprinkle several droplets of beer onto Isla's sweatshirt, which smells just like Axel's signature cologne this close.

Well, *smelled* like it.

"Now, if you'll excuse us, oh great followers of the rules, *we* will be going to bed," I say, turning on my heel.

Aspen wiggles her fingers in a little wave over her shoulder as she sing-songs, "Good night, guys!"

The three of us cackle in laughter as we race back to the dorms, and halfway there, I finally take off those torture devices, not caring that my bare feet slap against the grass as we run.

"Oh, that was *great*," Aspen breathes when we burst into the back entrance of our building, clutching her side. "I so did not expect you to play along, Whitney."

"Or for you to pull that move with Axel," Martina says, nudging me with her pointy elbow. "*You're* not as uptight as you make yourself out to be, missy."

Maybe I'm not, or maybe I am. I'm not sure I know exactly who I am anymore, just that I don't hate this version of myself.

And that's all I need to know.

CHAPTER SEVENTEEN

Early the next morning, I have the bathroom to myself again as I get ready, and the mirror draws my attention more than usual.

I rest my hands on the countertop, finally forcing myself to take a real look at how my appearance has changed since I arrived at camp. There's a light but uneven tan on my arms, still pale where the sun doesn't reach, and a few highlights in my hair that definitely weren't there last month. My face seems slimmer, or maybe it's all the healthy food I've been eating keeping away the puffiness from my usual greasy, salty diet. When I slip off my shirt, I take in the small indents in my bulging biceps when I flex them—a far cry from Axel's bodybuilder arms, but even he'd be proud of this progress.

As I change into a pair of tight black athletic shorts, I notice that even my thighs, the one place where all the carbs in the world seem to go to, feel firmer to the touch.

On the whole, I'm still same old Whitney, but these little changes are the proof I needed that I'm more capable than I thought, although I don't want to get too hung up on them. I never came here to look any different, so if anything, this is the added bonus, and not the goal.

The true goal? To finally *run* a mile.

Fortunately, it's a balmy seventy-five degrees outside, so

Axel can't force me into the gym again for our morning session. The warm sun bathes my exposed shoulders in my tank top as I make my way across campus after breakfast. I pass by Willow and Joanna sitting together on a bench, talking. They look up and wave as I pass by, and warily, I wave back.

"Hello, my favorite little trespasser," Axel says when I approach him. "Sleep well?"

There's a mischievous look in his eyes, and I know I usually pay the price of whatever idea is brewing behind them.

"Wait a second." I back up and cock my head to the side, like a suspicious puppy. "Did you spare me yesterday so you could make this workout even worse?"

"No. Contrary to popular belief, I don't exist only to torture you, Whitney."

"Aw, how *sweet* of you. Honestly, I'm starting to think it's my job to torture you."

"You wouldn't even know," he mumbles, and I swear his cheeks tint the slightest bit pink.

We warm up and set out down the same road leading to the beach, but the stretch of pavement is far less daunting. Although Axel has a certain swiftness to his movements that I probably won't achieve for another five years, with his steady form and long, deft strides, I don't find myself speeding to catch up to him every few moments.

"I noticed you walking back to your dorm with Willow the other night," he says out of the blue, turning to look at me.

I open my mouth to question how he even noticed that, only to realize that's the least of my concerns. "It wasn't really by choice. She and Joanna came to the pool at the same time as me and my friends, and we all left together."

"You two don't get along better now? I figured cleaning tables together could've brought you closer."

"Would *you* get along with the person who ruined your life, Axel?"

"I wouldn't," he says, and I think that's settled, until he goes ahead and curses me with his wisdom. "But did she *really*? I'd be careful how much power you give to one person."

I mull over his Cindy-esque words for the next quarter mile we run, deciding it'd be better not to throw something snappy back and ruin the mood. Because in a way, he's right. While Willow did ruin portions of my life—the social part, most glaringly—there are still many parts she could never taint, like my grades or my family. And there are still problems there that I could never rightfully attribute to her, like my relationship with my dad.

"Fine," I say, almost too late for the conversation to still be relevant. "Maybe you're right."

"I wasn't quiet this whole time waiting for you to say that."

"But are you mad?"

"Got me there." He smiles cheekily and tilts his head thoughtfully again, his curious eyes scanning my face. "You tired yet?"

"Nope." I square my shoulders and pick up the pace. "Let's keep going."

He does a double take at the fact it's *me* uttering his signature phrase, but he doesn't question it. We turn right at the intersection and continue along the road parallel to the beach, affording us some scenic views and cleaner, salty air. I make sure to focus on my breathing as I run, realizing I'm usually out of breath before my legs are leaden and sore.

Filtering all thoughts from my brain, I let my world become the sun, the ocean, and the sound of my sneakers pounding the pavement, a rhythm that sounds better than music to my ears. I only stumble to a stop when I feel fingers wrapped around my bicep. Wiping the sweat from my brow, I look up and meet Axel's intent gaze.

"I said your name three times," he says, letting me go with suspicion. "I don't think I've ever seen you in the zone like that before."

"Wait, how long did we go?"

He holds his watch out instead of answering me, and my eyes practically pop out of my head at one point two miles. Hell, a couple weeks ago, I'd have been happy with just the point two. "A-are you sure that thing is accurate? I've heard they tend to exaggerate."

"This baby was a whole paycheck the first summer I worked here. I'd believe it before I'd believe my own mother."

I smile wide, letting it sink in that I really did that, and in that moment, it feels like maybe none of my goals are all that lofty. I try not to let my elation show too much around him, knowing a one-mile run is all but a warmup to him, but it's practically written all over my face as we start walking.

He leads me to an open and seemingly neglected field, with patches of yellow and brown and clusters of crabgrass crunching under our sneakers as we walk. There's a run-down soccer goalpost in the distance and unfittingly, a baseball in a glove lying inside of it. Scattered across the dead grass are footballs and small flags and a random plastic water bottle, reminding me of the aftermath of recess as a kid.

"Why are we here?"

"Figured we could cool down a bit before running back," he says and picks up a busted football. He tosses it between his hands before sending it sailing my way.

I shriek and duck down, covering my head, and there go my five seconds of feeling good about myself.

"Jesus, Whitney," he laughs. "It's a football, not a bullet."

I pick up the supposedly harmless object from by my feet and roll it in my hands, remembering how Poppy and Dad would always throw one in the backyard on Thanksgiving growing up, while Mom and I would try to replicate my Grandma Jean's world-famous apple pie recipe. I've long convinced myself I enjoy baking more than sports, but I would always steal a glance at them through the kitchen window, wondering why I'd never ask to join them, or why they'd never offer.

"Throw it back to me," Axel calls, breaking me out of my thoughts. He backs up about fifteen feet, hands up by his face waiting to catch it. "What are you waiting for?"

The ball slips out of my fingers and bounces twice on the grass. "I don't know how, Axel. Football's not my thing."

"I already told you it's not mine either," he says, and it takes me a moment before I recall his former rapper dreams. Reading my mind, he holds up his palm and warns me, "Don't you dare start."

Fighting a smirk, I gear up to throw the ball, having no idea what part of the pigskin my fingers should be touching or how much force I need to chuck it across the field, but I figure if it feels like I'm dislocating my shoulder, I'm doing it right.

Or not.

It sails about ten feet before bouncing three times on the ground and falling flat.

How dramatic.

"Try again."

"No thanks. Like I told you, I don't do football. It was actually my grandfather's thing. He was an NFL coach before—"

"He was a fucking *what?*"

"I know, right," I laugh, throwing my hands up in the air. "And then I of all people turn out to be his granddaughter."

He doesn't say anything back as he jogs ahead and picks up the ball and then gets into position. It emphasizes muscles in his arms I've never even seen before, and I duck down, bracing myself. When the ball spirals and slices through the air, I realize I should've known Axel and I have two *very* different definitions of being bad at something.

Yelping, I dart to the side again and let the ball bounce several feet behind me.

"Okay, how about we run back now? I'm not tired anymore."

"You're not taking the easy way out this time," he says, and it takes all my power not to laugh that he called *running* the easy way out. "I have all day, Whitney."

His insistence will be the death of me, but I know it gets me places, so I pick the ball up and hurl it again without thinking. Instead of cutting through the air in that perfect spiral fashion, it sails up in a near-vertical line before crashing down to the ground.

"Come on, Axel," I grumble, looking away. "I didn't need to feel like a failure *right* when I started getting good at this camp thing."

"Just because you're not good at something doesn't make you a failure," he says, like some washed-out motivational speaker. I roll my eyes so hard I give myself a headache. He fetches the football from the grass and tucks it under his arm. "You know you don't have to be good at everything, Whitney. Quite frankly, no one is good at everything—even me, as hard as it is to believe."

"I'm pretty aware." I drop down to a patch of crabgrass in defeat and observe the tiny ant crawling up my shoelace. "My whole motivation to apply to this camp was because I'm bad at *many* things." I pause and then clarify, "Specifically tennis in that instance, but that's beside the point."

"I won't ask for the story, then," he says, lowering himself down on the other side of the field. It's comical talking with this much distance between us, but I think we both know things start to happen when we're too close to each other. "But was that really why you wanted to come here?"

The question sinks right into the void in my heart, the one I've been trying to fill up my whole life. "No," I say quietly. He looks like he's waiting for me to continue and reveal the real reason, so I shake my head and say, "But it's stupid, so I'm not saying it out loud."

"The only stupid thing to say is a lie." We lock eyes from a distance, and my heart skips a bit. "You know you can trust me at this point."

"Promise you won't laugh?"

"I don't make promises I can't keep."

"You *asshole*."

"Kidding, kidding," he laughs, holding his hands up.

I take a moment to gather my thoughts, but the longer I wait, the more intent Axel's expression becomes, so eventually, I blurt out, "I thought becoming more athletic would make my dad love me more."

The silence that follows is exactly why I can't say this reason out loud, but I realize he's not stunned or weirded out. He's contemplating my answer like it makes any sense, but when his eyebrows knit into one continuous line, I realize even he's struggling to find the logic in it.

"Why would your dad's love be based on that?"

Been asking myself that question all my life.

"I mentioned my sister, Poppy, before, right?" He nods. "She was good at everything growing up. Not just school, but all kinds of sports: lacrosse, track, golf, you name it. It's not that I was very different from her, since we'd both collect academic awards at the end of the year, but she also had banquets, trophy ceremonies, endless praise from her coaches, more things that could connect *her*, not me, to our sports-crazed dad."

His jaw is more tense than it was when I first began talking. Maybe he's caught up thinking about his own dad, who's dead, not just emotionally absent. I suck in my cheeks and lower my eyes.

"My dad's in finance, so he worked a lot growing up. And I'm grateful obviously. I grew up really privileged and always had everything I could ever want. But I couldn't help but notice how he'd use those precious few hours he had to himself on the weekends to play a game of tennis or a round of golf with Poppy. Or the way his face would light up when she won a championship or a race. It was that fatherly kind of pride too. The, '*Yeah*, look, that's my kid up there' kind." My voice drops as I say, "He's never been like that with me, not even during my valedictorian speech in June."

"Have you ever talked to him?" he asks, skipping straight to the point. "You still have a chance." He looks away, shoulders slumping. "I don't. And I haven't for eight years."

"I'm sorry. My situation doesn't compare to yours."

"That's not what I'm saying. I'm saying you're not out of options yet. You don't realize . . ." He pauses to collect himself, running his fingertips mindlessly over the surface of the football. "You don't realize until someone's gone how pointless it is to leave things unsaid. Saying them to a gravestone doesn't quite hit the same."

He's right, if only I knew *what* I would say. I doubt Dad has ever spent longer than three seconds thinking about the same thing that's eaten at me all my life. What if I confront him, and he gaslights me into thinking it's all in my head? Or cuts me off midsentence to go hop on a video call? Or worse yet, what if he admits he *does* love Poppy more than me?

The more I entertain the worst-case scenarios, the more I want to flee my mind, so I scramble to my feet, looking around for refuge. My stomach sinks with the realization that there's no place to escape myself, only this situation, so with the speed I can attribute only to the man behind me, I take off down the field and back onto the main road. To any onlooker, I'd appear the pinnacle of athleticism, bare legs cutting through the air like jackknives, but they don't have to know it's all a façade.

"Whitney, *wait!*" Axel calls, and I hear the pound of his footsteps from twenty feet behind me. "Where are you going?"

"You'd better catch up!" I yell over my shoulder, fighting a smirk with all my might.

Because damn, does that feel good to say.

CHAPTER EIGHTEEN

For the next team challenge, we're all the way on the other side of campus by the athletic fields. Instead of Cindy, eight female trainers meet us in the middle of the field. They stand in a neat line, hands behind their backs, heads tipped down, staring at us through their eyelashes. As we draw closer and my stomach roils, I finally understand the intimidation of those contestants on *Shark Tank* as they'd stand before a row of people with their fate in their hands.

"Good morning, girls," May greets us. Her short hair is pushed back by a neon-green sweatband, and her jersey falls over the hem of her shorts, making her appear nearly a decade younger. "Welcome to my personal favorite part of the Camp Campbell experience: the trainer-camper face-off. By popular vote, this year we'll be playing a game of soccer."

Isla steps forward from the center of the pack. "Since there are eight of us, we need eight of you, so choose your team wisely. In case it wasn't obvious, we're *very* tough competition."

"Oh, give me a break," Willow mutters under her breath from behind me, and for once, I couldn't be more in agreement.

"Over to the right, you'll find Ryan—he'll serve as our referee."

He sends us a huge wave and then completes a convoluted

air-handshake with Martina, which makes me realize Axel and I need to up our game.

"We also have Axel with us," Isla says, tone rising in merriment. It darkens again when she clarifies, "He's here to make sure no one tries to kill each other again."

He shoots me and Willow a hard glare from across the field, and we both burn holes into the grass below us.

"Good luck, and may the best team win . . . which will probably be us!"

The trainers cackle as they jog to the other side of the field, but Adriana calls out for them to stop. "So, wait, let me get this straight. *Our* team is made up teenage girls at a fitness camp—some of which still can't even run a mile—and *yours* is entirely made of certified personal trainers. How, exactly, is that *fair?*"

Isla throws her head back and laughs. "And who ever said anything about fair?"

Face scrunching up, Adriana storms off to the other side of the field, and we reluctantly trail behind her. She elects herself team captain and huddles us together, and for once, no one tries to temper her overcompetitive tendencies.

"We're taking them down, do you understand?" she says through her teeth, driving her index finger down towards the ground. She looks up and beckons to her sister. "Marti, you're a no-brainer. You played for, like, three years."

"Yeah, in middle school," Martina laughs, jogging up to her. "But at your service." She salutes her, and it's probably the first time they've ever been in accord since I met them. It feels as odd as the prospect of me and Willow getting along. "Anyone else play soccer?"

Kennedy steps forward, telling us she only plays defense.

Adriana rounds up the rest of the athletes among the sixteen of us—representing field hockey, dance, and volleyball—and ignores Noelle, who reminds us all she plays tennis.

"Get back to me when you make varsity," Adriana snaps. She looks back at the rest of the group, resting her hands on the hips of her hot-pink shorts. "Now, who of the athletically challenged here wants to help us win? We need a goalie and center midfielder."

It's crickets among the ten of us left. When no one volunteers after a minute, Adriana resorts to picking players herself, which is how I end up the team's goalkeeper: the perfect position for someone with a very recent but undisclosed history of getting hit in the face with an airborne spherical object.

"You got this, Whitney!" Martina calls as she jogs to the center of the field, and I flash her a gloved thumbs-up.

As I slide on a neon-yellow T-shirt over my tank top, I figure this can't be *that* hard. I've watched the World Cup before— once. All I have to do is dart from left to right and look a little constipated as I do so, and whatever I do, don't use my hands outside my little white cage.

Should be a piece of cake.

Ryan blows his whistle, and the game begins. For the first few minutes, I hunch over, palms to my knees, on high alert for a flying ball or a striker gone rogue, but it doesn't take long before I realize all the action is happening on the other side of the field. I pace the length of the grass between the two goalposts, gloved hands to my hips, and look at Axel. He sits slumped over on a small chair with his phone in his hand, not even glancing at the game.

The sound of cheers rips my gaze away. Martina's racing

across the field, arms high in the air, as the rest of the team runs and cheers behind her.

"*Yes*, Martina!" I call, jumping up and down. "We're gonna crush 'em!"

The trainer team grows noticeably disjointed as the game continues, clearly not used to us being better than them at anything, but it's too early to call this game a win. I fire up all my senses and track every movement of the ball, watching it go from May to Danielle then to Isla, who sends it sailing towards me.

I jump up and slam the ball backwards, seeing it soar over the net and out of sight.

"Hell yeah, Whit!"

"Let's frickin' *go*!"

"Go, Whitney!"

My head starts spinning trying to take in this foreign-sounding praise, even though I know I deserve it. I glance at Axel for reassurance, but he's still hunched over nose-deep into his phone, like a moody teenage babysitter. So, I try it. I pat myself on the back, a tiny, unremarkable touch to my trapezius muscle, and it feels *glorious*.

"Yeah, Whitney," I whisper to myself as I get back into position, "let's frickin' go."

As the game drags on, the tension mounts with it, and I start to feel it in my quads and shoulders, stiffening every time a trainer gets close to a shot on goal. Bodies slide across the grass and grunts fill the air, sheer frustration and anger driving every pass. For a second, I feel like I'm back in fifth grade watching two teams of rowdy tween boys face off at recess.

The ball is back in Isla's possession again, and I hunch over, squinting to track every one of its movements, but Kennedy swoops in and sticks her leg out to sweep it away. Isla stumbles and wavers in the air before falling flat on her face, letting out a shrill cry, louder than I ever was after getting hit in the eye by a tennis ball going sixty miles an hour.

Ryan blows his whistle long and hard and points to the ground where Isla has rolled over onto her back, grasping her shin held up in the air.

Martina whips around. "She's faking it, Ryan!" She jogs across the field and grabs his arm when he shakes his head. He says something indistinct, and her face breaks, like all the trust built between them shatters in that moment. "Come on, Kennedy *barely* touched her. You can't give them a penalty kick for that!"

"Ugh, I knew this game was biased!" Adriana screams, kicking at the air. She turns to me of all people and asks, "Why are we still playing again?"

The field breaks out into angry accusations, curse words thrown left and right. We're one step away from a full-on trainer-camper war when Kennedy shoves another trainer and she shoves her back, but before Ryan can blow his whistle again, Axel's voice booms across the field.

"That wasn't a penalty."

Ryan shoots him a suspicious glance, and Isla's eyes turn to saucers, but Axel says nothing and begins walking in a slow menacing line across the field. The world falls silent, and all I can hear is the crunch his stiff Nike sneakers make over the sound of my own heartbeat, each step crushing the grass some more.

At last, he stops before Isla, grabs her hand, and yanks her up to her feet.

"Stop embarrassing yourself," he says before stalking away.

For the next minute, no one knows how to react. Maybe, just like me, they're waiting for Axel to laugh and tell us we're being punked, but he doesn't turn around until he's all the way back on the sidelines. Between two blinks, I start questioning if everything I've ever seen and believed about him and Isla was all in my head.

After a silent moment, during which the eight of us exchange equally confused glances, I speak up. "Okay, but does anyone *actually* want to continue this game?"

It's a bold question to ask when I know, unlike me, most of these girls' first inclinations aren't to quit when things get hard, but I'm tired of fighting my true nature today, especially when Adriana is right. This game is as rigged as ever, another power trip for the same people who already make our lives miserable enough.

When I look around, I expect some glares or maybe to be ignored entirely, but slowly, girls start shaking their heads. And then a couple use their voices. And then, bolder than them all, Willow tugs off her Camp Campbell T-shirt and throws it to the ground.

"I'm with Whitney," she says, chin held up high. "I'm out."

One by one, the rest of the team pulls off their T-shirts and tosses them into the growing pile, and then even the girls on the sidelines join in. I almost can't believe I started this mutiny myself, but I don't double back. I take my sweet time pulling off my gloves and then my yellow T-shirt, and when my tank top comes off with it, I don't care that I'm standing there in the same ratty polka-dot sports bra I wore to that 5K.

Willow smirks when she catches sight of it and tugs down the thick strap of her tank top to reveal a strawberry-themed one.

"This is ridiculous," Isla breathes, staring between all the silent trainers around her. "Is *no one* going to do anything about this blatant disregard for our authority?"

More silence answers her, and I send her a tight smile of pity.

"I really do hope you feel better, Isla," I say and take a wide step back, eyeing all the open green space behind me. "I heard ice and a painkiller work wonders for a bruised ego."

I break into a sprint before she can lunge at me, and soon enough, I can barely hear myself think over all the sneakers pounding the grass around me, following my lead off the field. When I pass Axel on the sidelines, there's no missing the approving smirk on his lips.

In that moment, it feels like the greatest win of them all.

CHAPTER NINETEEN

"You do push-ups like a girl," Axel says, crossing his broad arms over his chest.

I drop down to the exercise mat, the backs of my hands resting on the sand above my head. *Who invented this exercise, and how can I get a word with them?*

"Isn't it surprising that I, Whitney Carmichael, a biological female, do push-ups like wait, what? A *girl?*"

"That's not what I meant. Let me demonstrate again." Axel lowers himself to the cold, firm sand, not even bothering with the mat. After a few seconds, he glances back at me with a frown. "Are you even watching?" He waves a hand in front of my face to get my attention.

"Yes, of course," I lie, pretending like I wasn't just ogling his back muscles.

He gets down on his hands again, kicking his feet back into the proper push-up position. He completes about seven in a matter of seconds, his arms pumping up and down like there are springs secretly implanted under his muscles.

"There," he says, brushing his hands together and creating a cloud of sand. "You try it."

I plant my hands firmly onto the mat again and kick my legs back behind me. I shift my feet and move my arms closer together, making sure my hands are directly underneath my shoulders. I bend my arms down and back up again, feeling the strain on my chest. The first few tries mimic his form, but by the fifth push-up, I'm inventing some combination of a plank, push-up, and belly flop.

Axel exhales, digging his fingers into the bridge of his nose. "Let's not waste any more precious time." He orders me to get up and then asks, "Do you know what a burpee is?"

"A *burpee*? What kind of dumb name is that?"

"Oh yes, because I invented the exercise." I laugh again, unable to control my immaturity, and his expression softens. "All right, looks like you're gonna make me work today."

Axel jumps up and does a complicated series of motions that consist of some half push-up and an awkward jump squat that ends with him standing before me again. I stare at him wide-eyed in the dim light of the evening.

"Hold on a second. You decided that, since I suck at both push-ups and jump squats, it'd be the perfect idea for me to try them *together*?"

"I was hoping the whole would be more impressive than its parts," he says, but even he looks like he knows I'm going to disappoint. "Let me break it down a little further, before you give one a shot."

When his series of detailed demonstrations ends, I maintain a vivid mental image of how this "burpee" works and attempt it myself. Surprisingly, I don't fall over on my face, but by the third one, my thighs and arms feel like they're on fire, burned out from all the squats, lunges, and planks I completed before Axel came up with this brilliant idea.

"Finish this set, and you're done for today."

"O-okay," I stammer, dropping down the ground. "But let me warn you: this might not be pretty."

And boy, was I right. I'm a pile of crumpled limbs and shattered hopes by the end, unable to even pick myself up off the sand. I stare up at the golden-blue sky until my heart stops rattling and Axel's three heads merge into one.

After a few moments of contemplation, I sit up and frown. "Do you love making me feel like shit right after I begin feeling good about myself?"

"Come on, don't be so hard on yourself. I'd give your performance a solid . . . five out of ten."

"*Rude.* Why are you no fun today?"

"You want fun? I'd planned on it earlier, but maybe I'll change my mind."

"*No,* Axel." The uncontrollable desperate plea leaves my lips, and he smirks. "Come on, spare me for once."

"Say please, and maybe I will."

I come to my senses and shoot up to my feet. "I take back my desperation now."

"I'm just messing with you," he says, but my heart sinks to my stomach when he grabs one of my arms.

I barely have time to react when his other hand snakes behind my knees. He lifts me up with ease, keeping the slightest distance between our bodies as he jogs towards the water.

"Axel, no!" I cry, grabbing on to his bicep. Insecurities start flooding my brain, making me wonder if I'm too heavy or if I smell like sweat or if he can see how fast my heart is pounding through my shirt. "You can't *carry* me."

"I can bench-press twice your weight," he says, even though I wasn't implying he couldn't. As if to prove his strength, he adjusts his grip and throws me over his shoulder. He holds my body up with just one protective arm around the backs of my thighs, and my heartbeat hits new heights. "This is a warmup at best."

As he trudges through the water with me up in the air, I've never felt so weightless and scared and exhilarated all at once. I drive my palms into the hard planes of his back and lift myself up, seeing the world from a new elevated angle. When he's in the water up to his knees, I accept my fate and toss my sneakers and socks to shore. But then the first few droplets of seawater pellet against my skin like freezing cold bullets, and I'm clawing at his muscly chest, hoping he never lets me go.

Axel has a mind of his own today, and without warning, he chucks me into the ocean. I don't even have time to process the paralyzing shock of the chill that follows before my head pops back up, and I spit out salt water and wipe my stinging eyes. I stand frozen in place as I stare down at my soaking white shirt, realizing the padding in the sports bra underneath was just an illusion. I look up, and Axel floats on his back with a wide grin, clearly finding this escapade much more enjoyable.

"How have you lived in this part of the country your whole life and still aren't used to the ocean? Tolerating the cold is a rite of passage here."

"I don't usually swim in the ocean." Because I hated the way I looked in a swimsuit, a sorry excuse now. "Whatever's under this water is none of my business."

When a wave forms in the distance, I grab on to any part of him on instinct, fingers curling around his right forearm, letting me feel the bulge of his veins as he tenses. An apology forms on my lips, but he doesn't seem mad, especially not when his other hand travels down my lower back and pulls me closer to him. Heat pools in my belly when I feel his hard muscles pressed up against my front.

Right when he eyes my lips with thinly veiled desire, the wave crests and splits us apart. Feeling myself being dragged under, I kick my legs and claw at the water, but my strength is no match for the forces of Mother Nature. The wave tosses me around and drags me to shore as it crashes, so far under the surface my stomach skims the abrasive ocean floor.

My body battered, I drag myself up to my feet and tug down the hem of my shorts, wincing as a handful of sand pours out of them.

Axel jogs through the water, calling out, "Jesus, Whitney, are you okay?"

My throat burns as I try to yell back an answer, but no words come out. As I clear it to get rid of the feeling, some salt water dislodges, and soon enough I'm bent over at the waist and having the coughing fit of an old man diagnosed with COPD. Wiping my mouth on the back of my hand, I look up and say through a grimace, "Now do you get why I don't swim in the ocean?"

Lips flattening with either realization or regret, he picks me up and hauls me out of the water on his back, and this time, I don't fight him; I *welcome* his services. We make it to shore, and he sets me down on our exercise mat and tells me to wait for him. He jogs up the sand and turns to a speck in the distance, and I hope at the very least, he'll bring me back a towel.

Five minutes pass, and I'm still shivering alone on the beach, and I know it's too soon to surmise that he's forgotten about me. Another five minutes, and I prepare to trek back to my door alone, soaking wet and with half my dignity, but I finally spot

Axel in the distance. Sure enough, he has a towel in one hand and a brown bag in the other, the contents of which are unclear from this far away.

"Sorry," he says when he finally makes it back to me. Instead of handing me the towel, he drapes it over my shoulders and pulls the two ends together. "Didn't mean to make you almost catch hypothermia."

"You could've thought of that before throwing me into the ocean," I laugh, though my tone doesn't indicate I'm mad, *especially* when I catch a whiff of whatever's in that bag. "Did you—"

"Finally get you a proper fucking meal?" He opens the brown bag and fishes out its contents: two burgers and a side of fries that spill out of the large cup. "I did."

"Damn, you really are the best trainer ever." The compliment escapes me without thinking, and I open my mouth to take it back or phrase it in a more professional way. I don't say anything when I catch the way Axel's eyes light up, like he cares about my praise. "This definitely makes up for the almost-hypothermia."

He laughs, and we sit down together on the small exercise mat. He hands me a burger, and I unwrap the foil in seconds, my mouth watering as I consider sinking my teeth into a fatty, juicy mess.

"All right," I say, speaking through a mouthful. "How many push-ups am I gonna have to do tomorrow after this meal?"

"I'm not trying to ruin your relationship with food, Whitney. But, to answer your question, fifty."

"You know it'll be miracle if I can even do ten." His eyes narrow, like he doesn't even believe that, so I correct myself, "Okay, more like five."

As we continue eating, I'm not sure what seems more forbidden: being this close to him or the greasy fast food we're eagerly consuming. All I know is this workout session shouldn't have lasted this long, if this moment even counts as part of it at this point. If anything, this feels an awful lot like a first date, and the thought both thrills and unnerves me at the same time.

"Did you ever do this with your other trainees before?" I ask, finally entertaining my curiosity around this subject.

"No. I've never done this with anyone before, trainee or not."

"Neither have I." When he doesn't respond, my cheeks flush, and my defenses start firing up, which always leads me to start rambling like an idiot. "Obviously, I've never had a trainee before, not that I'd ever want one either. I'm pretty much a disaster to deal with, so I can't imagine being stuck with someone like me for over a month. But anyways. It's also obvious my social experiences were as limited as my athletic ones before I came to this camp, because no one wants to date someone like—"

"Whitney," Axel says, dropping his palm to the mat with a declarative thud.

I jolt, looking up. "Yes?"

"Stop talking."

"Okay," I squeak.

"And Whitney?"

I nod, not trusting myself to open my mouth and actually say anything socially acceptable.

"A lot of guys would want to date you. Trust me on that one."

"You're blushing," Martina teases when I make it back to our dorm.

When I untie my hair, the tangled, wet strands slap against my back. Shivering in the arctic air-conditioned air, I search for a clean towel so I can finally take a shower and wash all this sand and seawater from my skin.

"It's probably sunburn," I insist.

"No, no. There's this weird"—she waves her hand in a circle in the air—"*glow* to your skin."

"That's called sweat, Martina."

"You *can't* deny your clothes are soaking wet." She drags her eyes from the thin white shirt clinging to my sports bra and my bunched-up shorts. "*You* are hiding something, Whitney."

Too cold at this point, I wrap the towel around myself and hope I have another clean one somewhere. "Okay, so just because I come back here and don't give you a word-for-word recount of my last workout session, I'm *hiding* something?"

"Right, exactly," she says, like it's the most obvious thing in the world. Because maybe it is. Maybe there's a sticky note plastered to my forehead that reads, *Hello, my name is Whitney, and I'm hopelessly attracted to my personal trainer. Please send help.* "Because you weren't working out. Wait a second," she says, wiggling her eyebrows, "did you and Axel sneak over to the camp's pool and finally fuck each other's brains out?"

"Martina, what the *hell*? I would never consider doing that . . . in public."

She shrugs and holds her palms up in defense. "Hey, no shame in exploring your raunchy side. There *are* other workouts besides running, after all."

"There is some shame when that could get him fired or this

place sued," I scoff, sitting down on the edge of my bed.

"Oh, so you *wouldn't* be opposed to fucking him, then?"

"No one would be, okay? Why else do you think Isla acts like that around him?"

She grimaces. "Ugh, not Isla. He definitely didn't seem into her during the soccer game the other day."

"Right, exactly," I say. "But I'm getting so many mixed signals. Last week I saw her come up to him out of the blue, and she asked if he wanted to go out. I don't know if he said yes, but the next morning at our workout session, he looked all worn-out and stuff . . . like he'd had a long night with her. To top it off, I saw him texting her on his phone, smiling like a goofy idiot. Then that time in the woods, she was wearing *his* sweatshirt . . ." I drag a palm down my face and look up. "I'm reading too much into everything, right?"

Martina doesn't say anything for a few moments, staring off at our doorway and picking up and dropping her phone in a rhythm. When she turns to me, her eyes crease up at the sides, and I can't tell if she's in pain or pitying me.

"Whitney, this might sound mean," she says, but I know it won't. Martina is the bluntest yet kindest person I've ever met, the slap of reality I always need. "But you're not with him yet. Technically, whatever he does, even if it's fucking Isla's brains—"

"Please stop. I'm begging you."

She laughs softly. "Look, whatever he does is none of your business. I've been here before if that helps." Her gaze grows pensive as she continues. "Liking someone, thinking I'm entitled to their affection, all while they're in a relationship and figuring themselves out . . . It's like sitting on the sidelines of a game that never ends."

"Did you get him eventually?" I ask after a moment.

"Not him," she says, shaking her head. "*Her.* And no, I didn't."

"I'm so sorry for assuming. I just thought—"

"No, it's fine." She stands up, stretching her arms above her head and revealing a tattoo I didn't know she had. "I was gonna drop that I was bi eventually. It's not some secret."

"Do you still like her, then?" I ask as she walks towards me.

"Not really. Even if I still did, she's in college in Colorado now, has this successful art business, and a bunch of new friends. I'd be stupid to chase after her when I have more options here at this point in my life." She throws herself down next to me and props herself up on her elbow. "You will too, you know, in college. Even if you and Axel don't become a thing."

I fall to my back, covering my face with my hands. "Ugh, I swear I sometimes miss my life before this camp."

She lies down next to me, and I'm starting to wonder if this is our routine now. I know I'll miss this when I go to college, maybe even more than my fleeting moments with Axel.

Her phone buzzes in her pocket, and she flickers her eyes to the screen. I make out the name Aspen before she tosses the phone to her bed on the other side of the room.

"Yeah, sometimes I do too," she murmurs back.

CHAPTER TWENTY

"Whitney, *Whitney*," Martina hisses, nudging my side. "Stop zoning out."

I pry open my leaden eyelids and remember where I am—the yoga studio. It's already hard enough to focus during these "relax and recharge" sessions, and with the dull ache building in my muscles over the past day, oddly different from my usual post-workout soreness, I'm in a whole different universe in my mind.

Preferably with a bed but can't be too picky, I guess.

"And take a deep breath in and exhale as you bend down to touch your toes," Cindy says gently.

I barely graze my knees before my eyelids start drooping again, and I jolt back up to a standing position. Willow shoots me a concerned look over her shoulder in her half-bent position, which probably says something about how rough I look right now.

"All right, let's stop here," Cindy says at last. "Before we move on to the heavy stuff, we're going to have a little fun, so gather into a circle on the ground."

Everyone stands up and shuffles past each other in an attempt to form a somewhat circular pattern. I plop down at the last minute right between Willow and a girl trying to get something stuck in her teeth out with her finger.

"This camp is about exercise, but it's also a social experience. And I realized that since you've all seemed to form your own cliques, another icebreaker could help you expand your social network here." Soft groans pop up across the room, echoing my own sentiments about these kinds of forced games, sure to haunt me again in college. "I'll throw this ball to one of you and ask you a question, and then you'll answer and throw the ball to someone else you don't usually talk to, who will do the same thing. We'll continue until everyone has a chance to speak. Make sense?"

We nod, and she throws the inflatable beach ball to Joanna.

"Least favorite exercise?"

"Jump squats, for sure," she answers, and a chorus of yeses erupts across the room. Joanna looks around and tosses the ball to Neha, who deftly catches it.

"Who's your role model in life?"

"I don't have one," she says. "All human beings are flawed." A couple of girls laugh, thinking she's not being serious, but after hanging around Axel, I've gotten used to philosophical answers. Neha squints and then throws the ball to Adriana. "Do you like being a twin?"

"Eh, it has its perks. It's useful when I want to see how an outfit looks on me and I'm too lazy to try it on." Martina rolls her eyes, but Adriana shoots her a wry grin. She passes the ball to a redhead named Sophie. "Do you think I'd look good if I dyed my hair red? I've been debating the decision for years."

"That's not the kind of question we want to be asking, girls," Cindy cuts in, but Sophie holds her hand up.

"I don't mind," she says, "because you absolutely would *not*."

Adriana's lips part in shock, but even Joanna and Willow drop their foreheads to their hands. Sophie chucks the ball to

Willow. "What's it like being the daughter of the icon who runs this place?"

Willow fiddles with the ball in her hands, running her fingers over the smooth surface. Before Cindy can cut in and tell us that's also not a question we should be asking, Willow forces out, "I've had worse experiences in my life." Shoulders tensing, she tosses the ball to Martina and steals Neha's question. "Do *you* like being a twin?"

"I didn't have much choice in being one, did I?" she says, evading it, and throws the ball to Noelle, who jumps up to catch it. "How much wood would a woodchuck chuck if a woodchuck could chuck wood?"

"Martina," Cindy warns, but we can barely hear her over the sound of our laughter.

"I don't know, let me ask my pet woodchuck first," Noelle snaps. I laugh at her response, but the sound fades when she trails her brown eyes across the room and pauses on my face, the edges of her lips curling up into a mischievous smirk. The ball comes flying at my face, and I lunge forward to grab it, not wanting to replicate my experience playing tennis last time, even if this ball would do far less damage.

"Did you really come here because you sucked at gym and everyone always made fun of you? Like who actually sucks at gym class? It's the easiest shit ever . . . especially for someone who somehow graduated valedictorian." All eyes land on me, and my stomach churns with my mounting horror, heat fanning across my cheeks. Noelle shrugs, her devilish smirk growing as she finishes, "But that's what Willow told me, so I could be wrong."

Willow gasps and turns to look at me, her eyes pleading, as if someone like her could be above those remarks.

"Noelle, that is simply—"

"I, um, I . . . I . . ." I try to cut Cindy off, but I'm stammering, not even knowing what I did to make Noelle say that. Or why I *can't* say anything back to her. My throat feels like it's closing up in anaphylactic shock, and I claw at it, trying my best to swallow.

Martina jumps in before Cindy can say anything again. "Are you really one to be talking, Noelle, since you've been following my sister and her friends around like a lost puppy this whole time at camp? I wouldn't be surprised if you're just projecting right now."

"You know what that means, right?" Aspen supplies, and a couple of girls snort. "It might be a big word for someone not nearly as smart as Whitney."

Noelle's jaw drops, and now the giggles and leers around the room are directed at her and not me. I finally breathe out a sigh of relief as I shakily climb to my feet, knowing I was too astounded to come up with anything remotely snarky on the spot.

"Can I be excused from this game?" I ask Cindy.

Before bothering to hear her reply, I chuck the ball at Noelle's head, and it ricochets off her forehead and strikes Willow in the face, an equally satisfying target. Hearing the door slam shut behind me, I run down the hall with the dwindling strength I have today, while my humiliation grows with every step.

I burst out onto the grass and suck in a lungful of humid air, calming my fiery nerves. After collecting myself, I continue trekking to my dorm, replaying that moment over again and cringing. That's the way I always was in high school. The pranks, the jokes, the hurtful words, they came and went, but I never said anything, hoping someone else would defend me. I thought

I'd finally built a backbone at this camp. Hell, if Axel hadn't stopped me, I would've done far more damage to Willow during that fight.

I'm too tired to even think by the time I make it back to my room. When I throw myself down on my bed and tug the sheets over my head, I'm back at square one, wishing I'd never come here in the first place.

—

The next morning, after consulting the camp's nurse and sleeping a choppy yet invigorating thirteen hours, I woke up feeling a lot better. Whatever sickness those symptoms amounted to was clearly short-lived, making me wonder if the exhaustion from this experience simply caught up to me all at once.

I climb back into bed after a quick lunch and chug the rest of my water bottle. My phone rings as I finally get into a comfortable position on my side, and I groan. I stick my arm out without looking and fish for the device somewhere on my side table and almost knock over the lamp in the process.

I hold the screen up to my face and do a double take. *Dad?*

I click the green button.

"Hi, Whit, how are you doing?"

I sit up straighter in my bed and hug a pillow, pressing the phone to my ear. "I'm okay, Dad. How are you?"

"Your mom tells me you texted her that you're sick. What's going on?"

"Oh, yeah, sadly I've come down with one of those weird summer colds. How convenient, right?"

"Have they let you take a day off, at least?" I hold back

a laugh. The concept is unheard of in his world, where work always goes above all, even your health.

And me.

"Yeah. You caught me right before I was going to take a nap."

"Should I let you go? You should rest up as much as possible."

"No." The word almost comes out in a yell, because there's nothing more I want than to finally have a real conversation with him. "I . . . I mean, I've already slept a lot. Distract me, what's going on in your life?"

"Currently packing for Chicago. I'll be there for a conference for a few days. Then your mom and I want to take a little trip. God, I don't even remember the last time just the two of us went somewhere exciting, but then again, your mom isn't one for adventure."

"Hope you guys have fun, then," I say. "Chicago, huh? Are you looking forward to going, or is it just work as usual?"

"No, I probably won't see much more than the inside of a hotel and a couple of air-conditioned conference rooms . . ." His voice fades, but when I hold the phone closer to my ear, I realize he's just talking to Mom. "Wait, isn't Chicago the city you've always wanted to visit? Or am I off?"

"Way off," I say. "It's actually San Diego." The two couldn't be more unalike, but I guess the thought was what counted.

He changes the subject. "How have you been holding up with all that exercise? Your mom tells me it's a lot more intense than you thought."

I open my mouth to rattle back a lie before I realize I don't even have to fake it at this point. "Actually, Dad, working out now isn't nearly as bad now as it was in the beginning." I wait a beat. "I'm kind of liking it."

"Ah, that's great, Whit," he says, and my heart swells. "Deep down, I always knew you had it in you, just like Poppy."

I freeze in place, my phone slipping a few inches in my hold, as I take in my three least favorite words: *just like Poppy*. I bite the inside of my cheek to prevent a snappy reply, knowing he didn't mean it like that.

But that's just this time.

"Hey, Dad, tell Mom I say hi, okay? I think I'm going to take that nap."

He sighs. "All right, kiddo, sleep well."

We hang up, and I stare at the ceiling, not even knowing what to think anymore, just that I'm not going to fall back asleep anytime soon.

———

"She's back from the dead!" Aspen cheers when I join her and Martina at dinner.

"Hey, guys," I say, sliding into my spot at our usual table. The dining hall has thinned out by now, and even Martina and Aspen sit in front of empty plates, clearly having waited for me. "What'd I miss while I was gone?"

"Not much," Martina says, resting her chin on her fist. "Well, Noelle has sat alone for all three meals today. Maybe Adriana and her friends do have a conscience."

I picture the sight for a moment, her small, sad self hunched over a table eating a sandwich alone, and a weird pang of sympathy grips my heart. Willow at the beginning of high school flashes in my mind, that taste of a warm, likable person she used to be. I'd never thought about all the similarities between her and Noelle before, but, unlike Willow, maybe Noelle is lucky her attempt at becoming another malicious queen bee failed.

She at least has a chance to become someone better.

"I don't know, guys . . ." I say, lifting a spoonful of chicken noodle soup to my mouth. "I kind of feel bad for Noelle."

"*What?*" Aspen's jaw drops. "You feel *bad* for her after she humiliated you in front of everyone?"

"No, that still sucked—though still not the worst thing anyone has ever said to me." I laugh at the thought. "What I mean is everything about her is so . . . pitiable? She's younger than us, desperate for attention, and probably thinks being mean is gonna make her this cool, likable person."

"That definitely didn't work out," Martina snorts. "I'd tell my sister to knock some sense into her, but I don't think she's one to lecture people about making good friends."

"Maybe Whitney should talk to her instead," Aspen says. "That'd make her feel guilty at least."

The thing is, I don't want to make her feel guilty; I want to make her *understand*. But confronting her feels very low on my priority list and almost out of character. I've barely been able to get in Willow's head this whole time, and she has years of being a bitch to me to make up for, unlike Noelle.

"You know what, forget I mentioned her," I mutter, telling myself I'll think through this idea later. "What are everyone's plans for tonight?"

"There are some activities going on around the camp," Aspen says.

"Like what?"

"They're screening a movie in Room 100," she says, and I wait for the catch. "But it came out ten years ago, and it's rated PG."

Martina and I snort. "Next option."

"Some girls are playing beach volleyball tonight." Aspen looks at me. "Do you know how to play, Whitney?"

I laugh through another spoonful of soup, spewing a few droplets of broth across the table. "You have too much faith in me, Aspen. Far too much."

We settle for a lazy evening on the beach, which is the best option given today's energy levels. After nearly twenty-four hours holed up in my room, the rough sand below my bare feet and the cool breeze blowing against my face make me feel like a whole new person. I lower myself to my towel with a blissful sigh and tuck my arms behind my head.

"Do you want to go for a walk?" Aspen asks, unzipping her hoodie. She tosses it on top of Martina's crumpled shorts on the corner of the towel. "I get it if you're still tired."

"I'll sit this one out. But have fun on my behalf."

They walk away and halfway to the rocky shoreline, Martina's hand gravitates towards Aspen's. Their fingers brush for a moment before Aspen pulls her hand away. I think something of their proximity for a moment, recalling my conversation with Martina in our room a couple of days ago, but they would have told me if they had something going on between them . . . right?

"Hey, Whitney."

I jump at the sound of Joanna's voice and sit up on my elbows. She appears nearly twice as tall from my low angle, in a white bikini and tiny athletic shorts with the logo of her high school on them. "Oh, uh, hey."

"I was wondering if you wanted to play beach volleyball with us."

I turn my head around to figure out who *us* is, but I shouldn't be surprised to see Adriana and Willow standing on opposite sides of the net, with Noelle nowhere to be found. "I'm good, thanks. Still feeling a little under the weather."

"Hope you feel better soon," she says and begins to turn away. "If you change your mind, we'll be over there. We're missing a player in case you didn't notice."

I shoot her a smile as she walks away, while my head spins, wondering when I entered the timeline where I'm being voluntarily invited to hang out with them.

I scroll through Instagram to distract myself and catch up on Ava's life. There's a big family photo at her cousin's wedding and some shots of her playing tennis at her parents' beach house in Florida. I notice Willow liked that photo and click on her profile and scroll through the perfectly edited and filtered shots of her at school, in skimpy bikinis on the beach, and at swanky dinners with her mother. Scattered among those are dozens of dance photos, of her in leotards and pointe shoes and her limbs tangled up in poses that I didn't even think were humanly possible, and I notice how big and genuine her smiles are in all those pictures.

I've almost hit the end of her page when I find one photo that sticks out among the rest: it's much, much older. Willow looks about eight and is almost unrecognizable: full cheeks, dirty-blond hair, gap-toothed grin. Squinting, I focus on the tall man she hugs, taking in the gray-speckled hair and the wrinkles by his eyes when he smiles.

My heart sinks at the caption: *Rest in peace, Dad. No one will ever support me like you did.*

When Willow starts feeling strangely human again, I toss my phone into the bag holding down the edge of the towel and force myself to take a walk to decompress. Shoving my hands into my sweatshirt pocket, I amble along the firm sand of the shoreline, taking in the feeling of being here without having to drop down and do a burpee or ten push-ups. As I continue down the beach, I overhear some shouting, and I freeze, debating whether to continue or jog back.

"Come on, Ryan, let's go!"

With just a few more steps, it becomes clear the trainers, just like us, are unwinding after another long day. Ryan and May form a team on one side of the net, and although their backs are to me, it doesn't take a great amount of deduction to realize Axel and Isla form the other team. I know they're just coworkers having fun but seeing them together in any circumstance always awakens the green-eyed monster inside me, especially when Isla jumps up to return the ball and her boobs bounce in her skimpy blue bikini top. I can't see Axel's face from here, but I'm not sure I'd blame him for stealing a glance.

They play for a few moments, the sound of hollering and cheering fading the more I zero in on Axel and Isla maneuvering around each other, moving with the same vigor of two players in the Summer Olympics. After a forceful serve from Ryan, Axel dives down and slides across the sand on his front to make contact with the ball but misses altogether. Booming with laughter, he stands up and brushes the sand off his front, facing my way now.

It's the first time I've seen him shirtless, but I don't have time to ogle all the grooves and indents in his bronzed abdomen. I zoom down the beach, kicking up sand on the backs of my legs. I almost race right past Martina and Aspen in the water, but maybe I should've, because the two are practically brushing bodies. Between two breaths, Martina pulls Aspen in for a kiss, and I gasp, covering my mouth with my hand to conceal the noise, even though there's no way they can hear me over the crashing waves.

The kiss lasts three seconds—or maybe four—before Aspen breaks away and runs back to the shoreline. Martina calls her name to no avail and then slaps the surface of the water while mouthing something that's probably a curse. She locks eyes with me on the way out and ducks her head down.

"Martina!" I call, meeting her halfway. "Martina, hey. It's okay."

"No, it's not," she says, pushing her wet black hair out of her eyes. "I just got rejected, and you're telling me it's *okay?*"

"Maybe Aspen was caught off guard," I reason, trying to catch up to her as she marches up the sand. "O-or maybe she's still figuring herself out. It doesn't mean you did anything wrong."

She holds her palm up, and it feels like a slap in the face. "With all due respect, Whitney, stay out of this one."

I stand frozen on the sand as she stalks away, naively thinking she's going to turn around and apologize, but she soon becomes a speck in the distance. With no one else to turn to, I fight all logic and trudge up the sand to the volleyball net on this side of the beach.

"Hey."

Willow and Joanna turn to me, and after a moment, Adriana tears her eyes away from the pathway Martina just marched away on.

"Do you guys still need another player?"

They look between each other and then back at me before nodding in unison.

"Yeah, actually," Willow says, tossing the ball to me, "that would be great."

Week Five

CHAPTER TWENTY-ONE

On Monday, we have to be outside by six in the morning for a sunrise retreat in the woods, which is a bit of a misnomer, considering the sun rises at five thirty. It streams into my puffy and stinging eyes as I begrudgingly drag myself over to the group of girls gathered outside the Central Building.

This early in the morning, no one is in a sociable mood, which amplifies the sounds of nature: the calls of mourning doves, the crunch of our sneakers against dirt, the leaves on trees rustling as squirrels scurry up their trunks. I'm not sure if I'll ever be an outdoorsy person, but I know for sure I'll be seeing the inside of my room less for the rest of summer, already excited for all the different routes I can take in my neighborhood on my (not six-a.m.) runs.

Although Martina and I are still okay, she and Aspen haven't even acknowledged each other since their kiss in the ocean. I don't know how long they think they can keep arranging meals around each other in the dining hall or avoiding encounters in the hallway or the communal bathroom, but the silent treatment has to end eventually.

I turn to Martina beside me, whose eyes haven't left the dirt. "Hey." I nudge her lightly in the ribs. "You're supposed to be the optimistic one of us, remember?"

"It's six in the morning, Whitney."

"Okay, valid," I mumble, stifling a yawn at the thought. "But still, come *on*. We're supposed to be a team, Martina."

"Okay, and? I'm not saying *you* can't talk to Aspen."

"I mean the *three* of us. At least try to make up before camp ends. We only have a week left here."

"Eight days," she corrects.

"Actually, it's six." Aspen somehow heard us from ten paces ahead and turns around, looking somewhere between me and Martina's faces. "Just saying."

I wonder if this moment might be their breakthrough, but Aspen then turns around and disappears into the group of girls ahead of us.

Martina and I don't say anything to each other after that. By the time Cindy asks us to stop walking, we're at least thirty minutes into the woods. It's debatable if there's even cell service here; not that it matters, considering we had to leave our phones in our rooms.

I look up to find some sort of structure with a tarp covering it that's way too big to be another puzzle, a trash can in front of it, and a plastic bag filled with neon sticky notes and markers sitting atop a small white table. Slowly we look between each other, wondering what purpose these items could possibly serve, together or apart.

Martina leans into my ear. "Is this feeling a little culty to you, or is it just me?"

"We're beyond a cult at this point," I whisper back as Cindy rips the tarp off the object, revealing . . . a *mirror*?

"Today we'll be talking about insecurities." She stands in front of the full-length mirror and looks at her reflection. From my angle, I can make out the corner of my forehead, which thankfully isn't one of my many insecurities. "A lot of you might think that only teenage girls deal with insecurities, but the truth is, we're all insecure. Young and old. Male and female. Rich and poor. And everyone in between. Insecurities are truly the unavoidable plague of the human existence."

She turns around, and her body blocks the entirety of the mirror from our view. "But sadly, society has told all of you—you beautiful, young, and vulnerable women—that you need to *cure* this plague. And so, it feeds you diet culture and plastic surgery and thirty-day fitness challenges, and it takes body parts and facial features in and out of style, until you're stuck in an endless loop of fixing things that don't need a remedy."

Her face scrunches up, managing to create some wrinkles in her Botoxed forehead, which finally hints at her true age, somewhere between forty and fifty. "I would know this first-hand. Only when I left the modeling industry did I realize that standing in front of the mirror for hours a day and nitpicking every part of myself—thinking that a stranger was going to scrutinize the tiny zit on my chin or my crooked bottom tooth or care that I'm bloated because I just enjoyed a nice meal—*wasn't* normal. It was my own personal hell that I never thought I could escape."

Willow and Joanna are both staring at their sneakers, probably for different reasons. The rest of us look at Cindy with varying degrees of interest, but no one utters a word.

She walks down the row we stand in, silently assessing us. "But what I want you to understand today is that you *can* break free. Your insecurities may never go away, but they don't have to rule you. And you certainly don't have to change any part of yourself just because social media tells you that you should."

When she stops before me and Martina, I look up. "What if you still wanted to change yourself, anyway?"

"Maybe you should evaluate the 'why' behind the change. Is it really for you, or is it for someone else? And if you did change something about yourself, would you feel better . . . or would that change lead to a slew of new insecurities?"

I swallow that ball in my throat, realizing my answer isn't as black-and-white as she wants it to be. I didn't originally come here just for me, but I can't deny I already feel so much better about myself than I did before I arrived.

"What if it's not social media that made you insecure?" Willow asks, loud and bold, and even Joanna and Adriana do a double take. "What if it was someone much closer to you?"

Cindy sucks in her angled cheeks and doesn't directly meet her daughter's burning gaze. "How about you have a conversation with that person, then? And try to understand where they were coming from?"

"But what if they never want to hear you out? Or better yet, ever admit they're wrong?"

A couple of girls whisper confusedly behind me, but I'm not quite as taken aback, knowing by now that the issues Willow has with her mother must run deep, even if I don't know what caused them. Adriana whispers something in Willow's ear that seems to visibly relax the cords in her neck, but there's still that fiery rage in her brown eyes, the same kind I'd see whenever she'd hurl an insult my way in high school.

"Then maybe you have resort to other methods," Cindy says in a clipped tone, clasping her hands with a sense of finality. She looks up and blinks away her emotions, but it's funny she doesn't realize she might seem more credible if she showed them.

The empowering robot role is starting to get old.

"You're all right to think critically about a topic like this because quite frankly, it's not as simple as I'm making it out to be. But if we never acknowledge our insecurities, we'll never know how to deal with them." She picks up the plastic bag and fishes out some sticky-note pads and markers. She sets them down on the small table in front of the mirror before turning back to us. "I want you all, if you're comfortable, to participate in an activity I've named 'Trash Your Insecurities and Post Some Positivity.' The idea is simple. On a sticky note, write down an insecurity of yours." She bends over the table and scribbles something onto a sticky note and rips it off the pad. "Then, just like this"—she crumples the paper into a tiny ball in her first—"throw it into the trash."

From a few feet back, she chucks it into the trash can like she's shooting a basketball, and a couple girls cheer for her when it sails right in.

"Afterwards, write down a positive message on another sticky note and sign your name. Once again, it could be anything. Something you tell yourself in the morning when you look in the mirror. Or something you wish someone could tell you. Or even your favorite motivational quote." She jots down something in her half-cursive, half-print handwriting and picks the sticky note up. "Then stick it to the mirror right here." She slaps it on, the mirror shaking on its stand. Turning around, she asks, "Does anyone want to go first?"

Just like in a classroom, silence answers her question. Before she can call on some visibly uncomfortable girls, I volunteer to go first—mostly so I can read what she plastered on the mirror. I squat before the small table, tugging my T-shirt down over my backside. I draw a blank as I stare at a green sticky-note pad, rolling the Sharpie between my thumb and index finger. Hearing some whispers from behind me, I scrawl the first thing that comes to my mind.

I'm not good enough.

A load lifts from my shoulders just from writing it down. I'm not confident I'll make it in like Cindy did if I toss my crumpled note in from afar, so I hover my fist over the trash can before uncurling my fingers and letting the note go.

"Feeling okay?" Cindy asks.

I nod and decide not to overthink how trite my positive message is, choosing the opposite of my insecurity: *You are good enough.*

I post it above Cindy's sticky note and feel my heart tighten in my chest when I read her not-so-subtle message on a purple sticky note: *You are so loved.*

One by one, we stick our notes onto the mirror's frame, until its white color is lost in a sea of neon pink, blue, green, and purple. Cindy asks us return to the mirror one by one when the activity is over to take in all the messages at once, and when I do, I realize that none of us opted for subtlety.

Martina: *Love who you want to love.*

Aspen: *Be patient with yourself.*

Joanna: *Slay, tall queen! (And my short queens too)*

Adriana: *It's okay if you don't win today—there's always tomorrow.*

Kennedy: *Don't forget you're beautiful and smart! (By the way, I can read all your messages.)*

Willow: *I don't hate you.*

I look up, and Willow shoots me a soft smile from beside her mother, and for once, I smile back.

CHAPTER TWENTY-TWO

The next several sessions with Axel pass by in a blur, consisting of even more intense yet familiar workouts: trail running, boxing, and enough circuit training on the beach to make me hate the place. Axel has seemed to consider every session my last hurrah, which means I leave each one sorer than the last.

"Can't. Do. This. Shit. Today." Dramatically, I fall to the floor of the gym and stare into the spotlights on the ceiling until my vision blurs. "You're trying to kill me, aren't you?"

Axel looms over me, not even fazed by my theatrics. "That wouldn't be beneficial to me or you, so no, I am not." Crouching down, he asks, "How about we get some caffeine in you first?"

"I'm not drinking that nasty dining hall coffee."

He grabs my hand and hauls me up to my feet. "I'm not *suggesting* the nasty dining hall coffee. Stop talking and follow me."

We make our way down the hall. I think we're going to head out the back exit until he leads me up the glass stairs and clasps the door handle to Bob's office. "I can't follow you in there, Axel," I demur, taking a large step back.

He pushes the door open. "You think I'd even be coming in here if I wasn't on his good side?"

"Is it even humanly possible to get on that man's good side?"

"Shockingly, yes," he says and walks across the room. "You'll find out soon enough."

There seems to be something more to that statement, but I don't question it. I watch him fiddle with the coffee maker and then pull out some paper cups from the cabinet above it, and it all feels oddly domestic, like we're in our house and having a slow morning together.

He turns around, and I wipe that weird lovey expression off my face. "How do you take your coffee?"

"With some sugar and almond milk—if there is any. Skim milk is also good." He crouches down to the mini fridge under the table and pulls out a carton of almond milk. "How do you take yours?"

"Black with a spoon of sugar, usually."

"Doesn't putting anything in black coffee negate its existence as black coffee?"

"Are you always like this, Whitney?" he chuckles.

I draw closer and watch the way his eyes flicker down to the slight bit of cleavage showing in my tank top before settling on my face. "It's kind of in the name. Whitney . . . witty . . . it only makes sense."

"Should I start calling you that, then?" He hands me my cup of coffee, and our fingers brush as I take it from him. He draws out the syllables as he tries it out, and I can't decide if I tolerate it because it's not a bad new nickname or because he's the one saying it in that smooth, deep voice of his.

"If you want to, but then it's only fair if I give you a nick-name." I take a sip of coffee, my tastebuds finally rejuvenated after weeks of consuming fried motor oil. "I have lots of ideas after these last few workout sessions."

"I'll entertain them," he says, and when my eyes light up, he corrects himself, "to an extent."

"Okay, so first on my list is Ax Murderer. Clichéd, I know, but the name reference is already built in, so it gets some points for that." He frowns, eyes narrowing, but I hold up my index finger. "Next would be Axhole. I really like that one, but it doesn't roll that nicely off the tongue. You try it." He gives it a try before nodding in agreement. "My favorite would have to be Wheel, though. But apparently elementary physics humor isn't your thing."

"Because I failed physics in high school, Whitney."

I cup my ear. "Oh my god, is that a *flaw* I hear? Please continue."

"Finish your coffee, Witty," he teases, grabbing his own and walking to the door. Calling out over his shoulder, he adds, "By the way, you're paying for this today."

"*Axhole,*" I mutter under my breath as I follow him out.

———

At lunch, I sit alone with Martina again. She longingly eyes Aspen sitting in her spot at Kennedy and Neha's table. We're still friends with them, but now that the five of us can't sit together in a civilized manner, we naturally found our split.

"Hey. Can we sit here?"

I look up, mouth full of turkey club, finding Willow, Joanna, and Adriana standing in front of our table, trays in hand.

"Why would you want to sit here?" Martina asks.

"Come on, Marti," Adriana says, plopping down next to her and slinging an arm over her shoulder. "We shared a womb for eight and a half months. Me wanting to be near you shouldn't be that big of a shock."

"Yeah, and that was enough space-sharing for a lifetime," Martina grumbles, removing her sister's arm from her shoulder.

Willow and Joanna sit on either side of me, and I don't object to their presence. If anything, Martina is more annoyed than I am.

"What's gotten into you the past couple of days?" Adriana asks, stealing her fork. She pops a butternut squash cube into her mouth and adds, "You're usually the peppy one of us."

"Okay, why does *everyone* say that?" Martina snaps, dropping her hands down to the table with a thud that rattles our plates. "Never mind, sorry. I'm . . . I'm going through it, okay?"

"Does it have something to do with Aspen?" Joanna asks.

Martina's lips part in shock. "How—how do you know anything about that?"

"Oh, come on," Willow says. "We saw you guys in the ocean together." Martina's eyes fall to the table, and her shoulders slump with them. "We're rooting for you two, by the way."

"There's nothing to root for anymore," she grumbles and steals her fork back from Adriana. Through a reluctant mouthful of kale, she says, "Thanks, though."

We take turns trying to console her through the rest of the lunch, and by the end, she's back to being her usual jocular self, but I know the mood won't last long.

—

"Do you know if we have one of those try-not-to-throw-yourself-off-a-cliff-and-talk sessions with Cindy tonight?" Martina asks, dropping her headphones to her neck. She has on a men's burgundy sweatshirt with the hood tugged over her head and is already halfway under the covers, even though it's only four p.m.

"That's one way to put it." I shut the door behind me, still breathing heavily from my afternoon workout session with Axel. I fetch my water bottle from my side table. "Honestly, I don't know. I didn't look at the schedule closely enough."

"Could you please go look at it and text me back an answer? Preferably, no."

"Martina—"

"Thanks, Whitney, you're the best." She tugs on her headphones again and drowns me out.

After taking a shower and changing into some lounge clothes, I head to the Central Building, and, with one glance at the screen on the wall, I text Martina the answer she's looking for. As I make a beeline to the exit, I hear some music coming from Room 100, something low and classical, and for a second, I wonder if Bob has a soft spot for Tchaikovsky.

Slinking down the hall, I make out a thud, like feet landing hard against wood. Poking my head through the open crack in the door, there's a whir of spindly limbs and blond hair. Willow is dancing. She leaps and spins across the floor, seeming to defy the laws of physics that always work against me. On the last leap, she crashes down to the floor and stays there, palms flat against the wood. She breathes heavy as she stares into her reflection in the mirror, which soon becomes my downfall.

"What are you doing here?" she snaps, scrambling to her feet. She fetches her phone from the corner of the room and fumbles to turn off the music, her fingers working in a frenzy across her screen.

"You're a great dancer, Willow," I say. It's more of a fact than a compliment, but it's enough for her to eye me like a rabbit would a fox, waiting for the catch.

There isn't one.

"Thanks," she mumbles after a moment. She tugs a hand through her sweaty hair and lets it drop to her side. "Some people wouldn't say that, though."

"Who wouldn't?" I challenge.

"That doesn't matter," she mutters, shaking her head. "Just go, Whitney."

I don't listen to her and slip inside the room, looking at my reflection in the mirror next to her. We're polar opposites: my thick brown hair to her wispy bright blond, my curvy build to her waiflike figure, my baggy loungewear to her leotard and tight shorts. Our differences become even more apparent when I give in to my nagging desire to attempt a jeté with less than half the flexibility of a ballet dancer and come crashing down to the floor.

Willow winces. "That's not how you're supposed to do that."

"I know." I pull off my sneakers and kick them to the other side of the room. I spin around in my socks, close to whacking her in the face with my outstretched arm. "I've never taken a dance class in my life."

"Why are you trying to dance, then?"

"Have you ever heard of letting loose?" I can't believe I of all people am imparting that lesson on her, but I realize Willow may be even more uptight than I am. "You know, in high school, I used to always wonder if people like you ever got tired of putting on a mask every day. Wearing clothes you didn't like, laughing at things you didn't find funny, making fun of people you had no reason to hate . . . did the persona ever get boring?"

"Who said it was a persona?" she snarls. "Maybe it was actually fun."

I spin around again, and this time we're eye to eye. "If it

wasn't one, why haven't you been that way at camp? You could've had your own kingdom here. Wouldn't have been as big as the one you ruled over in high school, but it would've probably been enough for your ego."

Her shoulders tense, accentuating some of the tendons in her neck. "Where are you going with this?"

"Something broke you this summer, Willow," I say, thrusting a finger into her line of vision. "And I want to know what."

"What makes you think I'm going to tell *you* anything?"

"I don't think you will," I say, fishing my phone out from my pocket. I scroll through a playlist Martina sent me titled "IDGAF" and pick something pop rock that would work well at a karaoke bar. "But I think I can get you to dance with me."

I pull the scrunchie out of my hair and shrug off my sweat-shirt, chucking both in the vicinity of my shoes. The music blasts through the large, empty room, pumping the blood in my veins as I start moving. There's nothing elegant or graceful about the way I dance; one moment, I'm shaking my hips, then pumping my fists, then fluffing my hair and mouthing the lyrics like I'm onstage at my one-woman show.

While I unabashedly make a fool of myself, Willow eyes me with curiosity, arms still folded across her chest. Her defiance only fires me up more, and soon enough I'm down on my knees clutching my air microphone and whipping my hair back and forth. Willow waits a beat before she steals my imaginary micro-phone and sings the lyrics out loud instead. I beam like a fucking star as she shimmies around me, her fist up in the air and her hair spilling all over her face. We both start bouncing up and down and pointing at each other as we belt out the lyrics, our feet pounding against the wooden floor.

"How'd you know I frickin' love this song?"

"Everyone loves this song!" I yell back. "It's a classic."

We continue shimmying across the room, both our ears and our dignity an afterthought at this point. We bump backs right as the song ends, and we giggle softly in the silence that now bathes the room, looking at each other in the mirror. Our faces are flushed and our hair looks like a flight of pigeons flew through it, but the same contentedness wipes away the lines in our foreheads and the tension from our shoulders.

We slump down to the ground across from each other and soak in the silence for once, something I usually do everything I can to break. But silence around Willow means something different. It means she's not insulting me or trying to get into my head, and it means I'm not breaking down and seeking my pointless revenge.

But it also means there are still things left unsaid between us.

"You know it wasn't supposed to be this way, right?" She sighs, wrapping her arms around her knees, and rests her chin atop her forearm. "*I* wasn't supposed to be this way."

"Why do you say that?"

"I don't know. Or I guess—" She grimaces, shaking her head, and drops her palms to the floor. "Look, let me explain something. My mom might seem like this big old ray of sunshine to all you guys at this camp, but her female empowerment bullshit? It's all a façade. She's *never* practiced any of that with me. Instead, she's always been disappointed with me, comparing me to others, standing in the way of the things I love . . ." She chuckles softly and looks away. "But who here would believe me if I told them this?"

I would, I want to tell her, as all that harbored bitterness over my relationship with Dad starts suffocating me again.

I breathe out those feelings. "Has she always been like that?"

Her lips part in shock, like she almost expected me to shut her down. "Pretty much, yeah. When I was a kid, it was because I had no interest in becoming a model, no matter how many photo shoots she dragged me to or how many creepy old designers pinched my cheeks and called me pretty and angelic.

"And then when I was eleven or twelve, and she had her great big epiphany that the modeling industry is a toxic hell-hole, my grades suddenly mattered. But guess what? I'm *dumb*, Whitney. While you were sad if you got a ninety-five and not a hundred on a test, I was barely making Cs in the regular versions of all your classes. And dance? Yeah, I don't think I'm gonna get started on that."

"Dance might be the whole reason you're here," I say. I leave out where I got this piece of information, but I probably could've deduced it by now, anyway.

"You're not wrong. My dad was the one who always encouraged me to chase my dreams. I was his *petite ballerine* from my first dance class at two years old." She smiles distantly and blinks away some wetness from her eyes. "Then he died three years ago, and my mom has spent *every* waking moment trying to tear this piece of me away, down to this summer, when she forced me to spend it here at this camp so I would miss my audition for a professional ballet company and pass the time instead by listening to her tell us to *embrace* ourselves."

"But *why*?" I can't help but ask. "My parents would be over the moon if I danced. Hell, played any sport. My sister is a golfer of all things."

She lets out an airy laugh, tucking a strand of her hair behind her ear. "She thinks if I go professional, I'll develop body-image issues or an eating disorder or fall down some self-loathing spiral . . . But what she doesn't realize is the only person who could ever give me any of those issues is *her*." She works her jaw back and forth, her fingers curling into the wood below her. "So, yeah, Whitney. That's why I'm the messed-up person I am, and honestly? I'm sorry you had to suffer because of it."

I'm not even sure what to react to first: the information overload on her life or the passive apology at the end, so I finally ask the question that's been nagging me for years at this point: "But why *me*, Willow?"

"I don't know. You just . . . Gosh, you just *enraged* me, Whitney. You were everything I wasn't, except for athletic, which I guess is why I would pick on you so much. Otherwise, you were pretty and smart and kind and had a wonderful, loving family, and did I mention you're smart? Because every time the honor roll came out, and my mom would see your name plastered at the top of the list, she'd ask why I couldn't be more like *you*."

My eyes widen, and I think something of those moments in the past few weeks when she would seem to crumple in on herself any time Cindy complimented me and not her. "You mean, she'd compare you . . . to *me*?"

"Why wouldn't she? You're every parent's dream, Whitney. Me? I'm a walking disaster."

I sit frozen. This close and without her usual sneer and layer of foundation, she looks several years younger, almost like a lost child that I want to scoop up into my arms. She blinks away some more of the wetness from her eyes and looks out of the window, hugging her knees tighter.

"You're not a walking disaster, Willow," I say, reaching forward and placing my hand on her forearm, a soft, delicate touch. "You're a *dancing* disaster. There's a difference."

I expect her to snap something back, or maybe even storm away, but she just tosses her head back and laughs at my crappy humor. The bellowing sound echoes off the walls of this big, empty room and finally cracks the icy barrier between the two of us.

"You're so right, Whitney," she breathes. "I only realized what a hot mess I'd become after graduation, when the ceremony ended, and my popularity felt meaningless when I realized you were up there giving your valedictorian speech and literally all I'd accomplished was making random people hate me." She drags her knuckle over the corner of her eye. "You're right: it got boring real quick."

I fish out a tissue from my shorts pocket and hand it to her. She blows her nose before dabbing at her eyes with the same snotty side. "Maybe there's a reason we're both stuck here together, and it's so I can apologize to you. So, you know what? I will. I'm so, *so* sorry, Whitney. For every horrible word I said to you and stupid prank I played and all those ugly selfies of us in the newsletter. God, I had *so* many better angles than that."

"Jesus, Willow," I say, unable to contain my laughter. "Only you can make an apology about yourself."

"And you wanna know the biggest joke too? All that newsletter club experience, and I didn't even get into any of the colleges I applied to as a journalism major. Which probably is karma, but you have to admit, I do have quite the knack for it."

"At the expense of others' dignity and self-esteem? Oh, yes. Yes, you *definitely* do."

I laugh again with her, only stopping when I feel a stitch in my side. For the first time in what feels like forever, that heavy, suffocating weight lifts from my chest, and my next intake of air feels incredibly satisfying. I can see the girl in front of me in a different light, even if it's not that much brighter than before. And I can finally believe there'll be a version of me, sometime in the future, who doesn't think about what happened in high school anymore or about how many times I've been hurt, by her or anyone else.

"Look, Willow," I say, breaking the silence after a moment. "I don't—I don't know if we'll ever become *besties*." She cracks a smile with me when she remembers what I'm referring to. "But it does mean something to me that you've apologized. And at this point, I want you to stop thinking about me. You need to focus on yourself, because soon, I'll be off chasing my dreams, and you know what?" I wrap my hand around her bony wrist and pull her up with me. "I hope you get to as well."

Eyes welling up with tears again, Willow scrunches up her face and looks away, choking back a sob. Without warning, she throws her arms around me and squeezes me into her chest. I feel like I'm hugging a toddler, unsure where to even put my hands.

I leave them floating in the air as she falls apart against me, while I, at last, feel whole again.

CHAPTER TWENTY-THREE

Something in my world shifts after making up with Willow.

The air feels lighter and crisper as I walk out of the dining hall after breakfast, even if it's a muggy eighty-something degrees out. I didn't dread seeing her in the bathroom while getting ready this morning or avoid making small talk with her at our table, realizing she's become just like any other person in my life. I almost want to force Martina and Aspen to make up just so they can feel this same degree of bliss, but I know it's not my place, even if it meant consoling Martina through another misery session over shitty dining hall coffee.

I'm still not over how bad it tastes.

During our run down the beach a little while later, Axel notices my elevated mood, but he seems like he almost doesn't want to question it in case he ruins it. But when he instructs me to drop down and complete ten push-ups, and I don't complain, his suspicion hits its peak.

"Okay, something has *definitely* gotten into you today," he says. "Open to sharing?"

"Would I still have to do these push-ups if I tell you?"

"Ah. There's my Whitney again."

My stomach flutters at *my Whitney*, even if I know he doesn't mean it in the romantic sense. Or maybe he does. I still don't understand what we have going on between us—all I know is I don't want it to end anytime soon.

Although he doesn't answer the push-up question, I still tell him the truth as we begin walking down the sand. "Okay, the reason I'm in a good mood is Willow and I—yesterday we finally talked. And I got to understand her side of the story, which is pretty shitty, by the way. And I know . . . I know that doesn't *justify* the way she treated me all these years, but I finally got some closure."

"Did she apologize?" he asks after a moment.

"Yeah, she did. In her own way, at least."

"And did you accept it?"

I can't tell if he's curious or he's judging me, so I draw back and ask, "Was I not supposed to?"

"No," he says and stops walking. "That was the right thing to do. Honestly, accepting an apology benefits you a lot more than the person giving it."

I mull over his words as I get through the rest of the workout, realizing maybe that's why I feel like I'm on top of the world.

But I guess the high lasts only so long.

When we part ways with plans to meet later in the afternoon for a boxing workout, I spot Isla in the distance. She jogs over to Axel, her abs on full display in one of those tiny sports bras she wears, and I halt my bitter thoughts for a moment, deciding to be rational. She's probably going to talk camp logistics with him, or maybe she's conveying some important message. It's a lot better to convince myself of those options than the ones nagging my brain as I begin to walk away.

The pull of knowing turns me back around again, and there they are on the beach, engaged in deep conversation. I can't hear what they're saying from where I am on the main road, but it seems serious from the way Axel's eyebrows furrow together, and her frantic gesticulation.

And then it happens. She leans in, and her lips touch his and then . . . she *kisses* him. He doesn't push her away, or at least not quickly enough. Her mouth is moving by the time he pulls away, and I hate that I can't tell whether he loved or hated it.

Feeling my breakfast crawl up my throat, I turn around and begin running, blinking away the tears welling up in my eyes. It feels stupid to cry when Axel and I were never a thing, but he had to have felt *something*. Hell, I didn't make up that time in his room during that thunderstorm or when he carried me into the ocean or the many deep, soul-connecting conversations we've had, too many to even count on my two hands at this point.

"Whitney!" Axel calls, footsteps pounding behind me. "Whitney, *wait*!"

I should be flattered that he's chasing after me instead of Isla, but my humiliation only balloons, and I pick up the pace, tears blurring my vision. Eventually, his hand around my wrist tugs me back, but I yank it out of his hold and back away from him.

"Whitney, wait," Axel repeats, blocking my path forward. "That wasn't what you thought it was."

"So I just hallucinated you and Isla kissing each other on the beach over there?"

"I didn't—" Driving his teeth into his bottom lip, he drags his fingers through his hair, tugging at the damp ends. "She kissed *me*. There's a difference."

"Okay, great, that's settled, then," I say, throwing my hands up into the air. "Why are we having this conversation?"

He doesn't say anything as we continue looking into each other's eyes, our chests rising and falling in unison. His eyes flicker to my lips before they settle somewhere in the middle of my face, like a compromise.

"Come on, you know why things can't happen between us. I'm a trainer. And you're a camper." He looks off at the trees over my head as he forces out, "It's . . . wrong."

"But you're not going to be my trainer forever," I say, almost desperately. I'm starting to throw my dignity into the same landfill as my hopes at this point. "What then?"

My question silences him, and at first, it feels like a profound kind of silence, like I've said something that changes the game between us and will take this conversation in a different direction. But then his eyebrows draw together, and he clasps the nape of his neck, and his eyes turn stormy, like he's never once considered what we could be beyond this camp.

My heart plummets down to my stomach, and there's that burning feeling in my throat again, like I might throw up this time. Here I was thinking our little forbidden moments were a preview of a different kind of relationship, one devoid of his professional responsibilities and my restraint hanging on a thread.

"Look, Whitney. We're not supposed to feel this way about each other, and our lives are so different, and you're going off to college soon, and I—" He cuts himself off before he starts rambling the way I always do around him and shakes his head. "You really don't need to make this more complicated than it needs to be." His words drive the nail into the coffin of my hopes, and he only makes it worse when he grabs my hand, and I feel nothing when his thumb slides down my palm. "You get it, right?"

I swallow the lump in my throat, realizing he's right. This

isn't complicated. In fact, it's so simple that all I have to do is remind myself of the lesson life has been teaching me all along. It's never girls like me that win. It's the skinny ones. The tall ones. The athletic ones. The popular ones.

Willow in high school. Isla at camp. Poppy all my life.

I'll never be like them, and I don't know why I fooled myself into ever thinking otherwise.

"Yeah, of course, I do," I say, my voice barely there. "Thanks for the clarification."

When I've walked far enough to become a speck in the distance to him, I take off running down the road, and hot tears start flowing freely down my cheeks again. I use the collar of my T-shirt to scrub my eyes and face between strides, my heart aching more than my legs for once. I don't even notice how far I make it down this road until asphalt turns to gravel, and the wooden CAMP CAMPBELL sign in the distance is the only indication this area is still on the premises.

I collapse down to the grass and let out the cry I want to. Only when I'm hiccupping and gasping for air and running out of dry spots on my T-shirt to wipe my tears do I realize I'm not just crying about Isla and Axel kissing or his sugarcoated rejection of me. I'm crying because something seemingly so innocuous as not being good at sports is a brand that's marked me for life. It managed to ruin my relationship with Dad and Poppy and made my high school experience a living hell, and right when I thought I'd finally done something about it, I still ended up the loser in the end.

Collecting myself, I rise to my feet and dial Mom's number. The phone rings two times, then three, and right when I think it's going to straight to voicemail, she picks up.

Or Poppy does.

"Where's Mom?" I ask, skipping past the greeting.

"She's out on a run around the neighborhood and forgot her phone here in the kitchen." *Of course, she's out on a run*, I think, wanting to scream at the irony. "What's up?"

"The goddamn sky," I snap back, glancing up at the one cloud in a sea of blue, before I get a hold of myself. "I'm sorry. I'm just—I'm not having a good day, Poppy. Or life, really, but that's a separate problem. I was calling because I'm coming home today."

"Are you kidding me? How are you unable to power through the last *two* days of camp?"

When she phrases it that way, I realize how pathetic I sound, but I don't have the energy to justify myself. "Mom told me if anything ever happened, I'm welcome to come back home, and whelp, things happened."

She breathes a little louder on the other end of the line as she waits to answer me. "Look, Whitney. We're usually sympathetic, but unless you can prove to us you've lost a leg or are currently in a hostage situation, you're not coming home. Carmichaels aren't quitters."

"Maybe I'll be the first," I grumble, dabbing at my eyes with the damp collar of my shirt again. "I just . . . I . . . I think this was all a mistake, Poppy. I bit off more than I could chew coming here, and I've met too many people and learned too much about myself and opened my heart in the wrong way, and now I-I'm confused and heartbroken and u-unsure and—"

"Whitney," Poppy says sharply, using that same no-nonsense tone Axel uses. It snaps me out of my trance. "I want you to take a deep breath, okay? You're not making any sense."

I do as she says, breathing in and out with the rustle of the branches of the tree above my head, wishing I was as small and insignificant as the blue jay perched on one of them. "Okay."

"Good. Now what do you want to say?"

"I don't know," I whisper, my throat clogging up with tears again. "I really don't."

"That's okay," she soothes, but her tone wavers, like she knows nothing is okay. "Try to calm down, and call me back later, okay? We're all excited to see you again, especially Dad."

"He misses me?" I perk up.

"For sure. He can't wait for all the rounds of golf we can play together when you get back."

I hang up and sob even harder.

CHAPTER TWENTY-FOUR

After my falling-out with Axel, my eyes are set on one goal and one goal only: going home. Only one day stands between me and my parents' house, surrounded by the suburban peace and quiet I now crave.

I could barely crack my eyes open at the blare of my alarm this morning, having dreamt I was back holed up under my covers in my childhood bedroom after that tennis disaster with Dad, Poppy, and Levi. Still spooked, I checked my reflection in the mirror twice for any purple coloring around my puffy eyes as I got dressed, almost wishing I had to deal with a black eye and not a bruised heart.

Apparently, concealer only works on the outside.

"Hey." Martina slowly walks up to me in the middle of Room 100, where all sixteen of us have been waiting for the past ten minutes. "Are you mad at me?"

My heart cracks at her crestfallen expression. "No, of course not." I reach forward and pull her into a small hug. "I'm going through something dumb and didn't want to blow up in your face by accident. That's the last thing you deserve."

"Don't worry about it, Whit," she says, giving my shoulder a squeeze and letting go. "We should probably be more worried about what *he's* gonna tell us right now." She extends her thumb towards Bob, who's begun making his grand entrance.

He's developed more of a tan since I last saw him but still bears that same stony expression, slate gray eyes narrowed and judging us all. Without him having to say a word, we straighten up and smooth out the jagged line we stand in.

"Congratulations to all of you, first of all," he says, folding his hands behind his back. His tone is anything but congratulatory. "You definitely aren't the uncoordinated sloths you were five weeks ago."

We all look between each other and then back at Bob.

"As we approach the end of this experience, Cindy and I decided this would be the perfect time for you to obtain a concrete idea of your progress." He clicks a button on the remote in his hand, and it turns on the large screen behind him. "Here is a list of activities you've tried and skills you've developed while being here. Longer than you thought, right?"

We take a moment to peruse the listings. Most are familiar, apart from "rock climbing" for activities and "accuracy" for skills. I'm positive that, despite all the physical improvements I've made here, I still can't properly hit, throw, or catch a ball to save my life, despite what Dad might hope.

"To make it easier to conceptualize your progress, your final team challenge is quite simple: a 5K race. How you complete this race doesn't matter this time. You can run, walk, jog, sprint, or patent a hovercraft on your way from the starting line to the finish line for all I care. But if you put the effort in, some of you may be surprised by the results." His eyes move in the vicinity of where I'm standing, but I have no idea if he means me. "With that being said, we'll go through a quick warmup and then reconvene outside."

Ten minutes later, I've learned that Bob's definition of a "warmup" is a workout in itself and my stomach sinks with my hopes of running the whole race. After all, despite all the improvements I've made here, it's barely been three months since the last race of this kind I attempted, and the trauma still hasn't fully subsided. Worse yet, when Axel and I run, he doesn't usually fret over distances; most times, I end up dead and out of breath without him ever telling me how many miles I recorded.

"Okay, the race starts here," Bob says once we're outside, pointing to the yellow marker on the ground. "You're going to run down this road in a loop around campus until you get back to where you started. If you can't figure out how to do that, I wonder how you're still valuable to society, but I digress."

As we situate ourselves, I look off over Bob's head to check if he's recruited any trainers to monitor our progress. I find a couple scattered in the distance—Danielle, Ryan, another whose name I never learned—but no Axel.

"Race starts in five, four, three, two, one—*go!*"

I blink, and five girls have sprinted ahead of me. I take a few seconds to figure out a comfortable speed, knowing there's no way they can run that fast without slowing down eventually. Joanna and Kennedy have already started to regret their pace and relax it, and we all run in one neat line. I know thinking about my competition will only backfire, if this is even a competition.

Do I even have to try at all? The pessimistic part of my brain that's ruled over me this past day says I don't have to, but I know I can't let my training go to waste, so I charge ahead.

My sneakers pound the pavement, and my ponytail whips against my back, fueling my desire to make my steps defter and my strides longer. Minutes whir by, and I'm still going strong. I look behind me to find that I'm ahead of almost everyone, with only a few feet separating me from Joanna and a couple more from Adriana, whose face is already contorting in agony.

"Let's go, guys, keep going!"

I have no idea who said that, but all I know is it wasn't Axel. I realize I don't need verbal encouragement from him either, as with each heavy stride, it's my own voice in my head telling me that I can keep going and that I'm stronger than I think. I never imagined my own thoughts could feel like they belong to a stranger—a very peppy, upbeat, and self-assured stranger—but I could get used to her living in my head.

Halfway through the race, as my thigh muscles constrict and breathing starts feeling like a chore, I wonder why I'm trying so hard myself, knowing we even have confirmation from Bob that walking is acceptable. In that moment, Joanna passes me again, and I throw those thoughts into the garbage. I press forward and run as fast as I can, until I can't make out a single face behind me. At this point, my stamina is coming from no place other than spite and the competitive straight-A student in me that refuses to let me go out without a bang.

With this much distance over everyone else, I reduce my pace to a brisk walk and finally suck in a lungful of fresh air. I stare off at the majestic evergreens towering above my head, then close my eyes and allow the warm sunshine to beat down on my face and arms. By the time I open my eyes again, I spot a hint of a yellow line in the distance. Breaking into a sprint, I straighten my back, narrow my gaze, and allow that color to be all I see.

A couple more feet, a couple more feet, a couple more—

I open up and discover I've already crossed the finish line. That's all it takes for me to double over and calm my ragged breathing, reveling in the feeling of being done, in every way possible.

—

"Whitney, I'd like to have a word with you."

After lunch, Bob stops me in the middle of my walk up the hill with Martina, and I swallow a gulp, knowing whenever a person of authority utters those words, it never means anything good. Face scrunching up in horror, Martina looks one step away from giving me the last rites as I reluctantly agree to follow behind him, and I mouth *pray for me* over my shoulder.

Making some stiff small talk, Bob leads me to the Central Building and up the stairs to his office, the same one Axel and I enjoyed a cup of coffee in a couple of days ago. I peek my head in through the open door and expect to find it empty. To my surprise, Axel reclines in one of those club chairs in front of Bob's desk, his head turned to the right.

"Have a seat," Bob orders. He lowers himself into his black leather office chair and drops his folded hands down on his desk.

Axel looks up from his phone at the jarring thud. We exchange a dry greeting before I turn to Bob, finding it hard to make direct eye contact with his intimidating gray gaze. I distract myself with the picture frames on his desk, able to make out the photographs they hold from where I'm sitting. The word *family* is imprinted all over one of the frames, encasing a rare photo of Bob smiling. He stands behind a slim woman with dark skin, while a gap-toothed young girl holding a rainbow lollipop sits on his shoulders.

"Let me get straight to my point," Bob says, tilting the picture frame away from my view. "You, along with a few of your fellow campers, have caught our attention as potentially promising individuals in the world of fitness. You, Whitney, stood out because of your sheer willpower and constant desire to improve, which, in my opinion, is sometimes even more important than raw athletic ability. Right, Axel?"

"For sure," Axel says, nodding. Looking up from his phone again, he seems as forced to be here as he did during the trainer-camper soccer game. "She always keeps me on my toes."

"Compliments aside, we're here to propose an offer." Bob's following offer hits me like ten tennis balls to the face: "How would you feel about joining Camp Campbell as a trainer next summer?"

"Me?" I slap my palm against my front, as if he meant Axel. I clear my throat and amend, "Oh, wow, that definitely sounds interesting."

"I was hesitant at first after your fight with Willow, but I noticed you've worked out your interpersonal differences, a strong indication that you'd make a good leader. Now, logistically, you would need to become a certified personal trainer, but we would cover the costs of the course, exam, and necessary training. The only thing we'd ask of you is to be available in early June of next year to participate in our orientation and pre-camp training period."

Axel is busy staring at the stack of papers on Bob's desk. I squint and make out a printed-out version of my application at the top of the pile. A sticky note with the words *needs to put in effort but will probably survive* in Bob's scrawl stands out in bold.

If he wasn't currently staring me down, I'd probably laugh

out loud.

"How long do I have to consider this offer?" I ask him.

"Ideally, you get back to us within the next month or so." Bob leans his elbow over the stack, and Axel rips his attention away from the papers. "It might be helpful to read this packet outlining the full extent of your duties—which are a lot, I won't sugarcoat it." He fishes out a stack of papers from his desk drawer and pushes it towards me.

"Thank you," I say, knowing deep down the mere idea of this job isn't the problem. It's who I will be spending the next summer with, but I know I can't make the rift between me and Axel obvious. "To be honest, I never thought I'd come to like exercise this much."

Bob cracks a smile and stands up, extending a hand. "That's the goal here, Whitney. Do let us know when you decide." I return his firm handshake, and he nods at Axel. "I appreciated all your valuable contributions to this discussion, by the way. Feel free to add anything else."

Bob leaves the room, letting the door bang shut behind him. Maybe he thinks it'll make Axel more comfortable to speak, but we both continue staring at different corners of his office.

Axel notices my eyes lingering on the picture frame. "That's Bob's wife and his daughter, Remi."

"Bob has a *kid*?"

Axel chuckles, nodding. "She's nineteen now and probably the only person on earth besides his wife that can turn that man into a total softie. Not that he'd ever admit it, though."

Wow, Bob having a soft side. Who would've thought? For a moment, I question my ability to read people, realizing maybe I'm not as skilled at it as I thought.

Axel exhales. "Can we talk about yesterday, Whitney?"

"What's there to talk about?" My defenses fire up, and I rise to my feet, grabbing my informational packet and water bottle. "You made your point clear."

He opens his mouth to rattle something back before snapping it shut, curling his fingers around the nape of his neck. On my way out, I linger in the doorway, giving him a chance to speak again, to justify himself, but he says nothing and slips past me out the door.

And somehow, his silence feels worse than anything he said to me yesterday.

CHAPTER TWENTY-FIVE

"I can't keep living like this."

One day into my misery, and I'm already saying my thoughts out loud. Technically, I'm also telling them to Martina, but it's unclear if she's been listening to me this whole time, considering her only reaction to my recount of Axel's rejection was a dry "Fuck men. And women too." If I wasn't close enough to watch the rise and fall of her chest underneath her folded hands, I'd wonder if she's still even alive.

I sit up. "Wait, did you hear that?"

"Hear what?"

"That sound." I climb up to my knees on my bed and arch my ear towards the window, making out faint yells and a low beat, sounding like an EDM song is playing on a speaker somewhere. "There's a party outside."

Martina hmphs.

"Come on, Martina." I roll off my bed. "*We* cannot be entering a timeline where I'm more excited about the idea of a party than you are." I lean over the foot of her bed and press my palms into her down comforter, almost as flat as a pancake at this point. "The only way this friendship works is if *I'm* the loser, not you."

She releases a puff of air from her nose, but that's it.

I press my lips into a firm line, wondering if I've hit a dead end with her before I realize I've hardly exhausted all my options. No, instead, I simply have to be the peppy, fearless risk-taker of this friendship, and by taking risks, I mean go scope out my first-ever party at the ripe old age of eighteen years old.

I pry open our closet door and rifle through a small basket of unworn clothing until I find my gold mine. Martina doesn't even glance my way until I'm standing at the mirror on the back of our door and holding that ripped blue one-piece up to my front.

"You're not . . . *wearing* that, are you?"

I suck in my cheeks to conceal a smirk, already knowing it would be that easy, and swivel around with it held up in the air. "That depends. If you come with me, I won't. But if you wanna stay here and mope? Good luck stopping me."

It takes a ten-second staring contest before she shoots up ramrod straight in bed, and that lively spark returns to her brown eyes. She trades me a black square-neck bikini top for a spare linen shirt to throw over her top, and with a touch of makeup, perfume, and matching oversized sunglasses to hide our puffy eyes, we're out the door and ready to leave our miseries behind.

"There you guys are!"

Willow and Adriana run up the beach to us with a red cup in each hand, the liquid sloshing up the sides. Before I can even take in my surroundings, they thrust one into each of our hands and tug us towards the speaker blasting "Hips Don't Lie" by Shakira.

Down the length of the beach, it's a far cry from the

barren, sandy landscape from my workout sessions with Axel. Girls lie across neon-colored towels scattered across the sand, some trying to catch a last-minute tan in the dimming sun. Others contort themselves into questionable positions, sucking in their stomachs long enough for their friends to take another picture. Kennedy, Neha, and Aspen have unearthed two surfboards from who-even-knows-where and take turns trying to ride the shallow waves to shore. Joanna, currently in charge of the music selection, sips from a sweaty bottle of beer while Willow and Adriana shake their asses to the beat. She doubles over in laughter at the sight and dumps the rest of the bottle all over her feet, making me question how many she'd downed before that one.

"What. The. Actual. *Hell.*"

I can't believe Martina is fazed by the sight around us, still unmoving beside me. She looks between the cup in her hands and her sister, swaying her hips and mussing up her hair while Willow records her on her phone, and then back at me.

The muscles in her lips twitch as she fights a smile.

I grab her shoulder with my empty hand and give her a little shake. "You're defrosting now—I can feel it." She still doesn't budge. "Come on, you can't deny you're *enjoying* this, Martina."

"Actually, I'm thinking about how much trouble we're going to be in—"

I freeze. Martina worried about getting in *trouble*? I blink a few times to confirm I'm not actually back in bed and dreaming, but all I see are flashes of blue and gray and sweaty, moving bodies.

"—and how much I do not give a single *fuck.*"

She throws off her overshirt and charges ahead, and cheers

erupt as she climbs up onto a flimsy plastic table and downs her entire cup in one go. Watching her let loose, I stay off to the side and slosh my drink around in a circle, catching a whiff of beer. I don't bring it up to my mouth, but for once, the force holding me back isn't fear of breaking the rules.

It's the numbness. My mind has been a hazy white void ever since Axel walked out the door of Bob's office without a word, taking a piece of me with him. I thought a nap earlier would help, but after dozing off for an hour, the fog only thickened, until it may as well be San Francisco in my head right now. All I need is something to perk me up and reignite some of my hopes, not dull my brain even further, but I don't know what that could be.

I only know what I want, and he doesn't want me back.

Eyes stinging with tears that won't trickle down my face, I dump out the contents of my cup on the sand and then march ahead, hoping to take my anger and frustration out on a thousand pounding steps. Driving my feet deeper into the sand with each long stride, I close my eyes and attempt a variation of that stupid exercise Cindy made us try. I suck in a lungful of salty air and wait for the darkness to clear, and for an image of Axel to start expanding into every crevice of my brain so I can crush it into a million little pieces, but all I see is blond again. *Willow?*

I open my eyes, and she's standing in front of me, making me whip my head around to figure out how she teleported here. It turns out I've barely taken more than fifty steps up the beach. Hell, I can practically count all the little pathetic indents in the sand.

"Are you okay, Whitney?" she asks. "You stormed off out of nowhere."

A small genuine crease forms between her eyebrows, and she tilts her head thoughtfully, like she cares about my answer. I stand frozen, watching the golden rays of the setting sun bathe her in an ethereal glow. With her short white dress and blond locks down and framing her face, she almost looks like an angel.

"Depends on how you define okay. Physically, I'm at a ten. Emotionally? About a four. But if you average those, you get a seven, which I guess is a passing grade, right?"

Willow cracks a small smile, but it fades as quickly as it appears. "You know you don't have to do that all the time."

"Do what?"

"Deflect with humor. My mother would say it's an emotion-focused form of coping, a good thing. But to me? It's the cheapest way out of your feelings."

"All right, then. Do you instead suggest I find an innocent person my age and torment them for no reason until I feel better?"

She gasps.

"That was too soon, right?" I ask, wincing.

"Eh, probably deserved that one." I clear my throat to avoid saying anything else, and she exhales. "Look. All I'm saying is you deserve to feel your feelings as they are. They're supposed to feel pretty big and scary and stupid, and honestly, sometimes, they make you want to crawl out of your own damn skin. God knows that's exactly what grief feels like."

She tightens her arms over the scalloped front of her dress and glances wistfully at the ocean. I stand next to her and track the wave cresting and rolling to shore with my eyes. We're close enough that it sprinkles droplets of water onto our faces when it crashes, but I don't back away. Instead, I keep walking with her until we're in up to our knees, the icy chill of the water somehow feeling like a welcoming embrace.

This time, I try a different approach, deciding to take Willow's advice. I exhale and close my eyes and let those feelings pass, fanning my arms out and hoping the wind or a hungry seagull or a rogue wave carries them away. First comes the embarrassment, crunching my face up into a wince. Then anger, tightening the muscles around my shoulders. Then the sadness, making them sag again.

And finally, the *grief.*

I never realized I've been grieving this whole time, the old Whitney this camp erased and I won't get back. She had a lot of flaws and shortcomings and could barely handle anything life sent her way, let alone run a mile, but she got me through the first eighteen years of my life.

And she was pretty funny too.

"I get why the camp brochure said this place would change our lives," I say, opening my eyes. Willow is still beside me, running her fingertips mindlessly over the surface of the water. "Sometimes I don't even recognize who I am."

"Neither do I," she murmurs, dropping her arms. "But change is a good thing, right? It means we're moving forward and not back. And moving forward is good."

"Is that also something your mom says?"

"My therapist, actually. She might be worse than my mom, though."

We laugh and trudge out of the water, and by now, the sun is a dull orb in the pink-tinted sky. As we walk down the sand, it's almost like we entered a different dimension. Yelling has turned to talking, the music something soft and instrumental, and the dancing has dialed down to lounging. Willow and I sit down on a towel across from Joanna and Adriana, who pass around a family-size bag of potato chips. I grab a lime seltzer from the cooler and sip quietly as I scan the length of the sand, noticing that both Aspen and Martina are gone.

"To surviving Camp Campbell," Joanna says, pulling me out of my thoughts. We clink cans and glasses, but before we drop our arms, she throws in, "And to *never* doing jump squats again."

I don't have my phone on me to know how many hours pass after that, but by the time we pack up, the temperature has plunged at least ten degrees, and we can only make out each other's faces with the help of the moonlight. Wanting to make Poppy proud, I volunteer to stay behind to scan the beach for the last of our waste, but the already gray sand is nearly pitch-black.

Soon, the beach feels like a cold, disorienting void in the dark of the night, erupting goose bumps down my flesh. I button up my linen shirt and tighten my arms across my chest, but the hairs on the back of my neck still rise with that icky feeling that I'm not alone.

"Guess I'm not your trainer anymore."

My heart knocks against my rib cage at the sound of that low, gravelly voice, but I don't need a flashlight to know that tall and broad silhouette belongs to the exact person I don't want to see right now. Axel walks a couple of feet down the sand until we're standing face-to-face, angling himself perfectly under the moonlight. It shines down onto his straight nose and his angled cheekbones and those perfect lips, so soft and kissable this close to my face.

No, Whitney, you're supposed to be mad.

"Wow, Captain Obvious, thanks for that remarkable observation. Any others you want to make?"

He glances at the sand below my feet. "There's a beer bottle right by your ankle." I look down, eyes bulging, and kick it five feet to the side. "Are you drunk?"

"*Drunk?* No. I only had seltzer." When he quirks a brow, I huff. "The *non*spiked kind, Axel. I'm perfectly sober."

The truth motivates him to lessen the space between our bodies by a foot, but it should be easy to take a few steps back with how much empty space surrounds me. Hell, I could make a beeline to my dorm room and end this encounter before it's even started, but my feet are planted into the sand like it's wet concrete.

"Don't you have Isla to get back to right now?" I ask.

"*Isla?* You think I wanna be around her right now?"

"Didn't you kiss her the other day? Or did I make that up?"

His jaw ticks. "I didn't *kiss* Isla—*she* kissed me. There's a difference. But I think the reason you won't see it that way says something about you."

"Really now? And what's that supposed to mean?"

He doesn't tell me, taking another step forward until there's no space left between us. Without warning, he wraps his hand around the back of my head and tugs my face closer to his, so that our foreheads connect.

"Tell me you don't feel anything, Whitney," he pleads, voice falling a notch. "Please."

"I don't—" My breath hitches in my throat when he dips his head down and his lips graze my cheek, missing the corner of my mouth by a centimeter. So close to a kiss. But not a kiss. "I don't *not* feel anything."

"So stubborn," he murmurs against my skin and pulls away.

I think he's going to leave me, but he plops down on the sand and wraps his arms around his knees. Frozen at first, I give in and sit down next to him, leaving three feet between us for safety.

"You need to know something about me and Isla," he says. *I'm not sure I do.* "We've known each other since freshman year of high school. We dated on and off for years, and we got serious again at the beginning of college, and things were pretty much okay until May of last year." An awkward pause ensues, and I think that's the story, but then he continues, "One of my friends was going through a really rough time then. Her boyfriend broke up with her, her parents were divorcing, and her lease was up, so she didn't have a stable place to stay. So, I let her crash at my place for a couple of weeks until she got back on her feet."

I have a feeling I know where this story is going, but I keep my lips sealed shut. "Isla had this really shitty habit of showing up unannounced to my apartment, which is why I didn't tell her, figuring she'd be there before I could probably mention it. Well, that *did* happen, but that day she showed up, my friend was asleep on my couch, and her stuff was all over the living room. Isla saw her, and without asking me anything, she flew into this uncontrollable *rage*." He scrubs his palm down his jaw and winces at the memory. "Started screaming that I'd cheated on her and throwing stuff around the room and yelling all these nasty things. But I'm not completely innocent here. We got into a huge fight, and I said a lot of shit I shouldn't have, and so did she, and we ended things after that.

"Because we couldn't be within five feet of each other

without explosively fighting, we ruined a proposal—Ryan's to May, to be specific. He didn't talk to me for what? Six months, I think."

"But you guys seem like you get along now."

"Guys are a lot simpler than girls," he says. "You go to a football game and down a few beers and next thing you know you're hammered and best buddies again. But with Isla? It was never gonna be that simple, especially when we're coworkers every damn summer."

He looks me over and notices I'm shivering again, my thin overshirt not cutting it in the chill of the night. He unzips his gray hoodie and drapes it over my shoulders, and I whisper a thank-you.

"Earlier this year, when she realized how much she overreacted that day in my apartment, she started trying to get back together. It started with texts, then phone calls, then more unannounced apartment visits, and then that kiss you saw. And you know what? It's *my* fault for not driving it into her head that we were over after we broke up that last time. But I—" He gazes at the calm, rolling waves, beguiling him for a few seconds. The roar of the next wave crashing to shore makes him jolt and look back at me. "I don't know. I was too passive maybe. Because I was worried that we'd have one of those fights again, and I couldn't deal with that a second time. Especially this summer, when I realized I needed to give you my all." His voice falls again as he finishes, "You deserved that and so much more, Whitney."

I look down when an imaginary fist squeezes my heart. It's harder to be mad at him when he goes all mushy and soft, but maybe it's even harder to understand where he's going with this.

"Let me get this straight," I say, still staring at the sand. "You *don't* like Isla, and you *don't* want to date her." I look up and put two and two together. "What about us, then?"

A moment of silence follows my question, and when Axel presses his lips together, like he doesn't know what to say, I wish I could take back the word *us*. Us implies a thing. A thing implies dating.

Axel and I never dated.

Why the hell would I use the word *us*?

Right as I'm praying for a sinkhole to form in the sand below and swallow me whole, Axel answers me. "I don't want to hold you back, Whitney. You're a strong, brilliant woman with so much potential. You don't need to drag your worn-out trainer into this new stage of your life, which will be full of so many new people." He looks off at the dark ocean as he convinces himself softly, "I'm sure one of them will be the one."

I sit frozen beside him, unable to believe what I'm hearing. Of all the reasons he had to shut me out, his insecurities were on the very bottom of my list, especially when he's spent this whole time trying to rid me of my own.

"Hold me back," I say slowly. "You think you'll hold me *back*?"

"Pretty sure that's what I said."

I laugh. It's an airy, mocking laugh, one that even makes Axel shift uncomfortably. "Axel, you could *never* hold me back. Who made me realize I even have *half* of this potential? It wasn't me or my family, let me tell you that, and you're sure as hell not calling it quits before you can even see me put the rest of it to use." The muscles in his mouth twitch as he fights a smile, but they're as stubborn as he is around this topic. "Only *I'm* allowed to be the quitter, got it?"

Finally cracking that smile, he reaches forward and cups my cheek, his fingers slipping into my wind-tousled hair. I'm putty in his hands when his eyes drag down my face, and he slides his thumb down my bottom lip, like he's testing the waters. He tugs me closer until we touch foreheads, and my vision blurs, even more than it does from the tears pricking the corners of my eyes.

"How about neither of us quits, then?" he asks over my lips. He's so close I can almost taste the mint toothpaste lingering on his tongue. "Why don't we both win instead?"

Before I can answer him with a resounding yes, he kisses me. His mouth is slow and teasing, lighting the flames of anticipation in my mind, and his hands remain equally reserved. After several seconds, I run my fingers down his back, feeling the indents of his muscles through his shirt. Firing up, he tugs me over his lap, and his hands settle on my hips, his mouth never breaking away.

We continue to kiss under the moonlight. It's lips and clashing teeth and hands grabbing at whatever they can reach, and I like that I can't fully make out all his facial features in the dark, because what's between us has never been about looks. It's always been about what he says and how he makes me feel and how he almost understands me more than I understand myself.

When we let go, he turns me around, so my back meets his front, and we sit on the cold sand for a few moments, breathing hard and observing the crashing waves. I trail my fingers mindlessly down the veins of his forearm, and sparks reignite again when he snakes an arm around my waist and dips his head down. I giggle as he presses a line of kisses down my cheek, his rough stubble scratching my skin.

"You're so beautiful, you know that, right?" he murmurs.

I laugh, tipping my head back to make eye contact. "You can barely see me, Axel."

"Don't give a shit. Still said what I said."

Before I can argue with him, he kisses me again.

Post-Camp

CHAPTER TWENTY-SIX

"Oh, I'm really gonna miss you."

I pull Martina into a hug in the middle of our empty room, our beds two barren mattresses and our lives packed up into bags and suitcases again. She squeezes me back with equal force, and I try not to think about how we may never live together again. I wish she wasn't going to college in DC so I could already have my ideal built-in roommate.

"How far away is your town from mine again?" I ask. "Forty minutes?"

"You're in luck; Wilton is a grand twenty minutes away," she says. "We'll still text every day in college, too, right?"

"Of course, you idiot." I pull her into a hug again, and we stay like that for another minute, until Martina's phone vibrates. "Do you really have to go already?"

I expect her to hurry out of the room, but a figure looming in our doorway catches her eye. Aspen waits with a small, solemn smile, appearing like a different person in a pair of flowy pants and a pink blouse, her curly hair down and framing her face. Martina grabs her hand and yanks her over and squeezes the three of us into another suffocating hug.

"Wait a minute," I say, my voice muffled by Martina's shoulder. "Did you guys make up?"

"We sure did. When I noticed you and Willow had made up, I knew I had to one-up you." I burst into laughter, and Martina continues, "So, Aspen and I made some time to talk last night, and we both realized that neither of us is ready to date, each other or anyone else."

"*But*," Aspen continues, lifting her index finger, "we'd much rather be in each other's lives as friends than not in each other's lives at all. Because trust me, I need friends if I'm gonna survive college."

"Aw, I'm so happy for you guys," I say, clutching my heart. "I still think you would make a cute couple, though."

"That's what I've been—" Aspen cuts Martina off with another hug, and I join the embrace again, soaking up the last of these moments.

Someone clears their throat from our doorway.

"Oh, hey," Willow says, standing between Joanna and Adriana, both in jean shorts and crop tops. "We couldn't leave without saying goodbye."

"Get over here," Martina calls, but she holds up a hand when they're halfway across the room. "Actually, Adriana, you can sit this one out. I'll be seeing too much of you when we go home."

Adriana rolls her eyes but still shoves herself into the strangest embrace I've ever experienced. Kennedy and Neha join us soon after, then a few girls I've barely spoken to before, and we start to spill out into the hallway, laughing and hugging and crying like idiots.

After getting everyone's number, I'm left alone in our now lifeless room, and the only person left who I'll miss from this camp is Axel. We parted ways sometime after midnight, and I spent almost the whole night replaying our kiss and thinking about the very real possibility of returning here as a trainer next summer. Bob even stopped me for a quick chat after breakfast, seeming hopeful that I would accept the position.

Leaving my bags behind, I take a short walk to the trainer dorm and feel zero shame making a beeline to Axel's room. I poke my head into his doorway and find his room in the same state of disarray that mine was in earlier this morning, boxes and bags and papers galore. I can make out the top of his head from behind a stack of cardboard boxes, and I clear my throat to capture his attention.

He pokes his head up, and the stress lines in his forehead flatten when he sees me. Without saying a word, he walks across the room and pulls me into a bone-crushing hug, and all is right in the world again. I'm glad half my face is concealed by his shirt when a few tears start building in my right eye and dampen the cotton.

He tips my face up and brushes away the droplet that escaped with his thumb. "Hey, don't cry. This isn't a permanent goodbye."

"But what if it is? I still haven't told Bob yes or no yet."

He tips his head down and looks at me from underneath his eyelashes, his hard stare all but implying I have no choice but to say yes. At this point, with this new delusional love of exercise, I'd probably accept the offer even without the added bonus of a sweet hunky coworker, but no one needs to know that.

I flicker my eyes to his desk, finding a book sitting atop a pile of notebooks. Drawing closer, I realize the name on the spine is oddly familiar: *The Great Gatsby*. "Do you have a secret affinity for high school English class?"

"That's actually from my dad's old book collection."

"Oh, I'm sorry, I didn't—"

"He was an engineer, so I don't think he ever read a book past high school, though." The levity in his tone makes me laugh along with him and pick up the tattered copy of *The Great Gatsby*. He nudges his chin towards it. "Feel free to take it, if you want."

"I don't think I could do that," I tell him softly, putting it down.

"Really, Whitney." He closes his hand around mine. "I'd feel happier if someone besides me read any of these books. But let me add something first."

He hunches over his desk and scrawls something onto a piece of lined paper and then tucks it into the middle of the book. I would've never pegged him as the literary kind of romantic, let alone any kind of romantic, but it's safe to say nothing about Axel was as it seemed.

My phone buzzes in my hand with a text from Mom asking me what time I'm going to be home, once again reminding me that this experience is over.

An idea pops into my head. "Look, I know this is going to sound kind of random, and you can definitely say no . . ." He eyes me suspiciously as I trail off in thought, so I bite the bullet and ask. "My sister is getting married at the end of next month, and she expects me to bring a plus-one. So . . . Would you . . . Would you *mind?*"

"Jesus, Whitney, I was expecting something so much worse. But no, of course I don't mind. Text me the details."

He squeezes me into one last hug before I hurry back to my room to grab my bags and begin the solemn march to the parking lot. With leaden legs, I drag myself to my car and notice that Martina and Adriana's Lexus is already gone. As I'm loading my suitcases into the trunk—a slightly less arduous feat with some added arm strength—I catch sight of a girl sulking in an empty parking spot. Noelle sits hunched over her suitcase, fists under her chin, and looks wistfully at the main road every few moments. Her long hair is piled into a bun that sags down her head, and she's lost the makeup she started caking on her face by the second week of camp.

She looks small, sad, and lonely, and the combination tugs on my heartstrings hard enough to go to talk to her.

"Hey," I say.

Noelle snaps her head up, and her eyes widen as she watches me cross the asphalt. "Oh, uh, hey," she says, straightening up. "You heading out right now?"

"Yeah, that's my car over there," I say, pointing behind me. "Are you waiting for someone?"

"My mom. I still haven't gotten my license yet." She ducks her head down as her cheeks tint pink, and I can't tell if she's embarrassed because she can't drive or if it's because I'm still talking to her after what happened between us. "Look, Whitney, I'm really sorry about that comment I made in the yoga studio— about gym class and stuff. It was totally out of line, and it's okay if you think I'm a bitch. I deserve it."

I bristle as the humiliation of that moment washes over me again, but my feelings aren't why I came to talk to her. "Why'd you make that comment?" I ask her instead.

"Why?" Her lips part, and she traces a nervous line down her arm with her fingertips. "I don't know. I . . . I wanted those girls to like me, I guess. Which is stupid because that didn't work out, and now I have no friends from camp. And barely any back home, either, but that's a separate problem."

"You still have time to make new ones," I say, taking her by surprise. "But they won't be real friends if you can't be yourself around them—or if they turn you into someone you're not. You have a lot more to offer than you think, Noelle."

Her brow furrows, and she nods slowly, letting my words sink in. "You know what, I really needed to hear that. Thank you."

"I'm glad," I say and turn on my heel. Before heading back to my car, I look over my shoulder and shoot her a soft smile. "And Noelle?" She nods. "I hope you do make varsity this year."

I don't catch sight of her reaction the way I'm facing, but when I slip into my car, her mom has already pulled into the parking lot. Noelle rushes to the passenger side with a huge grin across her face and a pep in her step again, and that's all I need to see before I leave.

—

After a short traffic jam, the picturesque colonials of my neighborhood come into view, their manicured lawns just as green and driveways paved with a fresh layer of asphalt. As I pull into my driveway, Mr. Sullivan waves hello from deep in the trenches of pulling weeds next door, and reluctantly, I wave back.

Mom comes running towards my car in her post-Pilates gear, her short brown hair up in a messy bun and petite frame clad in yoga pants and a long-sleeve shirt. She clasps her mouth when she sees me. "Whitney? Oh my gosh, I almost didn't recognize you!"

"Mom," I breathe, tumbling out of the car. I wrap my arms around her and savor that familiar rush of warmth as she yanks me into her chest and practically lifts me a foot off the ground.

"What did they even do to you there? I can only imagine the stories you're going to tell."

I laugh with her as she helps me haul my bags out of my trunk, not even knowing where to start—or if I'm going to say anything at all. "It's been a long five weeks, Mom." I arch my neck towards the garage. "Where's Dad?"

"At work. He said he might be home for dinner today."

I say nothing else and drag my suitcase and duffel bag through the garage door and drop them off in the mudroom, not even wanting to think about unloading them. I inhale the scent of freshly brewed coffee in the kitchen and the fresh summer air wafting through the windows, smelling of mowed grass and pine, realizing at least something about home feels like camp.

Mom places a light hand on my shoulder. "Do you want to have a late breakfast? We have some leftover bagels and muffins from the bakery."

"Blueberry or chocolate chip?"

"Chocolate chip, of course," she says, giving my shoulder a teasing squeeze. "Your favorite."

When she leaves, I drop down to a barstool at the kitchen island and stare at the perfectly golden-brown muffin sitting on my plate. Before I can even break off a piece, the marble of the countertop blurs from the wetness clouding my eyes, and I go back to mourning the greatest experience of my life.

———

The only perk to working out alone is listening to music, which I blast during my one-hour morning jogs throughout the next week.

On jog number five, Dad bumps into me as I'm rushing down the stairs, with my earphones blaring an EDM remix of one of my favorite pop songs. I pull out one of my AirPods, and we both apologize at the same time.

"No, I'm sorry," he says, stepping out of the way. Before continuing up the stairs, he looks between the sweatband on my forehead and my matching green workout set. "You like running now?"

"I was at a fitness camp for over a month, Dad."

"Right." He clears his throat. "Do you want to go play a round of golf at the country club? I have the day off work."

That's a rarity. I know I can't pass up an offer to spend the day with him, but maybe this time, we should do it on my terms. "How about you join me on my jog instead? That'll be more fun for me."

His eyebrows knit together in confusion, but he doesn't question me, nor do I explain myself. I head outside and wait for him on the porch, feeling the humid August air settle into my pores. A butterfly lands on my arm as I drop down to the soft porch swing, and I observe it curiously before it flies into the distance.

Dad reappears in the doorway in a blue Yale cap and matching T-shirt that says YALE DAD. He gestures to his outfit, popping one of his legs out. "Had to make sure the neighbors know where my little genius is heading off to college."

"Oh my gosh, Dad." I laugh and steal his cap from his head, not even remembering when he bought the merchandise.

I thread my ponytail through the back and fit it on top of my head. "There. Now you look less like a campus tour guide."

We head out down the road of our neighborhood and jog in silence for at least ten minutes. Every minute or so, Dad turns his head my way, mouth opening and closing with some remark he wants to make.

At last, he forces out, "So, how was camp?"

"Good," I answer, though I know that's not much to work with. "Actually, it was more than good. It was kind of . . . *life-changing*."

"How so?"

"I met a lot of cool people. And changed my mind on some of them." Memories flash through my mind, with Martina and Aspen then Willow, Joanna, and Adriana. "I also . . . I realized there's a lot I can accomplish when I put my mind to something."

"That's not shocking to me or your mother," he says, slowing his pace. I do as well, almost having forgotten that at fifty-three, he's not as youthful and energetic as Axel. "You make any lifelong friendships?"

"I hope so," I chuckle, remembering the ten unread texts I have from Martina. "I also met— Actually, never mind."

"Met who?" His blue eyes twinkle as he leans into my personal space. "A *boy*?"

"No— I mean, yes. But we're not dating. We're just friends."

"Sounds good," he hums, not believing me in the slightest. "If you ever want to tell me more about this *friend*, I'm all ears."

My cheeks are flaming hot at this point, but the brim of my cap somewhat conceals my face from his view. We exit our neighborhood and weave into the next one over, with its brick McMansions and even greener lawns in the thick of the summer drought, some mark of achievement in upper-class suburbia.

"Dad?" He nods, giving me his full attention. "How come we've never done anything like this before?"

I can tell I've hit at something that hurts when he winces and looks away, dragging his fingertips down the graying stubble on his chin. His eyes catch sight of a young father chasing his two daughters down the driveway. When I peer closer, I realize they're carbon copies of me and Poppy minus fifteen years of age, one with long dirty-blond locks riding her bike and the other a somewhat tubby brunet toddling after her.

I know I shouldn't laugh when she falls over onto her face on the grass, but I do.

"I'm not sure I have an excuse—at least, not a good one. After that injury in high school"—he rubs his hamstring midstride like the pain is still there thirty-five years later—"I told myself if I ever had children, they would accomplish everything I couldn't. When Poppy naturally gravitated to athletics, I thought I had my side of parenting cut out for me, but I never thought about the other ways I could connect to my kids if they turned out *not* to like sports." We stop jogging once we approach a cul-de-sac, and he rests his hands on his hips with a heavy sigh. "There was never anything wrong with that, Whitney."

I swallow that hard lump in my throat and look away, blinking away the moisture from my eyes. "You know, I always thought I was a failure because of that. Because I *wasn't* athletic like Poppy."

"A *failure?*" His face scrunches up and his shoulders sag, like my words drive a dagger into his heart and not mine. "Whitney, you're my greatest investment. Don't you know how proud I am of everything you do?"

"No," I whisper, the tears dripping down my cheeks now. "I don't."

He steps forward and holds his arms out. I hesitate before melting into his embrace, and he squeezes me tight, resting his chin on the top of my head. "I'm sorry, kiddo. I never meant to make you feel this way."

I sniffle and pull away, dabbing at my eyes with my knuckles. "It's okay. You tried your best, I guess."

"I didn't, actually. But it's all you deserve from me right now. And if you want, we can start our own tradition—whatever you like."

I grin, looking up slowly. "Could this be our new thing?"

"It sure can. If we head out at six thirty a.m., we can jog together on the weekdays too."

I wince. "How about seven, Dad?"

"Seven it is," he laughs, and we take off down the road together.

CHAPTER TWENTY-SEVEN

"Hey, Whitney."

Poppy leans against my door frame with a smile on her face. She has on a pink floral minidress resembling the hues of the evening sky, making her legs seem ten miles long.

"Oh hey," I say, poking my head up from the third chapter of *The Great Gatsby*. "I haven't seen you in a couple of days."

"I was over visiting Levi's parents at their apartment in New York. I brought him back for dinner tonight." She closes the door and leans against it, releasing a long, satisfied sigh. "It's so nice meeting someone and knowing he's the right one. I don't think it matters how big or fancy your wedding is or how great-looking a couple you are if you don't truly love that person and aren't ready to spend the rest of your life with them."

"That was a lot deeper than what I was expecting."

"I'm sorry," she chuckles. "I sound all sappy, but I wanted to give you some advice you might be able to use someday. Mom told me you bought a dress for the wedding. Can I see it?"

I walk to my closet and carefully pull it out of the garment bag. After three hours of circling the mall, I went with the first midi-dress I'd tried on, made of a satin material with a cowl neck that emphasizes my collarbones. It cinches in a bit at the waist, hugging my hips just right.

I hold it up in front of my chest, striking a stupid pose, and her eyes widen. "Whoa, green is totally your color, Whitney." She thumbs the material and then swats at the arm I've raised above my head like a failing model. "You're going to look stunning."

"Nah, you're definitely gonna look prettier. Your dress made you look like a princess."

"A *princess*?"

"Oh sorry, a hippie, indie, free-spirited *princess*."

"That's better," she jokes and then throws herself down on my bed. She picks up my book from my bed and thumbs through the pages. "Wow, are you really missing high school English class already? It took at least three years for any nostalgia to kick in for me."

"Hell no. Someone gave it to me at camp."

"Who carries a copy of *The Great Gatsby* around with them at a fitness camp?"

"My personal trainer, apparently," I answer, turning around and walking back to my bed. "Who turned out to be a lot *more* than my personal trainer."

The underlying meaning doesn't register for her at first, but when I stare her down in that knowing way, she throws a hand over her mouth. "Oh my god, Whitney. You mean *Axel*?" She whacks my arm with the back of her hand, her diamond engagement ring practically stabbing a hole through my skin. "Shit, sorry. But still—I knew you'd meet the one at that camp! Give me all the details *now*."

And so I do, lying the opposite way down the length of my bed, my feet all up in her face. She slaps my foot away when I poke my big toe into her face halfway through the story of my first kiss, and we burst into laughter, transporting me back to our elementary school days.

She heads out the door when Mom and Dad call us down for dinner, but I linger by my bed, catching a ripped piece of lined paper in my peripheral vision. I pull out the note sticking out of the middle of my book, and I'm back in Axel's room, watching him write something down on paper. I almost can't believe I've waited a week to read it, but I'm very glad I'm alone when I do.

Hope you'll take me along on the rest of your thousand-mile journey. If not, I'll always be on the sidelines cheering you on. —Axhole

My lips curl up into a girlish grin before a tiny squeal escapes them, and I mask an even bigger one with a throw pillow from my bed. Just the catalyst I needed—I waste no time whipping out my phone and finally texting him that I'll be saying yes to Bob's offer.

I'm the last to sit down at the table at dinner. Levi is already talking with Mom, not seeming to notice that her eyes glaze over with all the medical terms he throws out. Dad holds two different wine bottles up to the chandelier, squinting at their labels. We settle in, and after a recap of today's stock market dip—very disappointing but not surprising to most seasoned investors, according to Dad—Mom dives right in.

"So, are you prepared to go back to New York after spending this summer in the suburbs?" she asks Poppy as she cuts into her filet mignon. "You accepted the offer at that economic consulting firm in Midtown, right?"

Poppy glances up from her heaping plate of vegetables, and her eyes turn into saucers. She takes a sip of wine to recover and swallows hard. "I lied that I was going to accept that offer." Even my eyes widen at how she easily she admits that, but I don't know if I should be surprised. "I'm going to be working at an environmental nonprofit next year. I figure it'll be a better use of my time before law school. If I decide to go, that is."

Apparently, none of us knew this besides Levi, who shoots our parents a tight smile.

"But that was a very prestigious opportunity to pass up, Poppy," Mom says, gripping the stem of her wineglass harder. "We didn't put you through Columbia for something you could've done anywhere else."

"Mom, as far back as I can remember, Columbia was *your* dream for me. And I got in and went, even though I would've been fine at any other college."

"But you talked about that college all throughout high school; it was all you wanted—"

"It was all *you* wanted, Mom. And sure, I'm very grateful for the amazing education and all your financial support, but what I do after is my choice. God, don't you realize that almost everything I've done in life is your dream and not *mine*?"

All of us have stopped eating. Levi tries to comfort Poppy by placing his hand on her forearm, but she pulls away, her fiery eyes burning into my mother, who shifts uncomfortably in her chair beside me.

"What about being a lawyer, then? That's a dream of yours . . . right?"

"It never was, but maybe I'll come back to it after I take

some time to discover myself. And I can definitely do that at this nonprofit."

Mom can't seem to find an answer for a few moments, and I wonder if she's finally understood Poppy's side of this argument, but her self-righteous reply doesn't convince me. "Okay, all right, I can get with that. But don't you see why I was against the wedding at first? You don't seem ready to make these kinds of big decisions at your age."

Poppy drops her palm to the table with a thud that rattles our plates, and I start to wonder if Levi should have a first-class seat to the unraveling of the Carmichael family. At least Dad and I managed to keep our drama and semireconciliation private.

"Okay, maybe I *am* young and clueless, but I'm young, clueless, and in love with the only man I'd ever want to be with. What's wrong with wanting to make our relationship official instead of dating for another ten years knowing we don't want to be with anyone else?"

"With all due respect, Mrs. Carmichael," Levi says before Mom can rebut, leaning over the table. "I love your daughter, and I know how much getting married means to her. I promise to cherish her with all my heart, but I think this decision is up to us. Even my mother is more than supportive at this point."

A long period of silence ensues, and while I'm aching to break it, I know that the only voice that matters right now is Mom's. After a minute, she finally speaks, her toned muted now.

"Wow, I . . . I almost don't know what to say," she murmurs, looking away with her palm pressed under her chin. "I guess I just always expected so much of you, and I maybe I never . . . I never questioned what *you* wanted in life."

Poppy nods and swallows tightly, dragging her knuckle into

the corner of her eye. "This is something I want, Mom. I've never been surer of anything in my life."

It seems like a boulder rolls off her shoulders when she stops talking and exhales loudly. Realization dawns on me, that I've always been so focused on all our physical differences that I never noticed how much my sister and I are alike on the inside. We've both been harboring so many hard feelings and things we've been wanting to say, knowing that one day we'd have to stop burying those feelings and confront them—and more importantly, our parents.

"How about a toast?" Dad says, breaking through the suffocating quiet. He lifts his wineglass up into the air. "To Poppy and Levi."

Hesitant at first, we all raise our glasses and clink them, but when we start to pull away, Dad keeps his in the air.

"And to Whitney," he says, winking at me.

———

It's remarkable in life how quickly one moment leads to the next.

I remember that day, winter break of my freshman year of high school, when my sister came home all flustered and anxious with a shy, lanky premed standing by her side, a boyish grin on his pink face as he held her hand. And now three and a half years later, my favorite and only older sister is about to get married to him.

Talk about commitment.

I shift in the solid white chair I'm sitting in, smoothing out the creases in my satin dress as I watch bodies fill up the seats around me. Poppy was serious when she said she didn't want an over-the-top wedding. There are no more than forty chairs in the middle of this green field in the Hamptons, part of the backyard of an oceanside mansion owned by one of Levi's relatives.

Though Mom's insistence isn't always welcome, I'm very glad she and Alice teamed up and urged against the barn idea.

I feel a tap on my shoulder and turn around to see Grandma Jean, Mom's mom—and the original owner of my very outdated middle name—looking precious in her yellow dress and floppy white hat.

"Whitney Jean, why is the seat next to you empty?" she asks, judgment coloring her green eyes. "Are you saving it for someone?"

I sigh, shoulders slumping in defeat. It's Axel's seat, only he hasn't arrived yet. I texted him twice this morning, making sure he was still coming, but he didn't respond, dampening some of my hopes.

"Yeah, it's actually saved for a special someone."

She clasps her heart, and for a moment, I worry I've sent the poor woman into cardiac arrest, before she tilts her head up and praises the heavens. "I've been waiting *all* these years to see you with someone," she says, like I'm forty and not eighteen. "You are the perfect girlfriend material, my Whitney."

I laugh. "Thanks, Grandma. You are—"

"He'd better be a good man though, or I will have a word with him. I may be in my seventies, but sass doesn't deteriorate with age."

"You'd better go get him then, if he doesn't show up . . ." I joke, but my voice fades to a whisper at the end.

The crowd, while small, has fully filled the seats now, and I glance at the time on my phone, noticing the ceremony will begin in just a few minutes. Right as I'm about to abandon my hopes, I catch a whiff of familiar spicy cologne, clouding my vision for a moment.

"Whitney," Axel breathes, scanning me from head to toe with those captivating hazel eyes of his. When my eyesight clears, I notice his hair has grown out more and is pushed back from his eyes, and he appears even more attractive than he could possibly be in a slim gray suit and gleaming dress shoes. "You look gorgeous."

"Gosh, I was so worried you were going to bail," I breathe, clasping my chest.

"And miss out on all this?" He sits down next to me and leans into my ear, murmuring, "I never make promises I can't keep, Whitney."

"So, this is the guy," Grandma comments from behind us. Axel and I both turn around, and her eyes widen as her palm flattens against the neckline of her dress. "My, aren't you handsome. Good taste runs on Whitney's mom's side of the family, by the way." She fluffs her short white hair. "As do the looks."

He reaches out his hand, and she shakes it firmly, and I try not to laugh at how of all my family members, he's first acquainted with Grandma Jean. "I'm Axel, Whitney's—"

"Boyfriend?" Grandma supplies, and he nods tightly.

"Something like that."

The buzz of the crowd fades to a hush, sparing us from any more awkward conversation, and when I check the time, I realize the ceremony has officially begun. We turn around to watch Poppy walk down the aisle with Dad. Her cheeks are a rosy shade of pink, and she looks breathtakingly elegant in her lacy long-sleeve dress, her blondish hair cascading down her back in loose waves.

I give her a discreet thumbs-up as she walks past. Levi's smile is so wide, tears seem to form in the corners of his eyes. Poppy looks away, giggling softly, before turning back to him.

"We are gathered here on this beautiful August day to celebrate the joining together of Poppy Carmichael and Levi Steele in marriage. Today is not only the marriage of two different people; it's the marriage of two different hearts, ready to spend the rest of their lives together in union . . ."

The ceremony carries on with all its formalities and rehearsed words, and it seems like the next time I blink, the officiant is uttering the much-awaited six words of every wedding: "You may now kiss the bride."

Levi goes all out, slinging an arm around Poppy's waist and dipping her down, and she has the biggest girlish grin on her face when he finally lets her go. We clap and cheer as the newlyweds walk back down the aisle, their joined hands high up in the air, seeming relieved that the hard part is finally over.

"All right then," Axel says as guests start to file out of their rows. "Is it time to meet the rest of your family? Your grandma elevated my expectations."

"There's still time," I answer him.

Following him out of our row, I can barely traverse the grass in my strappy heels, my steps as unsure as a baby giraffe's. Axel loops an arm around my back before I topple over onto my face. I look around for Mom and Dad, finding them deep in conversation with Grandpa Tom, who'll probably somehow find a way to change the subject to football at a wedding.

"My parents look busy with some guests right now."

"Great," he says, and I don't trust the mischievous twinkle in his eyes when he pulls away. "That gives me time to do this before you go introduce me to them."

Between two blinks, he drops down to one knee and opens his hands like a clamshell, with nothing inside his palms. "My *very* witty Whitney, will you be my girlfriend?"

Eyes going wide, I clutch his beefy bicep and try to yank him up to his feet, but it's like trying to lift a boulder with two fingers. "*Axel*, do you know how rude it is to pretend to propose to a girl at her sister's wedding?"

"And do you know how rude it is to leave a man hanging after he makes a fool of himself at said sister's wedding?"

He still doesn't budge.

"Yes."

The reply leaves me in an instant, and I can't decide if it's because I want him to *stop* making a fool of himself or because I really want to be his girlfriend. But one look into his eyes glimmering with some emotion that feels really close to love makes me realize I do want to be his girlfriend—and everything else to him.

"Of course I will, Axel."

Standing up, he pulls me into a bear hug and spins me around in a circle. My heel whacks into the chair behind it, knocking off my shoe before the chair flips upside down. I slip the other one off and run barefoot down the grass with Axel by my side and not ten steps ahead of me, ready to begin this new chapter of my life.

EPILOGUE

Poppy, Levi, Axel, and my parents surround me at our circular patio table on this balmy early-June night, where the sound of laughter hasn't ceased for the past hour. The golden sun descends farther behind the thick green trees enveloping the yard, slowly starting to be replaced by a bluish-purple sky. Wrapping my jacket tighter over my body as a breeze blows, I lean back into my seat and smile as I listen to my parents exchange a few jokes over now-empty plates of penne alla vodka.

Dad looks up and smiles tenderly at me, the corners of his warm blue eyes wrinkling. "When's the big announcement happening, Whit? We finished eating before you even breathed a word about it."

"Yeah, Whitney," Axel teases, nudging me with his elbow. He's the only one who knows what this announcement actually is, but he pretends like he doesn't. "When will you tell us?"

"It's not *that* big an announcement," I say timidly, feeling everyone's eyes land on me, "but I am kind of proud of myself." Mom and Poppy eagerly gesture for me to speak, so I finally go ahead. "As of this morning, I, Whitney Carmichael, am officially a certified personal trainer."

A series of congratulations echo around the table, and I feel my cheeks grow even warmer, unused to being the center of attention at these gatherings. I welcome the warm hug from Poppy sitting next to me and notice her husband waiting to speak, shaking his head in disbelief.

"I'm honestly shocked you managed to get certified during your first year of college. I never had time to set foot into the gym freshman year with those daily breakdowns over organic chemistry."

"Oh no, Levi—not *that* class," I groan. "I swear I still see hexagons in my sleep every night."

He chuckles over the rim of his glass of water and offers me a sympathetic smile. "I'll let you know if it gets any better in med school."

From the dead look in his brown eyes, I have a feeling he knows it won't.

Unlike Levi, Poppy stayed at her full-time job at the environmental nonprofit and put off continuing her education for another year, or maybe even five. Mom eventually got over the fact that law school isn't on her daughter's radar anymore, the end of a dream that wasn't Poppy's in the first place. It's a miracle what acceptance does to a relationship, as I haven't witnessed the two clash and quarrel ever since she got married. And best of all, instead of the stock market, we now discuss ways to reduce our carbon footprint before our meals together, which, after quite the battle to convince my dad that steak is terrible for the planet, are now mostly meat-free.

"Now is the perfect time for a toast." Dad picks up the sealed bottle of champagne from the corner of the table, eager to finally pop it open.

Poppy laughs. "You say that at *every* gathering, Dad. Just admit you want an excuse to drink fancy alcohol."

"We have a lot to celebrate this time, Poppy." He pops open the cork and grabs the first flute, looking between the five of us. "Whit's new job, your promotion at work, my son-in-law's start to a rewarding career, almost twenty-five years of marriage to your mother, *and* hopefully another wedding in the future."

"That's the first time you remembered our anniversary on your own, honey," Mom remarks, eyebrows raised in surprise. In a mumble, she adds, "I'll toast to that myself later."

"Wait," I say, cutting through the laughter that follows. "Did you say . . . *another* wedding? Who's getting married?"

"He means us," Axel says into my ear.

My eyes nearly bulge out of my head. "Dad. Some context, please."

"Did I say right now? I mean, sometime in the future. After graduating college would be great—just like Poppy and Levi."

I cringe into my hands, while Axel beams like a kid on Christmas morning along with Dad, always on his side. When I brought him home for dinner after the wedding, I shouldn't have been surprised that a personal trainer would fit into my family like its last missing puzzle piece. Golf, tennis, six-a.m. hikes, and 5Ks on Thanksgiving—all of it was right up his alley.

But what surprised me most was how close he and Dad have grown over the past year, much closer than Levi has ever been with Dad. Hell, maybe even closer than I am with him, despite the inroads we've made in our relationship since our first jog around the neighborhood, a tradition still going strong almost a year later. I know it has something to do with Axel's dad not being around, but I don't question it. Because I'm not upset.

In fact, my life is everything I could ask for as the six of us clink glasses, and the evening rolls into the night, marking the end of another perfect day.

———

"You move in today, right?" Mom asks when I step into the kitchen. I slide onto the barstool next to her, joining her for breakfast. "Are you excited to actually begin working soon?"

"To be honest, I don't even know *how* I feel." I pour myself a large cup of coffee, knowing I'm going to need lots of caffeine to survive a long day of Bob's orders. "I couldn't sleep last night overthinking everything, even though I'm pretty sure those campers have more reason than me to be scared out of their minds."

"Relax, Whitney, you've been training for this all year." She brings her mug of coffee to her lips and smiles before adding, "Besides, if you don't turn out to be all that good at the job, I'm sure there's been plenty worse before you."

I cut into a chocolate-chip pancake doused in syrup and shove in a larger-than-normal bite. "Thanks, Mom. Anxiety is *gone* now."

I keep a close eye on the clock as I linger at breakfast, grateful I already stuffed my car with everything I need to move in. With a tight parting hug to Mom, I hurry upstairs to survey my room for the last time and make sure I haven't missed any key belongings. When I confirm it's just my overthinking making me check again, I turn back down the hallway and bump into a passing figure.

"You're leaving already, Whit?" Dad asks, adjusting the collar of his white shirt.

"I don't have to, but my nerves are telling me I need to be two hours early." I return his warm hug and keep my head buried in his shoulder for several moments, until he finally lets me go with a melancholic smile.

"Sometimes I forget that you and Poppy are now full-grown adults. I remember when you were in kindergarten, you'd hug me like that every morning, rattling off a million reasons why you shouldn't have to go to school."

"You're going to have to try to keep me *out* of school now. Geez, I feel kind of old now, Dad."

"Trust me, I'm the only old one here. Now go kill it at the job, kiddo."

I load up my trusty Jeep and blast the AC to cool down my fidgety, overheating body, even though the nerves I feel now aren't even close to the vomit-inducing anxiety that gripped me before meeting Axel's mother and brother, Jake, in New York over winter break. That was, until I realized there's a reason Axel is the good man he is, with a mother that radiates pure sunshine and a brother that worships the ground he walks on.

That same week, Cindy invited me to one of her infamous brunches at the Gerard mansion, and there, Willow, Adriana, Martina, Ava, and I had the bonding session of our lives over one too many mimosas and servings of French toast. As she kept making up excuses to pop in and out of the room, even Cindy didn't know what to think of the five of us getting along so well, but how could she complain?

We all became besties in the end.

As I scroll through my messages, I glance at Willow's latest text in the Survivors of Camp Campbell group chat—a mirror selfie of her and Adriana in one of those inhuman ballet positions, all spindly contorted limbs and wide grins. Smiling softly, I text Axel back that I'll be at camp soon.

Soon becomes one traffic jam, two detours, and a near fender-bender later, but at last, I pull into the parking lot cut into the woods. I wait to start hauling out my belongings, wanting to find Axel first. On my journey across campus, I linger in the middle of the road leading to the beach, thinking about how this stretch of pavement once seemed so daunting, and now its length is all but a warmup to me.

"Hello, new coworker. Need me to show you around?"

Whirling around in a panic, I can barely register who stands in front of me before I feel myself being hoisted into the air.

"Axel," I laugh as he spins me around in a circle. After I urge him to put me back on the ground, he plants me on my feet and dips his head down. I cup his cheeks in my hands, running my thumbs over his rough stubble, sharing his same broad smile before mumbling, "That's one way to show me you missed me."

"I could also kiss you, but you've made it clear you despise PDA." He slides his big, teasing hands up my back, slipping his fingers underneath the hem of my shirt.

I flicker my eyes around the camp, not a soul in sight. "But who says we're in *public*?"

With a self-satisfied smile, he picks me up, wrapping my legs around his torso, and brings his mouth to my own. The kiss is shorter and sweeter than our normally long and passionate romantic exchanges, but that same toe-curling sensation rushes down my body, making me wish for more.

But, alas, we're now in public, and Axel practically throws me back onto the grass.

"You know, I've lived most of my life thinking that I need

a domineering career, going from the military to the fitness world, with a brief stint in construction in between, but now I'm starting to regret not becoming a professional matchmaker. Seems to be my specialty."

Neither Axel nor I have to turn around to know who those words belong to, spoken in the signature smug tone of Bob himself. Blushing like the shy lover he definitely isn't, Axel waves hello to his boss—well, our boss.

"Hope your summer's been good so far, sir," he says, unable to look him in the eyes.

"Oh, it's been *great*"—Bob walks up the grass with a pep in his step, his arms stretching over his head—"and it'll get even better when I have another sixteen minions to terrorize at the end of the month. Enjoy the last bit of your freedom, you two."

When Bob disappears, Axel turns to me again. "Are you ready for this summer?"

A confident smile pulls on the corners of my lips. "Bring it on, baby."

ACKNOWLEDGMENTS

I could not begin without a huge thank-you to my Wattpad readers, who saw something in this story when it was just a couple of chapters I drafted and posted online on a whim. I am forever grateful for your hilarious comments, sweet messages, and the love for *Boot Camp* you've shared with me all these years—I wouldn't be here without you.

To my parents, who have always believed in me and my (many) pursuits. To my mom, for instilling a love of the English language in me from such a young age. I wouldn't be half the writer I am today without all your effort (and especially those grammar lessons at the kitchen table). And to my dad, for telling me at eight years old that I'd become an author one day after handing you a short story on three pieces of copy paper stapled together. I finally did it, Mama and Baba.

To Terra and Charles, for your endless support, iconic sense of humor, and being the best siblings/travel buddies/ride-or-dies I could ask for. Love you guys forever. And to my friend Jewel—thank you for never letting a text go unanswered and for your always appreciated kindness and wit. The world needs more people like all of you.

To my editor, Deanna McFadden, for helping me transform this manuscript into something I'm so deeply proud of. Its strongest themes and messages would not have shined without you and your magic. To the rest of the Wattpad team, for all your hard work behind the scenes and for championing this story. And to Anne Dubuisson, for your many helpful insights prepublishing.

Finally, to the cast of the film for cheering *Boot Camp* on with me and helping bring its characters to life. What a wonderfully unexpected journey this has been.

ABOUT THE AUTHOR

Gina Musa is the author of *Boot Camp* and has been sharing her writing online since middle school. She grew up on the New England coast, where many of her summer romance novels take place, and enjoys taking long walks by the beach while daydreaming about her latest story idea.